A STOLEN KISS

"Sir, you may not realize it, but, quite often, a good name is all a poor girl has to cling to," Maura said.

"I realize that. I'm also sure that, by the time we get to Paradise, we'll have thought of some good explanation, something that will soothe most of those ruffled feathers. Like having you travel under an assumed name."

"It might work."

"You know it will." Tyrone stood up, grasped Maura by the hand and tugged her into his arms. "Why, you could do a great deal of misbehaving beneath the shelter of that name."

"Misbehaving?" she snapped, and started to push him away.

Pretending he misread her shock as confusion or surprise, he tightened his hold on her. Tyrone suspected he would pay dearly for stealing a kiss, but the temptation to do so was too strong to ignore. The look that briefly flared in Maura's eyes as he touched his mouth to hers hinted that she was as curious as he. . . .

Books by Hannah Howell

ONLY FOR YOU
MY VALIANT KNIGHT
UNCONQUERED
WILD ROSES
A TASTE OF FIRE
HIGHLAND DESTINY
HIGHLAND HONOR
HIGHLAND PROMISE
A STOCKINGFUL OF JOY
HIGHLAND VOW

Published by Zebra Books

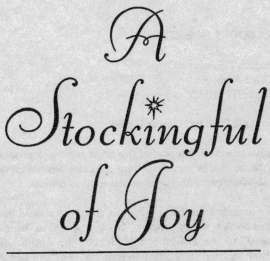

A Stockingful of Joy

Hannah Howell

ZEBRA BOOKS
KENSINGTON PUBLISHING CORP.
http://www.zebrabooks.com

ZEBRA BOOKS are published by

Kensington Publishing Corp.
850 Third Avenue
New York, NY 10022

All Kensington titles, imprints and distributed lines are available at special quality discounts for bulk purchases for sales promotion, premiums, fund raising, educational or institutional use.

Special book excerpts or customized printing can also be created to fit specific needs. For details, write or phone the office of the Kensington Special Sales Manager: Kensington Publishing Corp., 850 Third Avenue, New York, NY, Attn: Special Sales Department. Phone: 1-800-221-2647.

Zebra and the Z logo Reg. U.S. Pat. & TM Off.

First Printing: October, 2000
10 9 8 7 6 5 4 3 2 1

Printed in the United States of America

Contents

A Christmas
in Paradise

Prologue

Dunstanville, MO
October, 1882

"I CAN'T STOP THE bleeding," Deidre Kenney said in a voice choked with grief.

She looked over her father's pain-wracked body to her cousin Maura and saw the devastating knowledge of approaching death in the young woman's dark-blue eyes. In the hour since her father had stumbled into their small farmhouse bleeding profusely from three bullet wounds, Deidre had fought any acceptance of that cold truth, but she could do so no longer. Her father was going to die. It was probably a miracle and sheer stubbornness that had kept him alive this long.

"Ah, my two lovelies," Patrick Kenney rasped, opening his eyes and looking from Deidre to Maura and back again. "My tiny angels. None in heaven will look so lovely."

Even though she could see the dull glaze of death in his green eyes, Deidre said, "Well, you won't be judging the truth of that too soon."

Patrick smiled faintly and, shuddering with the effort, reached out and grasped each girl by the hand. "I will and we all know it."

"No, Papa," Deidre said, clenching his cold hand in both of hers.

"No, Uncle," Maura said at the same time.

"Yes, my pretties. Ah, I will surely miss you both. But, heed me now. I must tell you a few things and, I fear, I must ask you to finish something for me."

"The something that got you shot?" asked Deidre, fighting back her tears.

"Yes. There are some papers in my coat—deeds—and I have sworn to get them to Montana. 'Twas an oath sworn on my friend's deathbed and must be fulfilled."

"And this friend was also killed? It was Bill."

"I fear so. I don't want to put you children in danger, but . . ."

"But an oath must be fulfilled."

"And the money paid will be a fitting legacy for you girls."

"We would rather have you, Uncle," said Maura.

"And that warms an old fool's heart. Now, these papers must get to the Callahans at the Sweet Kate Ranch in Paradise, Montana, before the turn of the year. If the deeds aren't presented at the land office by then, they will lose everything. Don't forget to take that letter from Bill, too. It gives us Kenneys the right to finish this job and collect the money owed him. Can you do it, girls?"

"We will do it," said Deidre, and Maura nodded.

"Maybe I ask too much of you," he whispered. " 'Tis dangerous and you're just wee girls."

"Women, Da, and we will do it. Be at ease. We'll do it, if for no other reason than to make certain that the bastards who killed you and Bill won't win."

"That's my girl. How I hate to leave you, but, soon, I will be with my sweet Maggie again."

Soon came an hour later. Deidre and Maura still held his hands as Patrick Kenney breathed his last. They wept as they cleaned his body and dressed him in his Sunday best. It was hard for them to accept that they were alone now, the only surviving members of what had once been a large family.

The sheriff dutifully listened to their tale, but offered little hope of justice. The undertaker showed little sympathy for their loss as he charged them what both women thought an exorbitant amount for little better than a pauper's burial. As they prepared to bury Patrick Kenney, Maura carefully made copies of the deeds and letters that had to be taken to the Callahans, and Deidre made arrangements for the neighbor's oldest son to watch the farm while she and Maura were gone.

It was a gray, chilly day when they buried Patrick Kenney next to his wife, the love of his life. Deidre and Maura stood at his graveside holding hands, lingering long after the last of the mourners had left. They were packed and ready to go but neither was eager to begin what could be a long, dangerous journey.

"I am afraid," whispered Maura.

"So am I," said Deidre. "Terrified. Two men are dead. This is not a simple delivery."

"Well"—Maura took a deep, steadying breath—"we have helped Uncle and Bill before."

"Ye-es, but those jobs did not carry much risk. Until now, the most Papa and Bill risked in their detective and courier work was a punch in the face. These Callahans have some far more serious enemies than jealous husbands and disappointed heirs."

"Are you saying that we should forget about finishing this job?"

"No, we need the money and it's only right that Bill and

Da end their careers as winners. We can't leave it, can't have them dying for nothing."

"And, if the ones after these papers follow us, we might just find a chance for justice as well."

"Exactly. These papers could give us the killers, and I want them." She took a deep breath and looked at Maura. "You've made certain that you have copies of everything?"

"Yes, and that little weasel, Johnnie, made sure that they looked official."

"Maybe I should take the direct route. It could prove to be the more dangerous one."

"No. We tossed for it. It was all fair. Don't worry about me."

"Easier said than done." She hugged Maura. "Take care. I don't want to lose any more of my kin."

Maura kissed Deidre's cheek. "Neither do I." She stepped back, and, smiling faintly, saluted Deidre. "To success and Paradise, Montana."

Deidre saluted her back. "And to justice."

"He should be here by now," grumbled Tyrone Callahan as he scowled out of the window of his front parlor.

"Bill Johnson was highly recommended. Pa trusted him, too. Trusted the man's partner, Paddy Kenney, as well," said Tyrone's brother Mitchell as he sprawled more comfortably in a large wing chair as he closely watched his older brother. "Maybe he's slow because he is being very careful."

"He's a month late and there hasn't been a word. I think it's more than caution." Tyrone took one last look at the acres of the Sweet Kate Ranch spread out in front of the ranch house before turning his attention fully on his brother. "It's November. He should have been here by now, him or Paddy, and all of this nonsense sorted out. Time's running out now."

"What do you suggest we do?"

"Go look for him."

"And if he comes here while we're stumbling around in the cold?"

"Stephen will be here. He can turn the papers in at the land office. He's not only our brother, but a lawyer. He'll know what to do."

"It could be like looking for a needle in a haystack. Worse. We're not sure which needle we'll be looking for— Bill or Paddy."

"I know, but I can't just stand here watching the time slip away."

"Agreed. How do we do this then?" Mitchell asked as he rose, went to the sideboard, and poured them each a whiskey.

"You go the straightest route and I'll take the less direct one." Tyrone moved to stand next to Mitchell and accepted the whiskey. "We meet in Saint Louis at Johnson's office or our lawyer's."

"And if Johnson or Kenney can't be found?"

"Then we send Stephen a telegram and tell him to try and hold off the vultures."

"Damn it, why did Pa have to keep the papers so far away?"

"Maybe because he suspected that the Martins would try to steal everything. Be glad that he was such a cautious bastard. If he hadn't kept legal copies in another place, we'd be destitute and homeless by now."

"I'd still like to know how the Martins got rid of the deeds that were in the land office." Mitchell took a deep breath, pushed aside his anger and touched his glass to Tyrone's in a toast. "Well, then, here's to finding Bill Johnson or that cursed Irishman and spitting in the eye of that thieving bastard, William Martin."

"Here's to success and justice."

Chapter One

AS SHE STOOD QUIETLY waiting for the stage driver to set down her bag, Deidre looked around the town. She was so tired she needed a moment to recall where she was. When she did remember, her spirits were not improved by much. Only half the way there and November was already half gone.

"The hotel's just over there, ma'am," the burly driver said as he set her bag down by her side.

She glanced at the building he pointed to and inwardly sighed. There was one problem with traveling along a meandering trail to Montana, using stages and passing through small towns not considered important enough for trains: accommodations could be rough. Deidre consoled herself with the fact that they were also cheap. She picked up her bag and walked toward the large, plain building with the crudely painted hotel sign swinging precariously over the wide porch steps. At the moment, if the place had a clean bed and could produce a hot bath, she would consider it close to heaven.

Once in her room, Deidre breathed a sigh of relief. Not only was it clean, but it had a private bathroom. The owner clearly had hopes that the town would expand. Perhaps the railroad would indeed be arriving soon, she mused as she secured the door and the window. Clean or not, she was getting tired of hotels and would be glad to go home. It was also going to be nice to finish the job and be safe again, not to have to keep looking over her shoulder, and not to wonder if every stranger was an enemy. Deidre prayed that Maura was safe, that her brilliant idea to divide up did not turn out to be a deadly failure for them both.

"Watch your back, Maura," she whispered as she turned the dull iron taps on and began to fill the tub with water. "If you don't walk into Paradise safe and whole, I'll break your neck."

She laughed softly at her nonsense, but the brief flare of humor did not banish her concern over her cousin. Deidre prayed she had not asked more of Maura than the young woman could accomplish. Maura was not stupid, but she was sweet, trusting, and just a little prim, a little too susceptible to being shocked. A babe in the woods, Deidre thought with a grimace as she undressed for her bath, but that could prove to be protection of a sort. No one would suspect sweet Maura of doing anything daring. Maura could, at times, be so proper, so polite and unassuming, she could disappear in a crowd, pushed from view by the brighter and gayer. Deidre prayed that Maura was doing just that right now, that her cousin was at her most unobtrusive.

After her bath and once her hair was dry, Deidre dressed in a plain dark-gray gown and went down to the dining room. It took all of her willpower to step into the large and, to her dismay, nearly full room. A skinny young man, with a tuft of fair hair on his chin she supposed was a beard, hurried over to her and escorted her to a table. Deidre fought to hide her unease as she found herself seated in the far corner of the large room, a little too close to a large dark man who held the only other small table in the shadows. Even though they were not actually sharing a table, they were seated so near to each other they might as well have been.

While she told the boy what she wanted, she covertly studied her companion in the shadows. He looked big, dark, and dangerous. From his thick, nearly too long black hair to his finely hand-tooled boots, he was a long, leanly muscular and intensely alert man. Pure trouble, she mused as she let her gaze skim over his vaguely hawkish features, his long, patrician nose framed dramatically by high, wide cheekbones. The only softness on his harsh face was from the long, thick lashes on his eyes and the slight, sensual fullness of his mouth. Deidre suspected that could disappear in an instant if he became angry. She could almost see his straight, dark brows veeing harshly over his nose and his mouth tightening to a thin line. She inwardly shook her head at her own fancies as she forced her attention to the rest of the people in the room.

It was not easy to keep her attention fixed upon the others, however, as she waited for her food. She was irritated to find herself constantly glancing at the man, at the way his long fingers held the silverware, the way his black coat hugged his broad shoulders, even at the way his long, muscular legs straddled the stand of the small round table. He made her uneasy, yet she did not fear him, sensed no threat. It was a puzzle and she decided she was simply too travel weary to figure it out. Deidre was grateful when her food was served and she was able to turn all of her attention to eating.

"You Deidre Kenney?" asked a rough voice.

Hesitating only briefly in finishing the bite of tart apple pie she had just taken, Deidre looked at the two men who crowded up to her table. Big and ugly was her first clear thought after she pushed aside a blinding flash of fear. She was astounded at how bold her pursuers had become. Approaching her in a crowded room was bold indeed, and did not bode well for the rest of her journey. Deidre hoped this sudden audacity was not because the men felt safe to do just as they pleased. People had always told her that there was no true civilization and no law in the West, but she had always assumed such talk was no more than rumor or descriptions of a time long past. After all, Saint Louis was considered the West by many east of the Mississippi River and it was extremely civilized. Keeping her expression as sweetly blank as possible, she covertly slipped her hand into a pocket in her skirts, calming a little when she felt the cool metal of the gun she carried. It was only a derringer, but, at this distance, even that could kill a man. She smiled sweetly and plumbed her brain for any scrap of the French she had learned from Mr. Johnson.

"I do not speak English," she said in French, and took a steadying sip of her coffee, wondering if they would fall for the ruse.

The hairier of the two men scratched his gray-speckled beard and scowled at her. "They didn't say you was a foreigner. Deidre Kenney?" he said very slowly as if that would help her understand him better.

Deidre shook her head. *"Open the window."*

"Damnation, Pete," he grumbled to the soft-bellied man at his side. "They said she was from Saint Louis. They talk English in Saint Louis, don't they?"

"Yup, and her pa spoke it real clear, Jim. Hell, I can still hear him cursing us. Real clever with a cuss, he was."

A trickle of panic chilled Deidre's spine. These men had spoken to her father? It sounded as if the meeting had not been a friendly one. She suddenly realized that these were probably the men who had shot her father. Just the thought of it brought anger and grief rushing to the fore and she struggled to push those emotions aside before they showed on her face.

"Perhaps I may be of assistance?" said the tall, dark man seated at the next table.

Deidre looked at the man in horror, then quickly schooled her features. She had no time to let him know that these men could be a threat to her. There was still the chance that her fellow diner could also be a threat to her or, if some reward was offered for her, could soon become one. Worse, she only knew about a dozen French phrases, and many of those were risqué. She tried to calm herself by recalling that she had already replied to the rough men before her with pure nonsense and, if the man at her side truly understood French, he had to know that. Deidre prayed that he was simply trying to lend her a helping hand.

Tyrone Callahan could not believe his luck. Instinct told him that this was indeed Deidre Kenney, Patrick Kenney's daughter. She had the look of the man. He was not sure why she was here, but she could certainly be of some help. Her badly pronounced French told him that she was no foreigner and that she was trying to hide who she was from these men. Even if she was not Patrick's daughter, she clearly did not want anything to do with these men and that was reason enough to lend a hand.

He smiled to himself. Tyrone suspected that her beauty also prompted him to heedlessly jump into the midst of her troubles. She was tiny, with a small but shapely bosom and a very slender waist. Not the more fulsome figure he had always sought out before, but he had not been able to stop covertly watching her as she ate. Her flame-red hair was done up in a soft chignon so fat it looked ready to burst free of its pins at any moment. Huge light-green eyes, encircled by long, thick, brown lashes and set beneath delicately arched brows dominated her small face. Her delicate facial bones, from the high cheekbones to the hint of a point on her small chin, and a small, straight nose made for an enchantingly beautiful face, one that would probably stand the test of time. Her full, faintly pouty mouth gave that cool, elegant beauty a touch of sensuality. Tyrone wondered just how grateful she might be if he helped her.

"You know what she's saying?" asked the man named Jim.

"Yes, some," Tyrone replied, pulling his gaze from the small, long-fingered hand she had tightened around her cup of coffee. "She has told you that she doesn't speak any English."

"What's so hard about replying to a name?" Pete glared at Deidre. "Are you Deidre Kenney?"

"Your mother was a barge whore." Deidre forced herself not to blush.

"What did she say?" demanded Jim.

"That she doesn't understand you," replied Tyrone, biting back a smile.

Jim continued to idly scratch his beard as he watched Deidre with narrowed eyes. "I don't know. The bitch we're looking for is supposed to be traveling through here, this girl looks just right, and yet you're saying she doesn't understand us. Think she's playing some game?"

"Seeing as you just called her a bitch and she didn't flick an eyelash, I would say no," drawled Tyrone.

"Still, how many ladies look like her? Ain't that much chance you'd find two of them between here and Saint Louis." Jim suddenly pulled his gun and aimed it at Deidre's head. "Are you Deidre Kenney?"

As she stared down the barrel of the gun, held so close that she could smell the oil that had been used to clean it,

Deidre decided it would not be suspicious if she revealed her fear. Any sane person would be terrified to suddenly have a gun aimed at her face. She clutched at the arms of her chair, went cross-eyed staring down the barrel of the pistol, and pressed herself back against the chair.

"Why don't you stick that gun up your backside and blow your brains out?" She was not surprised to hear the tremor in her voice. She was so terrified she could not even blush over the taunt she had uttered.

Tyrone slowly closed his hand around the butt of his gun. He cursed himself as a blind fool for not having guessed what Jim or his rough partner might do next. Tyrone had to admire the little woman. She not only had guts, but the wits to know when it was safer to stick to her story.

"I do not believe there is any need to horrify the woman," Tyrone said carefully.

"A good dose of fear's sometimes all it takes to get folk to spit out the truth," drawled Jim, but his stance eased a little. "Don't seem to have worked with this little bitch."

"Then, perhaps, one should assume she is already telling you the truth. She simply has the misfortune to look like the woman you are seeking. You might also consider how most people will view your threat to harm a woman," Tyrone said, glancing around the silent, tense crowd watching them, then signaling with a jerk of his hand for Jim and his friend to do the same. "Not only are you not getting the answers you want, but you're making yourselves damned unpopular." Tyrone nodded when Jim looked around, then slowly reholstered his gun.

"Seeing as the little bitch even squeaked her fright in that foreign gibberish, I reckon she ain't the one we're looking for," Jim said and Pete nodded. "Good day, ma'am," he said, tipping his hat faintly before leaving.

Deidre just watched them leave, too taut and witless to

do anything else. It took her what felt like hours, but was undoubtedly only a moment, to start to ease her grip on her chair. Taking slow, deep breaths, she unclenched her hands, finger by finger, and struggled to loosen terror's rigid grip on her body and her mind.

Then anger began to break through the fear, gaining strength and heating her fear-chilled blood. The man had pointed a gun at her, then politely wished her good day and left? Deidre wished she had the chance and the strength to chase after the man. She desperately wanted to hurt him.

"Are you all right, miss?"

Slowly turning her head, she looked at the man who had tried to help her. Another complication. Although she was deeply grateful for his intervention, she was not in a position to make that clear. Anything other than a terse thank-you would require conversation, perhaps even proper introductions. Deidre could not afford even that fleet and understandable intimacy. She could not allow anyone to know who she was or where she was going and why. She thought Dame Fate especially cruel to present her with such a handsome man at exactly the time when she could not afford to do anything about it. This would forever have to remain only a brief, chance meeting.

"I will be fine," she murmured, absently patting her hair with a still-unsteady hand. "The upset already passes."

"Upset?" Tyrone grinned. "You call some hairy fool sticking a pistol in your face an *upset?*"

"Since I have never had anyone do such a thing to me before, I fear I lack the appropriate word for his extraordinary conduct," she muttered, a little annoyed at being the object of his amusement and yet finding herself made slightly breathless by the beauty of his honest smile.

"Perhaps you can find one in your vast French vocabulary, Miss Kenney."

"How droll, and I have not said that I am Miss Kenney. That fool was mistaken. He needs spectacles."

"Oh, I don't think so. He was right. You do have the look of your father."

"And you feel sure you know who my father is, do you?" Deidre idly wondered just how well traveled her father had been and just how this lean, much younger man might have met him. Unless, she mused, he was just another from the pack of jackals nipping at her heels and was simply far more clever in his approach. Deidre found that thought distressing and wondered why.

"I met Patrick Kenney a few times." Tyrone noticed that she did not reveal any recognition of her father's name. "Not enough to call him friend, but enough to know that you look a lot like him. What I don't understand is why Patrick Kenney has let you travel all alone."

"If Mister Kenney was my father, it would not mean that my business here is any of your concern."

"Oh, but I think it is. Allow me to introduce myself."

Staring at the big, long-fingered hand he held out to her as if it was a multiheaded hydra, Deidre shook her head. "There is no need."

"But there is. I am Tyrone Callahan of Paradise, Montana."

Chapter Two

❦❧❦

"ARE YOU READY TO talk now?"

That deep, drawling voice finally pulled Deidre free of her shock. Her eyes widened when she saw that they were both seated by the window in her hotel room and she held a brandy. Mr. Callahan, if that was really who he was, had taken quick and efficient advantage of her surprise. Deidre could not clearly recall leaving the dining room.

"It is not proper for you to be in my room," she said coolly and took a sip of brandy.

Tyrone almost laughed. She had sounded like the primmest of schoolmistresses. Until now she had looked lost, scared, and stunned. Deidre Kenney clearly had the ability to regain her footing quickly.

"You invited me in," he said, sprawling more comfortably in the chair facing her.

Since she could not recall whether she had or not, she did not argue. "Well, I believe I have adequately thanked you for your kind assistance earlier, so perhaps you might leave before my meager reputation is completely shredded."

"Sorry. Too late. After facing down two thugs and then being carried to your room by a handsome, gallant gentleman—namely myself—I fear you have little reputation left in this town." He smiled gently when she paled slightly. "I should not fret. It'll never get back to Saint Louis, especially since you signed the register with a false name."

Deidre tried to recall everything that had happened since he had introduced himself, but it was impossible. The last thing she remembered with any clarity was a roaring in her ears after he said his name. It was possible that she had fainted, and she inwardly cursed. It was a weak thing to do, something she had never done before. It also meant that she had been completely insensible throughout her first experience of being held in a man's arms. Dame Fate was definitely playing a May game with her. She steadied herself, for none of that was really important now. She had to concentrate on getting this man away from her so that he did not draw any more attention to her or, worse, himself. He had helped her once. Deidre was determined not to tangle him up in her troubles again.

"Why should you think the name I signed was a false one?" she asked.

"There is no need to continue this game, Miss Kenney. I am Tyrone Callahan."

"Am I to simply accept your word for that, sir?"

"Of course not, not Patrick's daughter." From inside his black coat he withdrew a collection of neatly folded papers. "These should give you enough proof."

Setting her brandy down on the small, delicate table between their chairs, Deidre read the papers. It was an odd selection, a few formal documents, one personal letter, a bill of sale for some horses, and a letter from her father

concerning the proofs of ownership she carried. The very
oddness of the assortment led her to feel certain the man
was exactly who he said he was. It was his timely arrival, the
fact that they had met at all, let alone exactly when she was
in need of a helping hand, that made her cling to a ghost
of a doubt.

"Pleased to meet you, Mister Callahan," she said as she
handed him back his papers.

"Are you?" Tyrone murmured. "I think I detected a hint
of doubt still."

"You probably did, as a few remnants do still linger. I
am headed to Paradise by a very confused route, yet, here
you are and at the exact time when you could gallantly
lend me aid and thus ingratiate yourself."

"Ah, yes, the coincidence is enough to raise a question
or two."

"Indeed."

"But, unlike the East, roads, stage routes, and railroad
tracks are not plentiful out here. There really aren't that
many ways to get to Paradise, at least not in any comfort. I
could not envision Johnson, your father, or anyone they
might employ, being the sort to ride across the land, living
rough like some trapper of old." He studied her for a moment as he took a bracing sip of brandy. "What I do not
understand is why are you traveling to Paradise? Where is
your father or Mister Johnson?"

"I fear they are both dead." The sharp grief she still felt
caused her voice to tremble slightly and Deidre took a
deep breath to steady herself. "Mister Johnson was killed
and then, a week later, so was my father."

"My condolences, Miss Kenney."

"Thank you. The loss of both men is still sharply felt."

"I am sure it is." He dragged his fingers through his hair
and stared blindly at the drink he held. "I knew there was
some danger involved. I had just not realized that the danger was a deadly one. Although I've always said the Martins

would do anything to get what they want, I hadn't really considered outright murder."

"The Martins are the ones who don't want you to be able to prove your claims?"

Tyrone nodded, then, suddenly feeling weary, slouched in his seat and rubbed his hand over his chin as he looked at her. "They don't own Paradise yet, but they want to. They've managed to buy, cheat, and steal a large part of it away from a lot of people. Each time they get another piece it adds to the power and wealth they can use to break someone else down."

Deidre nodded. "Such people are never happy with what they have, even when it's more than anyone else. You obviously have a piece they badly want."

"If they get the Callahan mine, they'll hold all the ore rights in the area. Getting my ranch would make them the biggest landowners in Paradise and one of the biggest cattle barons in Montana."

"I see. After they've worked hard to build their little kingdom, you Callahans are preventing them from donning the crown," she murmured, sickened that her father and their dear friend had been murdered for such base reasons. "If you've been in Paradise longer than the Martins, why is there any question of ownership?"

"Somehow they discovered that we didn't have the legal papers to back our claims."

"And there were none in Paradise?"

"There were, but they mysteriously disappeared."

"Along with other deeds, I imagine."

"Yes, but, unlike us, those poor fools didn't have a wiley father." Tyrone smiled faintly. "Pa took one look at the Martins when they arrived and, even though he was dying, made real sure there were copies of all of our legal papers made, signed, witnessed, stamped. verified, and secured far away. Unfortunately, Pa died before he explained exactly why he mistrusted the Martins so. I don't know whether it was a gut instinct or if he knew or had heard of them." He sighed and shook his head. "To be honest, I didn't see what he did until a long time later. It's a good thing that my brothers and I were of a mind to pacify the old man. We did everything he asked even though we thought it was a waste of time and money."

"Perhaps it wasn't the Martins themselves your father knew, but ones like them. But to kill for it all?" she asked, her voice softened by shock and an inability to understand. "I don't think my father and Bill knew how dangerous it all was, either. They weren't cowards, but they wouldn't have taken on the job if they had known people would be trying to kill them. My father always said he didn't mind a good dust-up, doing some running or hiding, or even a little genteel spying and thieving, but he didn't see any gain in putting himself in front of a bullet to get his pay."

"Smart man. I wish to God I'd had the sense to see that was what we were asking of him and Bill," Tyrone said quietly, his voice roughened by guilt. "I would've come after the papers myself if I had realized the Martins would stoop to murder. Who has your father bequeathed the job to?"

Deidre decided the man really was upset, was not just mouthing platitudes, if he had not yet guessed the answer to that question. Instinct told her he would fight it, would try to take over and stop her. She was sure he was who he said he was, and most people would just hand him the papers plus all of the trouble that went with them, but she could not do that. She had promised her father on his deathbed that she would get the papers to Paradise and that was just what she intended to do. There was also Maura to consider. Her cousin was working her way to Paradise as well and there was no way to get word to Maura to tell her to stop or turn around. There was also no way to stop the Martins, to let the enemy know that she and her cousin were no longer involved in it all. Tyrone Callahan could join her, but he would not stop her.

"He bequeathed the job to me and my cousin Maura," she replied, almost smiling at the look of utter shock that transformed his hard features. "I've taken this route and Maura is taking another. We planned it out very well."

Tyrone stared at her determined expression as he fought to put some order into his thoughts. It was impossible to believe that anyone would ask this tiny, pretty woman to take on a job that had already proven mortally dangerous. Yet, they had, and, worse, she looked as if she had every intention of completing her task despite the deaths, even despite having a gun held to her head just a short while ago.

She was fulfilling her father's dying request, he thought with sudden insight, and felt defeated before he had even begun to argue the matter. Her need to get the papers to Paradise was probably all tied up with her grief over her father's death, a grief she probably had not had the time to fully deal with yet. There was also another Kenney female to consider. She might not be easy to reach and thus stop. Tyrone had to doubt that Patrick had been in his right mind when he had thrust the job on to the slender shoulders of two young women. The man might even have thought the Martins would either not suspect women or not threaten them. What happened today proved that the Martins not only knew who had taken over the job but that they were not constrained by any chivalrous impulses.

"It's now obvious that the Martins know at least part of your plan," Tyrone said.

Deidre winced and fought to keep her fears tightly caged. "It would seem so. I can only pray that they don't know about Maura. Not that many in Saint Louis did. We lived just outside the city and only our neighbors knew my cousin had come to live with us. If the Martins' henchmen asked around about the Kenneys, not many would have mentioned Maura, and certainly not thought her one who would take on Da's work. Maura is very shy and sweet and rarely left home."

"If they know you left, they know she left as well."

"Perhaps, but there is nothing that can be done about it."

"There is no way you can reach her? Send a telegram, perhaps?"

"Not really. We decided that was for the best. After all, it might easily help our enemies find us."

He cursed softly, then shrugged an apology when she raised her brows slightly. She was right. In fact, she used the same reasoning he and Mitchell had when they had decided not to contact each other until one or both of them reached Saint Louis. The only way to possibly reach each other as they traveled was by telegraph. Those offices were easily watched and messages easily intercepted. Even without such help, the Martins' thugs were finding their victims easily enough. There was no sense in clearly pointing the way for them.

"How is your cousin getting to Paradise?" he asked.

"She will be riding the train for as long as it is safely possible," Deidre replied, seeing how annoyed he was, and idly wondering which aspect of this miserable tangle they were in irritated him the most.

"That is the way my brother is traveling."

"The chances of your brother and my cousin meeting are very small."

"As small as they were for us to meet?"

"Point taken." She returned his brief smile and then sighed. "They will both be trying to elude the same enemies. That could easily bring them together at some point, I suppose. Does your brother carry some proof of who he is? Maura is not as trusting as I am." She ignored his grin.

"Yes, he has similar papers to what I have. You do realize that the train route is the first one the Martins will check."

Deidre nodded. "They still have to find which train and which woman. Trains, the stations along the way, even the hotels the passengers might stop in, are a lot more crowded than anywhere along the route I am taking. I felt the crowds would offer Maura some protection. Maura is the sort people feel compelled to shelter and protect. Going by train gave her a better chance of gathering such well-meaning people around her. It's also the fastest route, putting her in reach of the enemy for the least amount of time. At least that is what I told myself after she won, or lost, if you prefer, the toss. We are to meet in Paradise."

It was clear that Deidre thought herself stronger and better able to protect herself than her cousin Maura. Tyrone wondered just what sort of young woman was riding the train to Paradise, expecting to elude the murderous Martins, and then deliver her packet of papers. The whole thing was ludicrous, yet he knew there was no stopping it. The best he could hope for was averting tragedy. He did not want his future prosperity bought by the blood of two young women. He was sure his brothers would agree.

"We will travel to Paradise together," he said.

Even though the man's expression and his tone of voice indicated that he would heed no argument, Deidre felt herself compelled to make one. Pure contrariness, she supposed. "We will, will we? I don't believe I invited you along."

Tyrone leaned forward in his chair, resting his arms on his legs and clasping his hands. "You didn't, but, to be blunt, you'd be a fool not to." The sudden spark that entered her fine green eyes told him that he was not endearing himself, but now was not the time to cater to offended sensibilities. "The Martins have tracked you down. They'll be nipping at your heels all the way to Paradise. You need someone to watch your back. Today proved that."

"Traveling with a single gentleman for days on end could seriously inhibit the smooth return to my life in Saint Louis."

"So could a bullet in the heart."

"Quite. Fine then, we shall travel together. We can watch each other's back."

"Good. I will send word to the lawyer Mitchell and I were going to meet in Saint Louis. Even if the Martins catch wind of it, it won't make much difference. They already know we are here and it won't take them long to figure out we'll be together from now on. Now, if you'll just give me the papers."

"And have you slip away and leave me behind? I think not."

It took almost an hour to get Tyrone to leave. He badgered her for the papers until they were both so angry it was impossible even to be vaguely courteous. As Deidre shut and locked the door after him, she breathed a sigh of relief even though she knew he had not given up. She did, however, look forward to some rest before having to go another round with the man. His stubborn refusal to concede had given her a headache. She smiled faintly as she prepared for bed. The man was obviously as hardheaded and stubborn as she was.

Once washed and dressed in her voluminous nightgown, she took a headache powder and crawled into bed. The events in the dining room had shaken her. Despite her arguments, she knew she would be glad to finish the treacherous journey with a strong man at her side. Tyrone was right. The Martins had tracked her down and would dog her heels every step of the way now. They wanted her dead, and the papers she carried destroyed. Deidre realized that, despite the murder of Bill and her father, she had not truly accepted the danger she was in until she had stared down the barrel of that gun in the dining hall. Her womanhood was obviously no protection at all and she wondered if she had truly been fool enough to think it would be.

Closing her eyes and forcing herself to relax, she reached out a little desperately for the peace of sleep. Not only would it give her some rest from the hard knot of fear in her belly, but she needed to keep up her strength for the days ahead. The race to Paradise was well and truly begun now. Not only were the Martins a threat, but instinct told her Tyrone Callahan could be one as well, at least to her peace of mind. That dark-eyed Irishman had stirred her interest in a way no man ever had, and she had just agreed to spend days, weeks perhaps, in close proximity with him. She murmured a curse as sleep started to tug her into its comforting hold. Maybe she was a fool.

Chapter Three

~~~

A DIRTY, CALLUSED HAND pressed tightly over her mouth yanked Deidre out of her pleasant, mildly sensual dream concerning a tall, dark-eyed man. She stared at the two men flanking her bed and screamed, even though she knew it to be a useless waste of breath. Her mind clearing of the last vestiges of sleep, Deidre sank her teeth into the rank hand that was nearly smothering her.

The bellowed curse of pain coming from her captor as he released his tight grip on her mouth was sweet music to her ears. She wasted no time in savoring her triumph, however, but lunged off the bed even as the men tried to grab her. It was Pete and Jim again, she realized as she raced for the door. It had been a mistake to think that she had fooled them or that they had given up. The Martins were undoubtedly offering the sort of reward that prompted such persistence.

Just as she started to open the door, Jim got near enough to slam his bleeding hand against it and close it. She ducked his grasp, punching him in the belly before she darted out of his reach. The bathroom was the only other place to go and she ran for it, tossing anything she could grab into the path of the two men stumbling after her and all the while screaming for help at the top of her lungs.

"Dammit, Pete, she's going to bring the whole town up here," snapped Jim.

"We still got a minute to grab her. They'll come to the door. Search her things."

Deidre cursed when she reached the bathroom, slammed the door, and locked it. It did not look strong enough to hold back two determined men. And it meant that she could do nothing to stop Jim from searching through her things. The papers were well secured in a hidden packet of the dress she had worn to dinner. It should not be easy to find, but there was always the chance that Jim would get lucky. When the door shuddered beneath Pete's assault, she pressed herself against it, looked around for something she could use as a weapon, and prayed someone had heard her cries.

Tyrone cursed as he struggled into his pants. It was startling enough to be rudely jerked awake by a woman's screams. Instinct told him who was doing the screaming and that only enhanced his sense of urgency. Deidre obviously had not stayed safe for long, he thought as he yanked on his boots, grabbed his gun, and hurried out of his room.

The manager and two burly men arrived at Deidre's

door at the same time he did. Tyrone looked at the thin, pale manager fumbling with the keys and snapped, "Hurry up! You're giving them enough time to kill her and make a clean escape."

"Do you know this woman?" The manager finally got the right key in the lock.

"Yes, she is my fiancée," Tyrone lied, his gut clenching with fear when he realized that Deidre was no longer screaming for help. "Met her here to take her back to Montana for the wedding."

"I hope your journey back home begins tomorrow."

It did not take a genius to know that he and Deidre had just been asked to leave town. Tyrone could not see how the manager could possibly think this was all Deidre's fault, but, as the door opened, he knew it was not time to argue. He pushed by the others, entering the room in time to see a man climbing out the window. Tyrone let the hotel guards go after him, knowing there was little chance of capturing the intruder, and looked around for Deidre. When he did not see her, he briefly panicked, thinking the intruder might have taken her with him.

"Is the girl with him?" he demanded, striding toward the window.

"Nope," answered the guard who had stayed inside while his partner had scrambled out on the roof of the front porch. "Two men. No girl."

"Deidre!" Tyrone yelled, looking around the room again, then striding toward the door that led to the bath.

"That you, Tyrone?" Deidre called back from behind the door.

"Yes. Open the damned door."

Relief washed over Deidre with such force she felt light-headed. Fighting the urge to sink to the floor and stay there until she could stop shaking, she struggled to unlock the door, her hands trembling so badly it took several tries. Finally, she got the door open, took one look at a fiercely scowling Tyrone, and flung herself into his arms. Guns with dinner and men trying to steal her from her bed was more adventure than she could tolerate with any semblance of calm. She had only just met Tyrone Callahan, but, even furious and half dressed, he looked like a pillar of strength and safety at the moment.

Tyrone stuck his pistol on the table near the door and wrapped his arms around Deidre. He had been startled when she had flung herself against him, but he was more than willing to offer some comfort. Turning slightly, he looked at the other men as he rubbed his hands up and down Deidre's slim back in an effort to still her trembles. He struggled to ignore the fact that, even in a nightgown he was sure could be wrapped around her twice, she was an enticing little bundle to hold on to.

"Did you catch them?" he asked, even though he saw the second guard climbing back in through the window empty-handed and breathless.

"No," replied the returning guard as he brushed himself off. "They got down into the side alley where they had horses waiting. It didn't look as if they had anything, certainly nothing that couldn't just be slipped into a pocket."

"Do you think it's worth calling in the sheriff? Did you recognize either man?"

"Nope," the man answered. "Both strangers."

"Unless you wish it, sir," said the hotel manager, "I see no need to disturb the sheriff. It could prove most embarrassing for your fiancée."

"Your *what?*" Deidre squawked, the manager's words shoving aside all of her upset, but her words were muffled because Tyrone put one big hand on the back of her head and shoved her face against his broad, smooth chest.

As Tyrone politely agreed that there was no need for the law to become involved, Deidre lost interest in the discussion. Her attention, indeed all of her senses, became fixed upon the chest she was so tightly pressed against. It was a distractingly handsome chest, muscular yet not too ridged and swollen by strength. He smelled nice, too, a mixture of a subtle, spicy cologne and something else. Eau de Tyrone, she mused, then wondered if being held so close to so much warm, male flesh had affected her mind. She struggled to listen to what was being said and not give in to the shocking urge to kiss that lovely chest, maybe even give it a quick little taste with her tongue. Then something the manager said as he was leaving fully caught her attention.

"It may have helped, sir," the manager said in a cool, polite, but chiding voice, "if you had made your relationship to this woman clear from the beginning. These sort of difficulties do not arise unless it is thought that the woman is alone, unprotected. Women today seem unaware of the troubles they cause with their unnatural bids for independence. In truth, I almost refused her a room when I thought she was traveling alone."

"You pompous . . . Mmph." Deidre glared at Tyrone over the hand he had clamped over her mouth.

Deidre considered biting Tyrone as she had one of her attackers, then contented herself with muttering her rather foul opinion of the hotel clerk under the muffling security of Tyrone's palm. Tyrone loosened the pressure of his hand, but did not remove it until the door closed behind the manager and the two guards. He then cautiously removed his hand and watched her as she strode over to the brandy decanter and poured herself a drink.

"I cannot believe that weasel thought that this was all my fault," she said after a bracing sip of her brandy.

Tyrone moved to pour himself a drink, then sprawled in the chair he had occupied earlier. "I will concede that it is grossly unfair, but this was not the time to try and enlighten the fool."

"Actually, I was not considering giving him a bracing lecture. I was going to punch him in his long, pointy little nose."

He laughed softly. "And that would have gotten us tossed out tonight instead of tomorrow morning."

"He has asked us to leave?" Deidre sank down into the chair facing him, not sure if she was more shocked or annoyed. If it ever got back to Saint Louis that she had been kicked out of a hotel, she would be utterly mortified.

"Yes. It doesn't really matter if he thinks it's our fault there was trouble or if we could ever convince him otherwise. The trouble came with us. He wants it gone."

"And, sad to say, it will indeed follow us when we leave. That little, pompous weasel will think himself all correct and justified in his nauseating attitudes."

Deidre looked at Tyrone and suddenly realized how scandalously they were behaving. He wore no shirt and she wore only her nightgown, modest though it was. Even her hair was loose. She told herself there had been no choice. In the midst of an attack she had had no time to don her dress and do her hair, and she was very glad that Tyrone had not been too concerned with propriety to rush to her aid. Deidre used those sensible thoughts to force aside the blush that was threatening to burn her cheeks.

"Why did the hotel manager think I was your fiancée?" she asked.

"Because I told him you were," Tyrone replied calmly, but watched her closely as he sipped his drink.

"Why would you tell that puffed-up little worm such a tale?"

"I was not sure he would let me inside the room to help you. A few things he said when I first arrived told me he was a stickler for the proprieties." Tyrone smiled briefly. "I think he might have insisted I return to my room, dress appropriately, and shave before he formally announced me."

She giggled and shook her head. "One has to wonder where he and his outrage were when those two men accosted me in the dining room and stuck a gun in my face."

"Safely behind his desk, I suspect. It was the same two men?"

"Oh, yes. I obviously did not fool them at all with my schoolgirl French."

"If I recall a few of those phrases correctly, I must take leave to doubt that any schoolgirl would know them."

This time she did blush, but only faintly. "Riverboat French then, the tutor being Bill Johnson. Well, I thank you for rushing to my rescue yet again, Mister Callahan, but I believe I will seek my rest now. I suspect I will not be allowed a leisurely breakfast and departure in the morning."

"Fine. Your room or mine."

"Excuse me?"

"Do you want to stay here or will you come and stay in my room?"

Although instinct told Deidre that he was not proposing some sordid liaison, she was still outraged by the suggestion. "You will trot off to your room like a good boy and I will stay right here."

Tyrone set his glass down and stood up. He leaned toward her, placing a hand on each arm of the chair, and effectively caging her there. Her eyes widened slightly, but he was pleased to see only wariness and not fear. Even though she refused to give him the papers, she obviously trusted him to some extent. Although, he mused as he studied her with her glorious hair rippling over her slim shoulders in thick waves all the way to her gently curved hips, she might be wise to fear him just a little bit. Despite her extremely virginal nightgown, the sight and scent of her, the proximity of her full lips, had his body hardening with keen interest.

"Now, Miss Kenney, I have been a patient man," he said, and ignored the soft derisive noise she made. "I have accepted the fact that you have taken over your father's obligations. I gave in to your insistence that you hold on to the papers that are rightfully mine. I have agreed to allow you to accompany me to Paradise despite the added danger and difficulty that will arise. However, after what has just happened and what occurred in the dining room, I insist that we stick close together. If that offends your delicate sensibilities, then I am sorry."

"No, you're not," she muttered, then pressed her lips together when he scowled at her.

"If you must go to Paradise with me, then you will accept my protection and not complain about the form it takes or any inconveniences that may result."

"We are talking about more than inconveniences, sir. We are talking scandal, the complete blackening of my name should any of this ever reach the ears of anyone in Saint Louis."

"You would rather they hear about your untimely death?"

Deidre clenched her hands into small, tight fists and glared at him, fighting the urge to punch him squarely in his firm, beard-shadowed jaw. He had already used that threat to her life to bend her to his will once. It was evident that he intended to use that particular cudgel as often as necessary, and she was already heartily sick of it. What truly upset her, however, was the thought of being in his company day and night. He stirred all of her senses, and that frightened her. There would be no time for her to step back, to get away from his increasingly intoxicating presence and restore herself to some state of calm, to regain some distance from him. That was not something she could explain to him, however. She would have to cling to the argument concerning the impropriety of it all, and it was clear that he was not about to heed any of that.

"Sir, you may not realize it, but, quite often, a good name is all a poor girl has to cling to," she said.

"Oh, I realize that. I'm also sure that, by the time we get to Paradise, we'll have thought of some good explanation, something that will soothe most of those ruffled feathers.

That is assuming there will be any need to do so. I think the chances of any news of your adventures reaching those you know in Saint Louis are pretty small, especially since you are traveling as Mrs. Irene Williams. In fact, if you stick to that name whenever we may stop, or another, it will give you a perfect chance to deny it all."

She had not considered that, and she frowned at him, annoyed that he had. "It might work."

"You know it will." He stood up, grasped her by the hand, and tugged her into his arms. "Why, you could do a great deal of misbehaving beneath the shelter of that name."

"Misbehaving?" she snapped, and started to push him away.

Pretending he misread her shock as confusion or surprise, he tightened his hold on her. Tyrone suspected he would pay dearly for stealing a kiss, but the temptation to do so was too strong to ignore. The look that briefly flared in her eyes as he touched his mouth to hers hinted that she was as curious as he. It could explain why she had not yet fought herself free of his firm but easily breakable hold.

"Misbehaving," he whispered. "Like this."

Deidre went still in his arms as he pressed his lips against hers. She knew, to her shame, that it was not all shock or uncertainty that kept her from shoving him away or hitting him. A part of her, a dangerously large part of her, was eager to be kissed by him. She had accepted a few chaste kisses from beaux in Saint Louis and fought free of a few mauling ones, but never had a man as heartwrenchingly handsome as Tyrone Callahan ever shown an interest in kissing her. One quick kiss, she mused, could not hurt anything, especially if she followed it with a hasty retreat and the appropriate show of outraged modesty. As he began to nibble at her lips, Deidre realized there could indeed be a great deal of danger in even one stolen kiss.

She slid her hands up his chest to clutch at his broad shoulders as he nudged her lips apart with the gentle proddings of his tongue. When he began to stroke the inside of her mouth, she trembled, her grip tightening slightly as unknown yet thrilling sensations tore through her. It terrified her and confused her to discover that a man's kiss could affect her so completely and deeply. What truly worried her was that loud, demanding part of her that did not care, did, in fact, relish it. There was clearly a devil inside her, and Tyrone Callahan was what was needed to draw it out.

"Ah, now that is sweet," he murmured as he began to kiss his way to the soft hollow at the base of her throat. "Sinfully sweet."

It took every scrap of scattered willpower she could pull together, but Deidre heard the word *sin,* planted it firmly in her mind, and used it to rally her strength. Still tingling from his kiss and a little unsteady on her feet, she pulled free of his hold and hurriedly put some distance between them. The man was ruination and temptation on two long legs. She was almost tempted to give him his papers and run back to Saint Louis as fast as she could. Only the thought of Maura, the danger her cousin might be in, and the need to meet her in Paradise kept her from doing just that.

Tyrone fought to control the urge to drag her back into his arms. She enflamed him, and her response to his kiss, brief and untutored though it was, told him his passion was returned. He wanted to explore and satisfy it in all of its promised glory, but he could see that he had at last frightened her. Deidre had obviously never had her passions stirred before, a thought that made his desire harder to control, but Tyrone held back. She would have to be seduced, carefully, slowly. It was ungentlemanly to consider the seduction of such an obvious innocent, but the way Deidre made him feel was far from gentlemanly.

"Get your things together and we'll go to my room," he said, watching her closely.

"Oh, we will, will we?"

"Yes. They know where you are now."

That made her stop and think. Twice she had been assaulted and the two men had escaped capture. She did not really want to stay and see if they would try for a third time. Tyrone Callahan might be a serious threat to her morals and her peace of mind, but Jim and Pete were a threat to her very life.

"Fine," she snapped as she moved to put on her robe and collect her belongings, covertly stealing a quick feel in the hidden pocket of her gown and pleased to feel the papers still there. "I really don't have any choice in this. But, there will be no more *misbehaving.*" She paused to glare at him. "Do I make myself clear, Mister Callahan?"

"Very," he murmured as he took her bag and gently pushed her toward the door.

He watched Deidre walk toward his room, his gaze fixed upon the gentle sway of her hips, a movement accentuated by the swish of her thick hair. The sweet, intoxicating taste of her was still on his tongue. If Deidre Kenney thought he would not be trying for another taste and a lot more besides, she was not as smart as he thought she was. The trip to Paradise was going to be long, hard, and fraught with danger, but Tyrone felt himself heartily looking forward to it.

Martins' thugs." She silently cursed, and left him to nego-
tiate with the man selling the horses.

She leaned against the side of the large stables and
watched the people of the town hurry about their business. It had always been her dream to travel, but this was
not what she had had in mind. Not only was it the wrong
time of the year, but the only thing she had time to watch
for was the approach of one or more of the men working
for the Martins. If there was anything else worth looking
at, she was too busy trying to get to Paradise alive to look
for it. Perhaps, when it was all over and the money for the
job was paid, she and Maura could take a small trip together somewhere.

As if compelled to, she looked at Tyrone, who was now
arguing over the price of the saddles, and sighed. He had
not kissed her again and she almost hated the part of her
that was sorely disappointed by that. Last night she had ignored his taunts and sarcasm and gone to sleep in one of
the chairs in his room. Sometime after she had fallen
asleep, however, he had put her into the bed by his side.
When she had opened her eyes this morning he had been
right there, staring at her, one strong arm encircling her
waist. To her embarrassment, she had squeaked in alarm
and moved away so fast she had fallen out of bed. His soft
laughter had followed her into the bathroom. Then, to further her sour mood, the hotel manager had only grudg-
ingly allowed them to breakfast before practically escorting
them out of the hotel personally. All in all, the day had not
begun well and she saw little chance of improvement.

What really preyed on her mind was what to do about
Tyrone or, more specifically, what he made her feel. She
could still taste his kiss. Even thinking about it was
enough to make her blood warm and her heart beat
faster. Deidre did not think it was just the newness of such
feelings that made them so hard to fight. They were proving too fierce, too tempting, to completely banish. She

tried to tell herself that it was so strong because she was lonely and afraid, her resistance weakened by that and a lingering grief, but her more sensible, honest self scoffed at that explanation.

The hard truth she fought to ignore was that she was afraid of the feelings he stirred inside her. They were too strong, too overwhelming. She knew nothing of this man except what little her father had told her or made note of, and none of those little insights had been the kind to help her much. They had not told her if he was the sort of man who would bed her then leave her, for instance, or if he was the sort of man who enjoyed many women. The biggest problem with Tyrone Callahan, however, the strongest reason why she should keep her wits about her and not succumb to whatever strange bewitchment flared between them, was who the man was. He was too handsome for any woman's peace of mind and he was rich, part of the growing society of powerful cattlemen and miners in the West. He was, in a word, too big a prize for a poor, skinny Irish girl from just outside of Saint Louis. Men like him built their futures with tall, well-shaped society women educated in the finest ladies' seminaries, ones with crisp accents, blond curls, and big blue eyes. Ladies with fashion sense and their own exclusive modistes. Ladies with two last names. Girls like herself were fondly remembered bachelor follies or that discreet little bit on the side. The Deidre Kenneys of the world only got burned if they tried to reach so high. Deidre feared it would not be too long before she risked that fate just to experience the fevered joy of being Tyrone's lover. It began to look as if Patrick Kenney's little girl would pay very dearly indeed to fulfill his dying request.

"Now we need to go and buy our supplies," Tyrone said as he stepped up beside her and hooked her arm through his before striding off toward the mercantile store. "Food, warm clothes, blankets."

"Are you sure we can't just take the stage or a train?" she asked. "Maybe we could just outrun them?"

"You haven't yet, have you?"

Deidre decided the way Tyrone could ask questions that shattered her arguments could become extremely tiresome. "No, but I'm not sure riding across country in the dead of winter will help much, either." She watched Tyrone out of the corner of her eye as they entered the store. "In fact, we could be helping the Martins. They'd certainly be pleased to know that they drove us out into the cold, barren wastelands and won't hear another word about us until the spring sun thaws out our pathetic corpses."

Tyrone bit back a laugh as he picked up a couple of thick blankets and thrust them into her arms. "Such a dour outlook. Not a hint of optimism. I certainly have no intention of leaving a pathetic corpse."

"A handsome one then." She grimaced slightly when he proceeded to hold up heavy, warm, and very ugly coats, trying to judge her size. "Although, it'll be unlikely if we're wearing something like that."

"We seek warmth, not style."

"A good thing, too, if that is all there is." When he moved to look at the women's clothing, she quickly shoved the blankets into his arms and snatched the coat he had been holding. "I will pick out some warm clothes myself, thank you." She nudged him toward the men's clothing. "You see to your own." She hastily tried on the coat, grimacing when the heavy wool coat, dyed a dull blue, actually fit. "Think it can repel snow?"

"We are having a very mild winter."

"That could change with a dangerous swiftness."

"Which is why I have plotted a trail that keeps us safely close to places where we may seek shelter."

She paused in looking over some flannel petticoats and eyed him with suspicion. "This is not a sudden decision, is it."

"Oh, it is, but I did plan for it before I left Paradise. Don't forget some thick, warm stockings," he said as he moved away to look over the selection of men's clothing.

A heavy sigh escaped her as she glanced toward the stockings. By the time she donned all of the warm clothes she was going to look like a walking lump of wool and flannel. What few curves she had would disappear after only one layer. These were not the sort of clothes meant to attract and hold a man's attention.

Then she cursed. Why was she worrying about that? Perhaps, she thought suddenly, because she was female and he was the handsomest man she had ever seen. He could also kiss her in a way that melted her bones and seared away every last vestige of good sense she had. There could well be an advantage to wearing so many thick, unattractive clothes, she mused as she snatched up a pair of black wool stockings and added them to her growing pile of clothing. If Tyrone tried to seduce her, there would be so much to remove, she would have plenty of time to come to her senses. Deidre just prayed that would happen, but had the sinking feeling she could just as easily help him with the unwrapping.

By the time they were done buying the clothes and supplies they needed, Deidre understood why Tyrone had bought a third horse, a rather homely but sturdy animal. While Tyrone packed their belongings on the docile beast, she was shown to the tack room so that she could change into her scratchingly new warm clothes. She put her other clothes away while Tyrone changed, surreptitiously tying the secret pocket which held the papers beneath her skirts.

As they rode out of town, Deidre decided that sometime soon she was going to have to tell Tyrone where she kept the papers. There was always the chance that something could happen to her and he would need to know. She was not exactly sure why she had not told him yet. There was still no doubt in her mind that he was Tyrone

Callahan and that he was as anxious as she to get the papers to Paradise on time, yet she hesitated to hand them over. She no longer believed he would take them and run, for he knew the men after her would not stop until they could see with their own beady eyes that she no longer had the deeds. All Deidre could think was that, in some odd way, she could still feel as if she was fulfilling her promise to her father if she held the papers even if she had, more or less, handed the problem of getting to Paradise alive over to Tyrone.

Deidre thought of the dangerous journey ahead, of the danger she had just barely escaped, and then thought of Maura. She prayed her cousin was having more luck than she was. If fate was kind, Tyrone's brother had stumbled upon Maura just as Tyrone had stumbled upon her. It was galling to admit that a man was needed to get the job done, but Deidre was not so choked with pride that she could ignore that truth. The closer she and Maura got to Paradise, the harder the Martins would try to stop them, and a set of broad shoulders plus a steady gun hand would not be amiss.

"Worrying about your cousin?" Tyrone asked as he paced his horse to ride by Deidre's side.

"Yes." She grimaced. "Despite the murders which set us on this path, I guess I never really considered such things as guns stuck in my face or men attacking me in the middle of the night."

"Unless it's something one's dealt with before, such threats are hard to consider."

"Perhaps, or, perhaps I was fool enough to think your enemies wouldn't think that a woman could or would take on the job."

"Or that they would have some scrap of chivalry in them and not actually hurt you?"

"That, too, I guess. A strange arrogance I didn't realize

I suffered from." She sighed. "And one that has set Maura in the sights of those killers. Well, there is no turning back now. I can't do anything for Maura, either, except to worry."

"And that won't help her much. Best to concentrate on yourself, selfish as that sounds; set your mind to getting yourself safely to Paradise. Once there, if Maura isn't there waiting, you'll have the freedom to do something."

She stared out over the empty land they had to cross and nodded. "And, if I get to Paradise, the Martins will know that they have lost and the threat to Maura should end."

"Maybe you should've warned us that you and Maura had taken on your father's job."

Deidre briefly considered that, wondering if she had erred, then shook her head. "The Martins discovered you were having the papers brought in by Bill and Da. They knew those two men were dead and that's why they now hunt me and maybe Maura. I suspect they would've managed to know if I had sent word to you, plus there would've been a delay while I waited for a reply or for us to sort out a new plan. Maybe the Martins were surprised that two women would take over the job and that's why I got almost half the way to Paradise before any real trouble started."

Tyrone hesitated a moment before reluctantly nodding in agreement. "Let's hope Maura got even farther."

"And then meets your brother?" She glanced up at the gray skies, the sun a weak, pale circle that only made it feel colder. "Does he also have an escape plan if the trains prove too dangerous?"

"He does. The routes we each chose are ones we've traveled before, many times. Have done for years. We have friends, relations, and even our own small cabins scattered all along the routes." He smiled at her expression of puzzled curiosity. "We traded horses for years, liked to hunt and fish, and also had business interests back East. Pa never liked the direct routes except for the simplest business. Felt it let too many crooks track you too easily."

"Well, we can now be grateful for his suspicious nature." She winced as an icy wind gusted around them. "Maybe."

Tyrone laughed softly and reached over to wrap her scarf more thoroughly around her neck. "We'll have shelter every night and if the weather turns poorly."

"This is nice weather, is it?"

Deidre silently cursed when he just grinned in reply. She hated the cold, always had, but it seemed she was now doomed to spend a long time suffering in it. It was a shame, she thought crossly, that there was no law which would allow her to make the Martins pay for her extreme discomfort.

The sun had almost set by the time Tyrone led them to a tiny cabin. She helped him settle the horses in the small but sturdy stable attached to the cabin, then stood slowly unwrapping herself as Tyrone built a fire in the stone fireplace. Once stripped to her heavy wool dress, she stood before the fire, soaking up its warmth and looked around. The cabin was surprisingly clean and well stocked with wood for the fire, but what made her frown was that it consisted of just one room and one bed.

"It'll warm up in here fast," Tyrone said as he filled a heavy kettle with water from the small sink pump set in a far corner of the room.

"Ye-es, it's very cozy," she murmured, wondering how one delicately approached the subject of their sleeping arrangements.

He grinned at her as he hooked the kettle over the fire and began to make coffee. She was so easy to read, her thoughts clear to see on her expressive little face. Although the cabin was a perfect setting for a seduction, Tyrone knew it was still too soon, Deidre still too wary.

"You can have the bed," he said as he retrieved some beans and bacon from one of his packs. "There's a decent sleeping mat in the chest at the foot of the bed. I'll use that." He concentrated on starting their supper, suspecting that what he was going to say next would discomfort her. "There's an outhouse a few steps outside the back door."

Deidre blushed faintly and hurried out the door. That had been her next question, but it had been stuck in her throat. Since she and Tyrone would be traveling together for several weeks, that was an awkwardness she was going to have to overcome. If nothing else, the man had better things to do than worry about catering to her modesty at every turn.

Supper was plain but filling. As Deidre cleaned the dishes and pans, however, she prayed she was not facing weeks of beans, bacon, and pan biscuits. It was good food, but it could quickly become tedious.

It was when she was ready to go to bed that Deidre faced her next dilemma. She did not really wish to sleep in her clothes. After a brief twinge of modesty, she decided her voluminous flannel nightgown was suitable enough, certainly nothing that would inspire a man's lust. Unfortunately, there was no place for her to change into it. She tugged it out of her bag, frowned at it, and was considering possible alternatives when she felt Tyrone's stare.

"I will turn my back," he drawled and, the moment she glanced his way, did so, facing the fireplace as he took a long, thin cigar out of his shirt pocket and lit it.

For only a moment, Deidre hesitated, then scolded herself for her lack of trust. Tyrone had already had plenty of opportunity to force himself upon her if he was so inclined and he had not done so. Nevertheless, she changed quickly, leaving her chemise and stockings on for added modesty as well as warmth. She carefully laid her clothes over the footboard of the bed, took her brush out of her bag, and, fighting a blush, went to sit by the fire to brush out and braid her hair.

Tyrone watched her as she unpinned her hair, his breath catching in his throat as the thick waves tumbled free. He knew Deidre had no idea how erotic it was for a man to watch a woman brush out her hair, but the fact that the temptation was innocently inflicted did not lessen its power. He ached to replace that brush with his fingers, to bury his face in those bright waves of soft hair. When a cross look faintly pinched her face as she struggled to braid her hair, he hastily grabbed the opportunity to indulge at least part of his fantasies.

"I can do that for you," he said, pleased at how normal his voice sounded. "You seem to be having a little trouble."

"Maura and I usually do each other's hair at night," she explained, blushing slightly as she considered how many rules she would be breaking if she accepted his offer. "If it would not be too much trouble."

"None at all." He tossed the stub of his cigar into the fireplace, took her hand in his, and tugged her to her feet.

"Do you know how to braid a woman's hair?" she asked as he turned her so that her back was toward him and took her brush.

"Can't be too much different from doing a horse's tail."

Deidre laughed briefly. "No, I suppose not."

A moment later, Deidre wondered if she had made a serious error in judgment. There was something upsettingly intimate about the simple act he was performing for her. She had always liked to have her hair brushed, but, when Maura did it, it was soothing. Feeling Tyrone slide the brush through her hair had her heart beating faster. It was even worse when he set the brush on the mantel and began to braid her hair. He stood so close she could feel his heat, a warmth that seeped into her, entering her blood and flowing through her body. As he slowly braided her hair, his fingers brushed against her, and each light touch sent a spark through her. She was mortified to feel her nipples tauten, and crossed her arms over her chest. Even more horrifying was the sense of aching fullness, even a light dampness, that formed between her legs. When he smoothed his hand down her finished braid and she felt him press a kiss to the back of her head, she trembled. Time to retreat, she thought, feeling a little frantic.

"Thank you," she squeaked, and hurriedly pulled away.

Tyrone watched Deidre nearly run to the bed and climb in, disappearing beneath the blankets until little more than the top of her head was visible. Amusement began to soften the frustration he felt. So did the knowledge that his hunger for her would soon be satisfied. He knew she was drawn to him, perhaps even as strongly as he was drawn to her. There was no misreading the subtle signs she had inadvertently given him as he had done her hair. Her breathing had grown uneven, she had begun to sway toward him, and she had trembled beneath his touch, light though it was. Deidre had just run away, not out of modesty, but out of fear of what he could make her feel. Tyrone was sure of it.

As he banked the fire, secured the door, and laid out his bedding near the fire, he decided he would allow her to retreat for now. There was time to slip beneath the barriers of modesty and maidenly reticence. As he stripped down to his drawers and slipped beneath his blankets, Tyrone hoped she did not make him suffer for too long.

"Good night, Deidre," he called.

Deidre silently cursed as she detected that hint of amusement in his deep, too attractive voice. The rogue probably knew exactly why she had just run away from him and hidden beneath the covers like a timid child. A man who looked as good as Tyrone undoubtedly had a lot of wordly experience. He could think what he wished, she decided, but it would be a cold day in hell before she ad-

Chapter Five

THE STRONG SMELL OF coffee crept through Deidre's nose into her sleep-clogged mind and she tried to force it away. After three days of travel, she was exhausted. She had barely stayed awake through the delicious meal the small-town boardinghouse had offered. All she had been able to think of was crawling into bed. Now someone was trying to tempt her out of her warm, soft haven with coffee. *Tyrone,* she mused, suddenly recalling that he had told the owner of the boardinghouse that they were married so that they could share a room, a plan she had been too weary to argue with.

A hand smoothed down her braid and she murmured with sleepy pleasure at the touch. Tyrone, the rogue, was obviously stealing a caress, something he did with increasing frequency. Deidre knew she ought to swat him for his impertinence, but she was too tired to lift her arm. When she felt something big and warm lie down beside her, however, she scowled and struggled to shake off the last vestiges of sleep.

"Get off my bed, Tyrone," she muttered, then drew her breath in so sharply she nearly choked when his warm, soft lips touched the hollow behind her ear. "Cut that out."

"I thought a little pleasant nuzzling might help you wake up," he said.

The way his deep voice rumbled against her skin as he kissed her cheek and then her forehead made her shiver. "The coffee was working."

"Was it? Well, the nuzzling got you talking."

She opened one eye and tried to glare at him. "Nuzzling could also get someone smacked offside the head."

He laughed against her neck and Deidre wondered if one's bones could really melt, for hers certainly felt as if they were. "This is highly improper. I am in bed and not dressed."

"Between that flannel tent you call a nightgown and all of these blankets, you are wrapped up like a mummy."

There was a disgruntled tone to his voice that nearly made her smile. "A good thing, too, if I'm to be plagued by rogues trying to sneak a little."

"A little what?"

He licked her ear and every thought in her head vanished. "What?"

"You said I was trying to sneak a little. A little what?"

"Sugar," she gasped, shuddering when he stuck his tongue in her ear and wondering how something so odd could have her feeling as if she were on fire. "Stop that." She struggled to free her arm from the bedcovers so that she could push him away.

The minute Deidre got her arm free and shifted

around to give him a good push, Tyrone nudged her fully onto her back and sprawled on top of her. Even through the thick covers, the feel of his body on top of hers made Deidre's pulses race. Although he pestered her, stealing kisses and caresses, he never really took more than she was willing to give. He coaxed and seduced, but seemed to know when her protests became heartfelt ones and stopped. The problem was, her heartfelt *stops* were growing fewer. She was growing more and more willing to give him everything he asked for. Very soon she was going to have to make a decision to either put a complete halt to this game or allow him to become her lover.

Tyrone brushed his mouth over hers and she sighed, trembling faintly as she wrapped her arms around his neck. There was always the option of just allowing him to seduce her, she mused as she opened her mouth to greedily accept the sensuous invasion of his tongue. With what few scraps of sense she was still able to grasp, she quickly rejected that idea. If she was going to take a lover, something that had far-reaching consequences emotionally and socially, she had to make the decision with a clear head. When Tyrone slipped his hand beneath the covers to cup her breast, such heat flooded her body, Deidre knew she could never make a rational decision while he was touching her.

"Tyrone," she said, trying to sound firm, but, even to her own ears, his name came out sounding like a husky moan of pleasure.

His warm, soft lips touched the too sensitive skin of her left shoulder and she realized he had undone a few buttons on her nightgown and was tugging one side down. She tried to move her hands to stop him, but could not seem to stop holding him close, savoring the feel of his thick hair beneath her fingers. Cool air touched her left breast and she heard his breath catch. When his far too

tempting mouth brushed over the already taut, aching tip
of her breast, Deidre did not think there was one inch of
her that did not feel it. She was rocked down to her toes.

"Ah, you were right," Tyrone murmured, his thick,
husky voice caressing her breast as he encircled it with
kisses. "Definitely sugar."

Deidre finally found the strength to pull away. She was
not sure if it was shock or a fear of the intense sensations
racing through her, but she made herself move, fast. She
scrambled out from beneath him until she was sitting on
her pillows, her back pressed against the rough headboard
of the bed. Fighting to catch her breath, she stared at
Tyrone, but it took a moment for the fog of desire to clear
her head enough to see that he was not meeting her gaze.
Deidre followed the direction of his gaze and gasped. Her
breast was still exposed, the nipple hard and her skin
flushed and damp from his kisses. Muttering a curse, she
yanked the front of her nightgown back together and
struggled to button it with unsteady fingers.

"I believe I will have that coffee now," she said, pleased
that her voice was steady even though the lingering huskiness revealed how he had affected her.

Tyrone groaned slightly and flopped onto his back. He
watched her get up, tug on her robe, and slip into the
bathroom, an added luxury that had cost him a lot since
there were only two rooms in the small boardinghouse
that had one. With her out of sight, it was a little easier to
calm the fierce hunger knotting his insides. It was a little
hard to believe he could want a woman so badly after
knowing her for so short a time, but there was no denying
that he did. He grimaced as he thought that, if he did not
have her soon, he would be so crippled with want he
would be crawling the last miles into Paradise.

A hint of guilt snaked through him as he sat up and
took his cup of coffee from the bedside table. Deidre was
obviously a virgin and he was asking her to give up a lot,

her good name as well as her innocence, with no promises of any more than a few nights of passion. He was, in fact, asking her to ignore all she had been taught was right after only a few days of acquaintance and a few kisses, bone melting though those kisses were.

"Well, hell," he grumbled as he stood up and walked to the table by the window where their breakfast waited. "If I have to, I'll marry her."

"Did you say something?" Deidre asked as she stepped out of the bathroom, collected her coffee, and walked to the table.

"Just complaining about the weather," he replied, and quickly turned his attention to his meal.

Even as she started to cut the small steak nearly hidden by the piles of scrambled eggs and pan-fried potatoes crowding her plate, Deidre glanced out of the window and gaped. "It's snowing."

"I think it started last night."

Hurrying to eat her meal before it got any colder, Deidre asked, "Do you think it'll end our journey?"

"Nope. Doesn't look like a bad storm. It's already snowing less than it was an hour ago." He briefly glanced at her over his mug as he sipped his coffee. "It does mean that we won't be leaving here until tomorrow, however."

Although that news made her nervous, she managed to give him a small smile as she salted her potatoes. "There are parts of me that'll be very glad of the short respite."

Tyrone grinned and nodded. "Despite all the riding I do at the ranch, even I'll be glad of a breather."

"Perhaps I will go out and see what shops there are here."

"Need something?"

"Not much, but it'll be Christmas by the time Maura and I meet in Paradise and I want to have a gift for her."

"Well, just so long as it isn't something big and heavy. I think I'll take a stroll around and make sure no one's followed us here. Don't leave the main road and, if you even think someone's taking an interest in you, get inside a shop or back here. People around you will provide some protection."

Deidre decided not to remind him that there had been a lot of people around her in the last place she had been accosted. She had not exactly noticed a stampede of good Samaritans eager to stand between her and that gun stuck in her face. So long as the snow remained light, she intended to go and look for that ever-elusive perfect Christmas gift for Maura. All things considered, it was especially important to find something special for her cousin this year. If she reminded Tyrone of how little chance there was of finding a hero to rush to her rescue if and when needed, he might take it into his head to keep her confined to their room.

Tyrone was gone by the time Deidre was dressed and ready to go out. Already used to his constant company, it felt a little odd to step out all alone. It was a good thing, however, she decided as she hurried outside. She needed time away from his handsome face and seductive kisses to decide what to do about the rogue.

The fact that he could so easily seduce her told Deidre that the man probably held a good piece of her heart already, if not all of it. She was sure her strict upbringing, her morals, would have proven shield enough against his seduction if passion was all she felt. There was not the slightest hint that he shared such deeper, more intricate, and confusing feelings. And that, she knew, was one very good reason to hold him at a distance. He could steal a great deal more than her innocence if she was not careful. She might be able to continue on to love, marriage, and children despite a lost maidenhead, but falling in love with the man could easily doom her to a cold, empty life after he left her. That seemed to be too high a price to pay for a few nights of passion, no matter how fierce and sweet that passion was.

And, yet, she mused as she studied the hats in the milliner's tiny window, maybe it was not. Instinct told her she would regret not ever tasting that passion, that it was rare in its strength, and that those regrets could be a lot harder to push aside than a broken heart or lost innocence. Tyrone's kisses could easily spoil her for anyone else, however. If she found someone to marry, there could well be a ghost in her bed whether she succumbed to Tyrone's seduction or not.

So why not simply enjoy? she thought as she entered the mercantile store and slowly surveyed what was for sale. There was always the chance that Tyrone's feelings could deepen, that what she suspected she felt for him could be returned by the time they reached Paradise. Maybe that was a gamble worth taking.

Pausing to finger some beautifully tatted lace, Deidre began to search deep within her heart to see exactly what she did feel for Tyrone Callahan, if it truly was enough to take such a risk. In truth, by traveling alone with the man and sharing rooms, even with a false name, she was already thoroughly ruined. If even the tiniest whisper of such impropriety drifted back home, she would be utterly ostracized. She would be condemned, treated as a soiled dove by all, no matter what she had or had not done. Would it really be such a sin to actually commit the crime when there was a good chance she would be condemned anyway?

"My wife does that all herself," said a gruff voice that carried a deep, endearing note of pride.

Deidre smiled at the balding man standing across the store counter from her. "It is quite beautiful. As good as, if not better than, any French import I have seen. I fear my mother was never able to teach me the skill."

She decided to buy some, for Maura loved to trim her

clothes with such subtle and delicate finery. She bartered with the man, but not too strenuously. The work was so fine she felt guilty questioning the price at all. Habit drove her, but she quickly subdued it. Deidre knew how much work went into such beautiful lace and did not wish to wheedle the woman out of what she had rightfully earned with such artistry. She added a camisole and pantaloons, each trimmed with the beautiful lace, and idly wondered if she had already reached a decision about Tyrone. There was no real reason to wear such exquisite underclothes if all she intended to do was hide them beneath too many layers of flannel and wool.

By the time she returned to the hotel, it was after noon. A hastily scribbled note from Tyrone told her that he had decided to get the packhorse reshod, one of the animal's shoes being a little suspect. Deidre ate a light lunch and took a long, hot bath. Dressed in her new underclothes, she donned her robe and sat on the bed to gently rub her hair dry with a towel.

"Ah, Maura," she said softly. "I wish you were here to talk to. I am so confused. Do I or don't I? Are my feelings true or have I mistaken lust for love? Is all of this simply an attraction for a handsome man made all the fiercer because I am running for my life?"

Cursing softly, Deidre flopped onto her back on the bed, her robe sliding open, and closed her eyes. Her thoughts were not getting much clearer. In fact, they spun so fiercely in her mind she felt almost dizzy. She felt sleep creeping over her, the gray skies, the hot bath, and a lack of anything to do making her doze. Perhaps, she mused, as she let sleep calm her, she would find the answer to her quandary in her dreams.

"This shoe could've gone a few more miles," said the burly blacksmith as he finally removed the shoe from the packhorse's left rear hoof.

Resting his arms on the side of the stall, Tyrone watched the man clean the hoof in preparation for the new shoe, ready and waiting to be put on. "Probably, but it's hard miles I have to travel and a lot of them. Just need to be sure."

"You're loco to ride across country at this time of the year."

"Can't be helped. Too many folk don't want me to get home. Riding like this makes it harder for them to get me." He shrugged. "We're having a mild winter."

" 'Pears to be so far, but that could change in a winking. If it turns sour you don't want to be caught out in it."

"Don't plan to be. My family's ridden this trail for years. I know where to hole up if the weather turns against me. Seen any strangers around?" He smiled faintly when the man looked at him and briefly raised his bushy dark brows. "Besides me."

"Just the few folk what are staying at the hotel. Don't get many passing through this late in the year. Even the stage stops coming here regular."

Tyrone nodded, pleased with the news. It confirmed what he had seen in his own explorations. He was glad he and Deidre would not be forced out into the snow, light as it was. The next place he knew of to stop at was nearly a full day's ride away and it would be impossible to reach it before dark. Snow and the colder temperatures that came when the sun set could prove far more of a danger than the Martins' henchmen.

As he watched the blacksmith put on the new shoe with a comforting skill, Tyrone cursed himself for a coward. Fixing the horse's shoe was not a total waste of time and money, but it could have waited. It simply provided him with a good reason not to go back to the hotel. Spending hours alone with a woman he ached for, but could not have, was more torture than he felt inclined to endure.

For just a moment he wondered if some of his problem

was that he had not been with a woman for a long time. There was a saloon in town and it undoubtedly had a woman or two willing to satisfy him for a fee. Then he shook his head, casting those thoughts aside as foolish. It was a weak excuse to blame his keen desire for Deidre on a lengthy celibacy. It was also foolish to think some saloon whore could give him what he needed even if his fastidious nature could be overcome enough to let him try. Tyrone suspected he would leave the whore's bed, take one look at Deidre, and be back to aching again. It would simply be a waste of time and money.

After paying the blacksmith and complimenting him on his work, Tyrone walked back to the hotel. He felt torn between a reluctance to spend hours alone with Deidre, something that only led to a gut-twisting frustration, and an eagerness for her company. It surprised him a little, but he had to admit that he liked her, enjoyed her company, even when she drove him to distraction. In an attempt to convince himself that that did not mean all that much, he tried to think of other women he had liked and produced a very small list, most of them relatives or the wives of close friends. He also respected Deidre, her bravery and her determination to fulfill her father's dying wish the seeds from which that respect grew. Tyrone did not even try to list other women he had respected, for he knew it would be the same short list. That should tell him something, but he was not sure he wanted to figure out what that message was. Tyrone also wondered when he had become so cynical about women. Too many unfaithful wives in the world and courtesans disguised as ladies, he decided.

He stepped into the room he shared with Deidre and almost turned around and walked out again. Deidre was sprawled on the bed, her hair a fiery carpet beneath her, accentuating the delicate paleness of her skin. Her slender curves were seductively clothed in a beautiful lace-trimmed camisole and pantaloons. Those pantaloons were bunched up almost to the top of her thighs, exposing her slim, perfectly shaped legs. Tyrone hastily closed the door and bolted it.

Taking off his coat, hat, and scarf, Tyrone tossed them on a chair and walked over to stand by the bed. Her full lips were temptingly parted, silently begging to be kissed. The soft swells of her breasts peeped over the lace-trimmed low neckline of her chemise, gently rising and falling with each breath she took. One slim arm was raised over her head, the other curled against her side, her delicate hand resting low on her belly.

"You're a bastard for what you're thinking," Tyrone murmured even as he yanked off his boots, socks, and waistcoat. "If you're lucky, she'll just shoot you." He took off his shirt.

A sleepy Deidre was slow to push him away, a fact Tyrone had quickly noted and taken advantage of before. Guilt pinched him each time he did, and it was pinching at him now. As before, however, his hunger for Deidre proved stronger. A half-dressed Deidre sprawled so enticingly on a bed was far more temptation than any man ought to be asked to resist, he thought as he cautiously settled himself by her side. He touched his lips to her sleep-flushed cheek and hoped that, this time, she would not only be caught unawares by her own passion, but stay caught.

Chapter Six

꧁⚜꧂

DEIDRE TILTED HER HEAD to the side, allowing the warm, soft lips better access to the sensitive skin by her ear. She purred her delight as she slid her hands over smooth, warm skin. Her dream was especially detailed and realistic this time, she thought, shivering with pleasure as a hot, wet tongue dipped into her ear. Strong arms wrapped around her, pulling her close to a big, hard body and she snuggled even closer.

A slight tugging and a coolness against her shoulders made her frown. That was more reality than her dreams about Tyrone usually carried. Big, warm hands cupped her face and soft, warm lips brushed over hers. Deidre slid her hands up Tyrone's broad back and combed her fingers through his thick hair. Her dreams were getting very good.

"Deidre," Tyrone said, touching a kiss to the tip of her nose.

His voice certainly seemed real. Deidre tried to cling to the safe haven of sleep, but her wits were stirring right along with her passion. A tart voice in her head scolded her for trying to cast aside responsibility for her actions by pretending she was still caught in a dream. She tried to ignore that voice. If she opened her eyes and accepted the truth, then she would have to make a decision. This was so much easier, so much more pleasant. She could just lie back and blindly let passion swamp her until it was too late to turn back, the decision gently taken from her hands. *Coward*, the voice taunted.

"Deidre, open your eyes," Tyrone said as he slowly undid her chemise. "I've decided I can't be such a sneaky bastard. I want you awake and looking at me."

"If I open my eyes, I might also open my mouth to say a very loud *no*," she replied, arching into his touch as he slid his hands inside her partly opened chemise and cupped her breast.

"How can you say no to this?"

The faint breath of cooler air told her he had opened her chemise, but no further touch of hand or lips came. Blushing, Deidre slowly opened her eyes. Tyrone was crouched over her staring at her breasts. She could read his desire in every taut inch of his long body, in the light flush upon his high cheekbones, and in the uneven pace of his breathing. It was a heady knowledge. She could also feel her own desire, flooding her body with a greed for him that curled her toes. Would it ever again be this strong, this compelling? Deidre thought not and knew her decision had just been made.

"I didn't think they were so small you couldn't find them," she murmured, blushing at her boldness.

Tyrone's startled gaze flew to her face and then he laughed. He slowly eased his body down on top of hers, growing serious again. In her eyes he thought he read willingness, but he could not be sure. He needed more than a look; he needed the words. As he had roused her from her sleep, he had realized that he wanted her to fully accept him, not to be just swept away by a passion she was too innocent to control. When he was sprawled, sated, in her arms later, he did not want to face tears and regrets. He did not want it all spoiled by anger and accusations.

"They are beautiful," he said quietly, brushing a kiss over the top curve of each breast and feeling her shiver. "I ache to taste them, to fill my hands with them." He looked at her. "I also know that if I did so, I would not want to stop there. I could have made you want that, too."

The arrogance of that statement almost made her contradict him just on principle, but she decided it was time for the truth between them. "Yes, you could."

He was a little surprised at how deeply those three little words moved him. "I decided I didn't want you simply dragged along with me, yanked from sleep into passion so quickly you could not say no even if you wanted to. I want no regrets, no blame laying. I want a yes, Deidre, a wide-awake, eyes-clear yes."

That was tossing the ball into her court with a vengeance, she mused. She understood, however. Since their first kiss she had been saying no; now, suddenly, she was not. The capitulation probably seemed a little too quick. He wanted some assurances and she could not argue with that. She would not, however, give him too many reasons for her change of heart. Some, such as the realization that she could be dead soon, would probably insult him.

Others would tell him far more about what lay in her heart than she wanted him to know. Passion was all he asked for and that was all she would offer, for now. If she left this affair with her heart in tatters, she would be the only one who would know it.

A little playfully, she opened her eyes as wide as she could as she wrapped her arms around his neck. "Yes."

A tremor went through him and he could not believe it when, out of his mouth, came the words, "Are you sure?"

"Callahan, I can't believe you mean to argue with me about this."

He brushed his lips over hers as he laughed softly. "I can't believe I am, either. A moment's madness."

"And, is that what this is, too?"

"God knows, it sure as hell feels like a madness."

Deidre had no quarrel with that and gave herself over to his kisses. She arched to his touch as he toyed with her breasts, his thumbs rubbing over the tips until they ached. Uncertain in her boldness, she tentatively touched her tongue to his as he stroked the inside of her mouth. His groan of approval was all the encouragement she needed to grow more daring, to become an equal partner in the mind-clouding kiss. She mumbled a protest when he ended the kiss, then purred her appreciation when his lips touched her throat. When he reached her breasts, stroking the too sensitive tips with his tongue, she clutched her fingers in his hair and lost all ability to think.

Tyrone could not believe what was happening to him, did not really understand it. He was no innocent. He had bedded women before, women with more beauty, more flesh, more experience. Never had he lost control as he was losing it now. He trembled like some boy ready to bed a woman for the first time. Deidre was a virgin, a woman who required skill and gentleness, Tyrone was not sure he could give her either, so desperate did he feel.

And Deidre was desperate, too, he realized with a touch of shock, as he had to nearly fight free of her hold to shed the last of his clothing. It was there to see in her flushed face, the restlessness of her movements, and the faint tremors shivering through her slim body. Tyrone hurriedly removed her clothes, blindly tossing them aside as he looked her over. She was all soft, creamy skin and slender curves. The sight of the fiery red curls at the juncture of her slim thighs hit him hard, like a fist to the gut. It took him a moment to realize that she had gone still, only the swift, uneven breaths she took revealing that she had not suddenly grown cold to him. Tyrone looked up and saw that she was staring wide-eyed at his groin and it was not a look of flattering appreciation, either. He quickly lay on top of her, and, even though the feel of their flesh touching sent him reeling, he struggled to cling to a few shreds of control.

The insanity that had gripped her at the touch of his lips and his hands upon her flesh fled Deidre almost completely at the sight of his naked body. He was beautiful, all lean, hard muscle. It was what jutted out of the tangle of black hair between his long legs that stole away some of the blind need passion had infected her with. Deidre knew the basics of making love, but no one had told her that the part the man was going to stick into her was so big. A tickle of fear took away some of the heat in her blood. Exciting though it was to feel his warm flesh pressed against hers, Deidre was unable to ignore the hard length pressed against her groin.

"It's all right, love," Tyrone murmured as he kissed her ear. "I haven't killed anyone with it yet."

Although she had already guessed that a man as handsome as Tyrone had to have had a lot of experience, Deidre was annoyed to hear him refer to it now while they lay naked in each other's arms. "I hope you are not suggesting that I ask for references."

Glancing at her and noting her faintly narrow-eyed look, Tyrone decided that annoyance was better than fear even though it was not what he had been trying to rouse. "I was trying to ease that fear I saw."

"It's fading," she gasped when he stuck his tongue in her ear.

"Thank God," he groaned as he caressed her stomach, savoring the faint tremors that began to ripple through her again as he edged his hand ever nearer to the bright curls between her legs. "I want to go slow and easy, to make you as mad for it as I am, but I'm not sure I can."

Suddenly, his hand was there, between her legs, and Deidre shuddered with the shock and delight of it. "I think I am already mad."

"Oh, yes," he said, his voice thick and hoarse as he peppered her small, perfect breasts with kisses and he stroked her with his fingers, finding a deep warmth that made him shake. "Hot and wet. Perfect."

Deidre was too caught up in the feelings rippling through her to respond. She arched to his touch, crying out softly as he eased a finger inside her even as he took the tip of one breast deep into his mouth. A sense of frantic need engulfed her, a throbbing, demanding ache growing stronger low in her stomach. One moment she would start to pull away, afraid of what his clever fingers were making her feel, the next she would open wider to his touch, silently begging for more. She clung to him, her legs shifting restlessly. A sane part of her mind whispered concerns about her nakedness, the fact that it was still alarmingly light in the room, that a man she had known for mere days had his hand on a part of her body she did not really have a name for, and even about the embarrassing wetness that was forming there. All of that was drowned out by the demands of the passion-crazed part of her mind, becoming a faint tickle at the back and no more. The Deidre in control now was frantic with desire, eager for Tyrone to give her what her body seemed to crave, and highly annoyed that she was not quite sure what that was.

His tongue seemed to be everywhere, caressing her neck, darting into her ear, plunging into her mouth, and tantalizing her breasts. He was muttering hot, erotic words against her fevered skin, words that should have shocked her, but only enflamed her more. Then, suddenly, the feelings building inside her burst free of her weak, untutored attempts to hold them back. Deidre cried out Tyrone's name as she sank beneath wave after wave of frighteningly pleasurable feelings. Then Tyrone was there, around her, over her, inside her. She gasped as he filled her, a sharp pain announcing his invasion. Even as her still-reeling mind recorded the fact that her virginity had just been taken, Tyrone began to move. The intense sensations his hand had produced had begun to ease, but were now reborn. Deidre wrapped her arms and legs around his lean body and clung to him, suffering a heady mixture of anxiety and greed.

She slid her hands down Tyrone's back and grasped his taut buttocks, not sure if she sought to hang on or push him deeper, but doing both. He groaned and moved faster, then slipped his hand between their straining bodies. Tyrone touched her, one brief stroke of one long finger near where their bodies were joined, and Deidre felt herself shatter. Even as she shuddered from the force of the pleasure cascading through her, he slid his arm beneath her hips, holding her as close to him as humanly possible. She held on to him tightly as he jerked inside her a few times, called out her name, and shuddered in her arms. He sprawled on top of her, his hot, swift breaths heating her neck as she tried to keep a grip on him despite the increasing lethargic weakness in her limbs.

"Hell, Deidre, I think *sugar* might be the wrong word," Tyrone said after a few moments, easing the intimacy of their embrace and propping himself up on his elbows so that he could look at her.

For one brief moment Deidre was embarrassed, recalling all they had just done and the fact that they were lying together naked as the day they were born. Then she shook aside the feeling. He was her lover now. Although she had no intention of becoming scandalously immodest, at moments such as these, too much modesty could easily steal away the beauty and the pleasure. If she was going to be his lover, she intended to be a very good one. It was one way in which she might be able to pull more from him than his passion. She was taking a big gamble here and she had to play her hand with skill and daring, holding back nothing. If she lost this gamble she would have enough regrets without adding a lot of *if onlys* to the pot.

"What would you call it then?" she asked quietly, idly sliding her foot up and down his hair-roughened calf.

"A frenzy."

She smiled, then laughed softly. "Oh, yes, it was that." Deidre trailed her fingers up and down his strong arm, enjoying the feel of smooth, warm skin stretched tautly over his muscles. "Definitely a fever of some sort."

"I didn't hurt you, did I?" he asked quietly, even though he saw no sign that she was in any pain.

"No, not really. If there was any, I believe the, er, frenzy we were both caught up in eased the blow." She grimaced faintly as she became aware of the dampness between her thighs and a mild sense of being chafed. "I do think, however, that I will slip into the bathroom for a moment. Did you see what happened to my robe?" she asked even as she started to glance around the room.

Tyrone reached down and retrieved her robe from where it had fallen by the side of the bed. He waited until she had disappeared into the bathroom before getting out of bed. It relieved him to see that there was not much blood on the sheet or on him. He moved to where a pitcher of water and a bowl were set on a table beneath a small mirror and washed up, then tossed the water out of the window. He poured himself a small glass of whiskey, walked back to the bed, slipped beneath the covers, and sat with his back against the headboard as he sipped his drink.

In all of his little fantasies about making love to Deidre he had not once imagined what had actually happened. The moment she had said yes, had let her passion run free of the bonds of innocence and modesty, he had lost control. That had never happened before. He had never been that aroused or that satisfied. Although it was glorious, his body already stirring in readiness for another taste, it was also troubling.

There was the possibility that it would burn out as fast as it had flared up, yet instinct told him that would not happen. It could also be the danger they shared, that constant threat of death adding a sharp edge to their passion. It could simply be because Deidre was so different from the sort of women he usually lusted after. A slender, sharp-tongued redhead was not what usually drew his eye.

Tyrone shied away from another possible explanation for the keen sense of oneness he had found in her arms. After two wretched, embarrassing, and painful entanglements in the past, the word *love* left a bitter taste in his mouth. He did not trust the emotion, did not like the way it could blind and weaken a man. It also did not seem quite sane to love a woman he had only known for a few days. Passion he could trust. So, too, a liking and a respect for the woman Deidre was. Tyrone decided to keep his mind fixed upon those. If the passion he and Deidre shared was still running hot and strong by the time they reached Paradise, he would consider all of his options before he let her leave him. As far as he was concerned, passion, friendship, and respect formed a firmer basis for a relationship than some elusive, deceptive emotion like love. If all three were still there when their trials were at an end, Tyrone decided he just might consider something else he had assiduously avoided for years—marriage. He knew he would be a fool if he allowed a woman who held his interest in and out of bed to get away.

Deidre dried herself off as she watched the few inches of hot water she had filled the tub with drain away. That brief wash and soak had felt good, easing the faint sting caused by the loss of her virginity. She was glad there had been so little blood, for she suspected too much could easily have killed her newly born passion. She had felt little pain at the loss of her innocence and no real shame over that loss now. No matter how deeply she searched within her heart, she could find no regret over the choice she had made. The only unease she felt concerned what would happen when the journey to Paradise was at an end, but she decided it did no good to worry over it. She would win her gamble or lose, and no amount of fretting would push the odds in her favor.

She donned her robe and moved to clean her teeth, sighing as she studied her face in the small oval mirror over the sink. There was no visible sign that she was now what many people would consider a fallen woman. Neither did she see any evidence of what was in her heart. It was curious, for Deidre felt there ought to be some look there which revealed the love swelling in her heart, a love she had tried to deny or ignore. The moment she had opened her eyes and looked into Tyrone's passion-taut features, she had known why she was going to say yes. It was love that had driven her to welcome Tyrone into her arms, into her body. She thought such a profound emotion ought to leave some mark upon her, but about all she thought she could detect was a gleam in her eyes, something that could easily be attributed to the passion she had just tasted. It was probably for the best, as she did not want Tyrone to guess all of her secrets.

As she walked back to the bed and saw him there, his lovely chest bared for her to appreciate, she felt the odd, almost painful skip to her heart that had become all too common. Deidre inwardly shook her head. She had it bad, was probably incurable. Several thoughts as to how she could pull Tyrone into the same snare that now held her so tightly passed through her mind and she shook them away as foolish. If she won him with tricks and games, she would have to play them for the rest of her life. It was best just to be herself and pray that would be enough.

"You are watching me very intently," she said, giving in to the urge to brush his tousled hair off his forehead.

Tyrone set his empty glass down on the table by the bed. "I guess I keep expecting you to do something."

"Something virginal or maidenly? Tears, outrage, hysterics?"

He smiled faintly and tugged her down onto the bed at his side. "Something like that."

"Why? I decided. If it turns out that I don't like the consequences of that decision, well, it is my problem."

"Consequences?" He slowly untied her robe, grinning when she blushed and quickly slipped beneath the sheets. "How are the consequences so far?" he asked, nibbling at her ear as he removed her robe and tossed it aside.

"Very nice." She murmured her pleasure and arched to his touch as he stroked her breasts. "Very nice, indeed." Deidre slid her arms around his neck and rubbed her body against his, smiling when he trembled faintly. "As you said, how can one say no to this?"

He kissed her and Deidre felt the heat of desire flood through her again. The greed she felt for this man was astonishing and a little frightening. It was certainly not going to be a chore to try to touch his heart. She just prayed she had the strength to survive failure, to walk away with dignity and pride intact and pick up the pieces of her life again.

Chapter Seven

"Is something wrong?" Deidre asked, frowning when a strangely tense Tyrone yet again looked over his shoulder.

They had lost time, over a week, locked in the boardinghouse by the weather. The light snow had been followed by bitter cold and occasional sleet. Such weather could have caused them as much trouble as the Martins' henchmen; so they had stayed put. It had been lovely in many ways, a moment out of time. She and Tyrone had come to know each other well, physically and emotionally. Even their arguments had taught her something about the man. She was even more in love with him, yet, sadly, still unsure of his feelings.

"I just get the feeling we're being followed," Tyrone answered.

"If we couldn't leave because of the weather, then certainly no one could have reached us for the same reason."

"Maybe. Maybe not. We needed a whole day to get to the next resting stop. The ones after us may have been a lot closer."

"Do we keep riding?"

"Not much choice."

"We really can't afford another long delay, either, can we?"

"Nope. I'd like to get to Paradise by Christmas."

So would she, but Deidre did not say so. Heartbreak might be waiting for her in Paradise, but so, too, might Maura. Thanksgiving had come and gone and she had sharply missed sharing the day with her cousin. She did not want to miss another important holiday with the last of her family.

She glanced up at the dull winter sky and sighed. There were still several hours left before they reached the next of Tyrone's stops. Deidre was chilled to the bone, her backside ached, and now she felt the constant urge to look behind her, certain that their enemies were right there. They were dangerously exposed as they rode along and she tried not to think about how easy it would be for one of the men after them to just shoot them out of their saddles.

"Tyrone?" she called, the return of the threat she had foolishly thought they had outrun making her think of something she had not yet done.

"See something?" he asked, glancing behind them again.

"No, but I just realized that this might be a good time to tell you what I have done with the papers."

Easing his horse up next to hers, he reached out and stroked his mittened hand over her cheek. "I figured you had them somewhere safe."

"I do, but . . ." She sighed. "Well, considering that we have who knows how many people looking for us and eager to stop us, it might be a good idea if you also knew where that safe place is. After all, the whole purpose of this trip is to get those papers back to Paradise. If anything happens to me, you will have to grab those papers and run with them."

Tyrone did not even want to think of something happening to her. It sent shivers down his spine and knotted up his insides with fear. At some time during their sensual days and nights in the last town, he had accepted that she was important to him.

"Nothing will happen to you."

"I certainly hope not, but I don't think I want to tempt fate by being too cocky, either."

"So, where are they then?"

"I have them tucked in a hidden pocket under my petticoats." She blushed faintly when he stared at her skirts and idly wondered how, after all they had shared, she could have a scrap of modesty left.

"I'm surprised I didn't find them at some time during the last week," he muttered.

She shrugged. "It's not that noticeable. It seemed the safest place. Bags can be stolen, rooms can be searched."

"So can you."

"True, but I felt that, if matters had taken that bad a turn, it really didn't matter much. I wasn't going to be getting to Paradise anyway."

"True. Thanks for telling me." It was a good thing to know, yet he wished she had not told him, for it made him far too aware of the dangerous circumstances they were trapped in.

"I was a little surprised that you hadn't asked again, after that first day."

"You said you had them and you were going with me. It wasn't all that important to know exactly where you had them."

Tyrone glanced behind them again, unable to shake the uneasy feeling that had dogged him for the last few hours. It would take them about two more hours to get to where they were going, and he began to feel that that was two hours too many. Something was not right, but he could not figure out what it was, or what he could do to try to protect them both. The danger was there, he was sure of it, but, unless he could see where it was coming from, he could not avoid it.

He nudged his mount to a slightly faster pace, glad to see Deidre quickly follow suit. If there was someone tailing them, moving a little faster would make little difference, but it did make him feel as if he was doing something other than scanning the horizon. He did know, however, that he would feel a great deal safer if he could get them behind the walls of the cabin he was heading for. It was a small hunting cabin of his uncle's, not intended to withstand much of a siege, but it would mean that their enemies would then be the ones out in the open.

When the attack came it was all over before Tyrone or Deidre could do anything to save themselves. The shot was still echoing in the cold air when Deidre saw Tyrone slump in the saddle. She screamed and tried to grab the reins of his panicked horse. Jim and Pete flanked her even as Tyrone's too limp body disappeared into the distance. The only clear thought she had for a moment was that it was odd he had not fallen off the galloping horse. Then she stared at the two men who had captured her and wondered how they intended to kill her.

"Damnation, Pete," grumbled Jim as he grabbed the reins of Deidre's horse. "We'll never catch him."

"Don't matter," replied Pete. "He ain't going to bother us now."

"So, little lady," said Jim as he turned his attention to her. "Where are them papers?"

"What papers?" she said, surprised at how calm she sounded, for inside she was screaming out her grief and fury.

"You can tell us now or wait for us to get you somewhere where we can have us a good time looking for them."

She did not really need to see the leers that twisted their ugly faces to know what they meant. Murdering her obviously was not enough for them, they meant to add rape to their many crimes. A hard, cold knot of fear began to twist her insides, but she fought to hide it from them. It was hard to stir any hope in her heart with the sight of Tyrone's limp body still emblazoned on her mind, but she struggled to grasp hold of some. At the moment, she was too numb to think of any way she could escape their plans, but, until they actually began their attack on her, she still had a chance.

"The papers are on Tyrone's horse," she said.

Briefly both men look dismayed, then Pete scowled at her, suspicion beginning to narrow his eyes. "I think you're lying."

"Do you now?"

"Let's argue this later, Pete," Jim said. "I'm freezing my ass off."

"Fine. We'll go to that little cabin a mile or two ahead and sort this out," snapped Pete.

"What do we do if she's telling the truth?"

"Then we'll have to go looking for that fool. He won't have got far. Horse won't run till it drops."

"Yeah, but there's a lot of country to look over. It won't be easy."

"We'll just look for the buzzards."

Those cold words horrified Deidre so much, she was unable to say a word as they led her away. The image scarred her mind and made it impossible to think of any plan for her own safety. A part of her wondered what the point was of trying to save herself if Tyrone was dead, but she found the strength to brutally silence it. There was a job to finish, for her father's sake and now for Tyrone's. She did not want to die, either, no matter how painful it would be to go on.

By the time they reached the cabin, Deidre had managed to calm herself enough to begin to think more clearly. Grief and fear made a hard, choking knot in her throat, but she had conquered the worst of it. Now was not the time to give in to it. It would only make her easier to kill.

Jim shoved her into the cabin, pushed her into a chair in front of the cold fireplace, and tied her to it. As she watched the two men unload the supplies and light a fire, she tried to think of some way to put a stop to their plans. At the moment she was completely helpless, but, if they truly intended to rape her, they would have to untie her. That would be when her chance might come. Although she was only one tiny woman against two burly men; she was not totally helpless.

Once the two men were in the cabin, the door locked, they untied her. It was a start, she mused as she rubbed her wrists trying to ease the chafing caused by the too tight ropes. There were still two somewhat meaty obstacles between her and freedom, but at least she could move now. She was going to need a weapon and she began to look around the small cabin in search of one.

"Get off your ass, woman, and cook us some food," said Jim.

Deidre stared at the man as if he was totally devoid of sense. "You expect me to feed you before you kill me?"

Jim looked sly and tried to make his voice sound honest, even coaxing. "Now, nobody said nothing about killing you."

"This is just a friendly meeting, is it?"

"All we want is them papers."

"Of course. I am sure the Martins would appreciate a witness to their crimes."

"No need to stir up trouble, is there? You just give us what we want and trot on back to Saint Louis."

"You have just killed a man. You killed two others in Saint Louis. You stuck a gun in my face and tried to kill me a second time that very same day. Forgive me if I question your sudden mercy."

"Just shut your damned mouth," snapped Jim as he yanked her out of the chair and shoved her toward the cook stove in the corner of the large room. "Make us something to eat."

Pete set some bacon, beans, and flour on the rough counter next to the sink pump and went back to searching through the bags. Deidre sighed and began to make some supper. There was always the chance she could find some better use for hot food and heavy pots than to feed the two men. The fact that they wanted to eat first also bought her a little more time, and she would be a fool to toss that away by being stubborn and argumentative.

As she prepared a pot of coffee, she found her concern for Tyrone rushing to the fore of her mind. She desperately wanted to believe the wound he had suffered was not a fatal one, that she had not watched his dead body being taken away to be left unburied in the icy woods. It was probably fanciful and self-deceiving, but she could not shake the feeling that she would somehow know if he had died.

Sternly telling herself that Tyrone's fate was not, and could not, be her concern now, she struggled to keep all thought of him from her mind. If he had survived, if he had only been knocked unconscious by his wound, he would take care of himself. He would also expect her to try to take care of herself. If some miracle happened, and Tyrone not only lived but was strong enough to come after them, she wanted to be strong enough and calm enough to be of some help.

Although she had no appetite, she forced herself to eat

with the men. Watching them shove the food into their mouths was pure torture, but she struggled not to let them see her disgust. They had kept too close an eye on her as she had prepared the meal, obviously seeing how easily she could cause them trouble with the items she had used to cook their food. Deidre was dismayed to see that they had enough wit to understand even that much. It did not bode well for her chances of making an escape.

"We didn't find them papers in your bags," said Jim as soon as he had finished eating.

"Looked through all of them carefully, did you?" she murmured as she cleaned the dishes.

"Real careful. So, where are they?"

"I told you, Tyrone has them."

"And I still don't believe you." He walked over to stand next to her.

"Then maybe you ought to search the bags again." She tried to edge away from him.

"I got me a few interesting ways of making you tell me the truth." He grabbed her by the arm, his hold so tight she almost cried out.

"Maybe I do know where they are. Why not take me to Paradise and let me tell the Martins myself? I didn't take on this job out of the goodness of my heart, you know. I had expected to get paid. Well, the Martins' money is as good as the Callahans'."

Deidre could not believe that he actually took a minute to consider what she had just said. She had found it nauseating simply to voice such sentiments, but it was clear that such treachery made perfect sense to him. Then his eyes narrowed and she feared there was some look on her face that told him she was lying. Or, worse, he had the wit to realize that not everyone was as crooked as he was. If he believed her to be honest, one who kept her word, there would be no tricking him with lies and evasions.

"There's a thought," said Pete. "Gotta admit, I ain't all

that comfortable with killing a woman, especially not one who could keep us both warm all the way back to Paradise."

"She could, but I think she's lying again," muttered Jim. "Them other two men weren't willing to deal even when they knew we were ready to shoot them and she's one of them. She's that fool Irishman's daughter, 'spect she is just as honest. Hell, if she was so damned willing to change sides, why's she been fighting us so hard all this time?"

"I didn't know you'd be willing to deal," she said. "I thought you just wanted to get the papers for yourself, the papers and all of the reward for them."

"Yeah, and we can still do that."

"If you kill me, you won't ever find those papers."

"You got 'em. I know you do, or you wouldn't be trying so hard to get to Paradise and Callahan wouldn't been trying so hard to get there, either. Now, you tell me where they are and maybe me and Pete will go easy on you."

Deidre knew it probably would not gain her anything, but pure frustration made her punch him in the nose. He howled, let go of her, and grabbed his nose. She made a dash for the door, but, even as she got it unlocked, Pete reached her. He shoved her away from the door and, as he locked it again, she kicked him, hard, in the back of his knee, then darted over to the fireplace to grab the heavy iron poker. Legs spread and the poker held firmly in both hands, she faced the two men. It gave her some small sense of triumph when she saw how Pete limped and Jim's nose was bleeding.

"Now, it ain't smart to be making us mad," said Jim as he inched closer to her.

"Why? You can't kill me twice," she snapped, swinging the poker at him and making him dance back a few steps.

"No, but it can make us feel real inclined to kill you slow and painful like."

"Dead is dead."

"A quick death is better."

"Well, I have no intention of dying. I have a few things I intend to make you pay dearly for. My father's death, for one. And Bill's. And Tyrone's. You two are long overdue for a hanging."

"You can't kill us both," said Pete, sidling around until he flanked her on the right. "Not with that, you can't."

"I can hurt you enough to let me get out of here," she said, and watched the man frown as he kept a wary eye on her weapon.

"No, I don't think so," drawled Jim.

She cursed when they both lunged at her. Although she got in a few good hard blows, raising curses and drawing blood, Deidre knew it was a lost battle. She should have waited, should have judged her time and chances better, but they had been closing in and she felt trapped. No clear route of escape had presented itself and she knew that now none would.

Jim ducked a swing of the poker and then grabbed her by the arm even as Pete threw himself at her. She hit the floor hard, her head grazing the hard brick hearth. Dazed, she stared up at Pete who was crouched over her, Jim peering over his shoulder, and she wondered how everything could have gone so terribly wrong. Unless some miracle happened, her father and Bill had died for nothing, and so had Tyrone, and so would she. The Martins had won. It seemed so terribly unfair.

Chapter Eight

A SEARING PAIN IN his side slowly pulled Tyrone out of the blackness. Then he became aware of the cold. He eased himself upright in the saddle, sweating with the effort and then shivering as the sweat was brutally dried by the cold air. He was amazed he was not dead, even more amazed that he was still in the saddle. With a shaking hand he patted the icy, damp neck of his mount, worried that the animal was close to collapsing, and tried to figure out where he was.

It took a moment for his pain-clogged mind to sort out the facts, but he finally realized he was not that far from where he and Deidre had been heading. He thanked God that their attackers had obviously not taken any time to come looking for him, for his horse had run only slightly off the trail. He would have been an easy target. Grimacing as he pulled a shirt out of his saddlebag and struggled to wrap it tightly around his waist to ease the bleeding in his side, he suspected he still was an easy target.

Deidre needed him, he reminded himself as pain and weakness made him sway slightly in the saddle. Tyrone prayed she was still alive, then pushed that fear aside, for it only added to his weakness, clouding his mind with worry when he needed it at its sharpest. The men would want the papers before they killed her and he was sure Deidre had the sense to buy as much time as she could. Glancing at the sun riding so low in the sky, he knew he had already lost about an hour, maybe more. Deidre might not be dead yet, but she might already be wishing she was.

Gently he turned his horse, riding back onto the trail he had originally meant to follow. Good luck was riding on his shoulder for now, he decided as he found the tracks of the men who had taken Deidre. They were headed straight for the cabin. It troubled him that they knew about the place. How much else did they know? Had the Martins somehow figured out the exact route he was taking? It would mean that, even if he was fortunate enough to get them out of this fix, he and Deidre would no longer have any safe haven.

Pushing aside all thoughts of future problems, centering his mind on the one he had to solve right now, Tyrone cautiously approached the cabin. He saw the light from one small window flickering through the trees and stopped. Softly promising his weary, chilled horse a warm stall soon, he dismounted and tied the horse to a tree. For a moment he sagged against the tree, fighting to quell the dizziness that had overtaken him. He was as weak as a newborn kitten. It was not going to be hard to save Deidre, it was going to be impossible.

"No, dammit, I can't let the bastards win," he muttered as he pushed himself up straight and took several deep breaths to try to stop the shaking of his body. "I should've never let her talk me into bringing her along, either," he grumbled as he started toward the cabin, careful to keep to the shelter of the trees.

It was not thoughts of the ranch, of his family, or even of losing to the Martins that kept him putting one foot in front of the other, however, and he knew it. It was the thought of Deidre in the hands of those two men. Although he had not seen who had attacked him, his gut told him it was Jim and Pete. Those two would not kill her quickly, even if they got their hands on the papers they sought. They would use her first, and the thought of either of the men laying a hand on Deidre gave Tyrone the strength to keep moving despite the blood that continually dripped from his side, staining the snow.

He paused at the edge of the wood, made sure there was no one outside on guard or standing in the window, and raced for the side of the cabin. Once there, he leaned against the rough log wall and tried to catch his breath. Tyrone knew he did not have much time to rest. Even in the dim light of sunset the bloody marks he had left upon the snow were visible. If anyone came outside, it would not take them long to know someone was there. The only chance he had was if he could catch them by surprise.

Inching along the side of the building, he made his way around to the back. A tiny window near the back door drew him. Before he could even try to get inside, he had to see how many were in there and how they were placed. Cautiously, he peered inside, and silently cursed. Deidre was trying to hold the two men back with a fireplace poker. He had to admire her bravery, but he did not think she could hold them off for long.

Even as the thought passed through his mind, they jumped her. Tyrone resisted the urge to immediately try to go to her aid. He hated it, but he knew he would stand a better chance of helping her if both men had all of their attention fixed upon her. That meant he had to let them start the assault they so clearly intended. He hoped she would forgive him for that if she ever found out.

Deidre cursed and tried to throw Pete off, but there was no moving the man. He simply pinned her to the floor more securely and then grinned. It was a disgusting smile, she thought with a mounting fear as she looked up at him, and not just because he had green teeth. It held both lust and violence behind it. She knew what these men were going to do to her and she felt herself begin to shrink inside with terror and a deep wretchedness. After what she had shared with Tyrone, the thought of either of these men putting one hand on her made her stomach clench with nausea. They would taint the beautiful memories she had of her time with Tyrone and she thought that might be the greatest of their crimes. Then she remembered that they would probably kill her when they were done and began to feel rage rise up through her fear and despair. She nursed it, pulled it forth with every ounce of will she had, for it cleared her head.

"Get off me, you great smelly swine," she snapped, and found some enjoyment in the way his eyes widened in surprise.

"You oughta think twice before you insult us, girlie," Pete snapped as he wrapped his hands around her wrists and pinned her hands over her head.

"It takes no thought at all. You are incredibly easy to insult."

"I'm beginning to think you're a stupid bitch," snapped Jim, his eyes so narrowed with fury they were mere slits in his pockmarked face. "You know what me and Pete are going to be taking now. I think you oughta be a little nicer. Maybe then we'd go easy on you."

"Make it easy for you to rape and kill me? Now, that would be stupid." She tried not to flinch as Pete tore at the buttons of her gown with his dirty fingers.

"We just mean to give you some of what that Callahan feller has."

"For you to compare what you're going to do to anything Tyrone has done has got to be nearly a blasphemy. Maybe if you took a bath, you could get a woman now and again without throwing her to the ground."

"Dammit, woman, you ain't got the sense God gave a goose." Jim shook his head, a look of amazement mixing unpleasantly with the fury twisting his coarse features. "Now, where are them papers?"

"Go to hell."

"Come hold the bitch down, Jim," said Pete, "so's I can get these damned clothes off her skinny hide."

Deidre shuddered as Jim took over the holding of her wrists and Pete roughly groped her breasts. She cursed herself for that sign of weakness. Although she was not sure how long she could keep up her act of bravado, pride urged her to try to cling to it. There was not much she could do to stop them from profaning her body, but she really wished she had the fortitude not to let them know how much it hurt her. Deidre knew there would come a time when she could no longer fight the horror of what was happening to her. She just prayed that they would not see it when she finally broke.

As Pete yanked her dress off, never missing a chance to grope her as he did, she felt herself retreating from it all. Her mind curled back, slipping into a dark corner to hide. She tried to fight that retreat of her senses even though a large part of her welcomed the chance to disassociate herself in some way from the violence she was being subjected to. If she let herself hide in that way, she might miss some chance to help herself, before or after the rape. Death would follow the debasement of her body and she wanted to have enough sense left to try to fight that, too. If that meant she had to be fully aware of the violation of her body, then that was the price she would pay to try to stay alive.

"God, she might be skinny, but she's got real pretty little titties," said Pete as he yanked open her chemise.

"I will see you dead for this," she said, as astonished by the coldness of her voice as Pete looked to be.

"And just how are you going to do that?" asked Jim, tightening his hold on her wrists until she had to bite back a cry of pain. "Gonna haunt us, are you?"

"Yes. If you succeed in killing me, that is exactly what I will do, for every day of your hopefully very short lives. Right up until the Devil leads you down into hell. But maybe you are forgetting the Callahans. I suspect they will be eager to make you pay for Tyrone. If I can't make you pay for this, they will."

"The Martins will take care of them," said Pete.

"Yeah, and they don't know who we are," said Jim.

"Don't they?" She was surprised when both men paused in their attack to scowl at her. "What makes you so sure of that? Are you positive that neither Tyrone nor I have gotten word to one of his brothers about you?"

"Don't matter," Pete finally said, after scowling in silence for a moment. "We took care of one Callahan. We can take care of the others if we have to."

"Stop arguing with the stupid bitch and get her drawers off," snapped Jim.

"Think her hair's red down there, too?" asked Pete with a chuckle.

"We'll know in a minute."

Even as Pete began to tug at her drawers, a loud bang sounded. Both men moved faster than she had thought them capable of. Deidre rolled out of their reach, then

quickly sprang to her feet. She gaped right along with
them when she saw Tyrone standing just inside the back
door. She could see the blood on him, see how pale he
was, and wondered where he had found the strength to
kick open the back door. Then she shook free of her as-
tonishment and looked around for a weapon so that she
could help him if he needed it.

She grabbed the fireplace poker again even as the first
shot was fired. Clutching her weapon, she pressed herself
up against the rocky side of the fireplace in an attempt to
shield herself from the flying bullets. Pete cursed as a bullet tore through his arm while he ran for the door. Jim
shot at Tyrone, who had taken shelter behind the heavy
cast-iron sink and kept him pinned down as Pete struggled
to unlock the door.

When Pete threw the door open, Deidre cried out in
dismay. It looked as if, yet again, the two men were going
to get away. Tyrone could not get an accurate shot because
Jim was keeping him pinned in his corner by the sink. She
wished she had a gun. When both men disappeared out
the door, Jim half carrying Pete and then slamming the
door shut behind him, Deidre waited for Tyrone to go
after them. When Tyrone finally appeared, making his unsteady way to the door, she changed her mind. Not only
did she not want him back in the line of fire, but he did
not look well.

"Wait!" she called, but he was already out the door.

Cursing softly, she hurried after him. The muted sound
of horses galloping over the snow reached her ears as she
stepped outside. Just as she wondered where Tyrone had
gone, a shot was fired close to her and she screeched in
surprise. After nearly throwing herself halfway back inside
the house, she then thought to look for who had fired a
gun. Since Pete and Jim were obviously riding away as fast
as their horses would take them, it could not have been ei-

ther of them. Peering out the door, she saw a shadowy figure slumped against the side of the house only steps from the door.

"Tyrone?" she called softly, her grip tightening on the poker.

"Lost the bastards again," he rasped, then stood up. "Got to get my horse in."

"I can do that," she said, but he was already disappearing into the shadows of the trees.

Deidre hesitated a moment, then hurried back inside the cabin. She quickly pulled on her clothes, knowing she could not go after Tyrone in her underthings, not in the cold and snow. Her body was shaking slightly but steadily and she knew she was finally reacting to all that had happened to her in the last few hours, but she fought against succumbing to shock. Later, she would give in to all the fear and horror bottled up inside her. Tyrone needed her sensible now.

As she stepped back outside, she caught sight of Tyrone disappearing into the small stable next to the cabin. Deidre quickly followed him. When he staggered as he took the saddle off the animal, she moved to take it from him. The man was near to collapsing, yet seemed compelled to go on.

"Tyrone, you've been wounded," she said as he clutched some hay and began to rub down his mount.

"It can wait a minute," he replied, the hoarse tone of pain in his voice putting the lie to his words. "It's not as bad as it looks."

"How can I know that?" she snapped as she grabbed some hay and worked on the other side of the horse. "I haven't seen it yet."

"I'm here, aren't I? And, I sent the bad guys running."

Tyrone did not know why he was being so contrary. He hurt and he could hardly see straight he was so weak and dizzy. Yet, he felt determined to stay on his feet, to tend to his horse, and then walk back into the cabin. He wondered if he was not only trying to deny the extent of his injuries to keep Deidre from worrying, but also to calm himself. Although he had been shot before, it had only been a flesh wound, easily mended and causing only the kind of pain that made a man curse a lot. He knew this wound was far more serious.

"Please, Tyrone," she said, her voice trembling with concern as she watched him stagger while trying to throw a blanket over the horse.

He sagged against the horse. "Almost done."

"Yes, you are. I don't think I can carry you," she said softly.

"Oh, I think you're a lot stronger than you look," he teased, but he knew his smile was little more than a grimace of pain.

She stepped up next to him and slipped her arm around his waist, gasping slightly when she felt the dampness there, for she knew it was blood. "Into the house. Now."

"Yes, ma'am." He draped his arm over her slim shoulders and tried not to lean on her too much. "I don't think the bullet is still in there."

"That would be the only good thing that has happened this afternoon."

She was nearly carrying him by the time they got inside the cabin. She dragged him over to the bed, then began to take off his clothes. The shirt around his waist was soaked with blood, and Deidre tasted fear. She was not without some healing skills, but the still too fresh memory of her father made her hands shake with uncertainty.

"Lock up the cabin," he said, his voice a mere thread of sound as she bathed his side, trying to get a good look at the extent of his wound.

Knowing he would not rest until she had done as he

asked, Deidre hurried to secure all the doors and windows. He nodded and closed his eyes as she returned to his side. To her great relief, the bullet had passed right through his right side. The loss of blood had been great, but it appeared that no serious damage had been done. If there was no infection or fever, he could well survive. Wishing he would hurry up and pass out, she busily cleaned his wound and stitched it. Taking a salve from her bag, she smoothed it over the wound, then bandaged him with a strip torn from her petticoat.

"Drink this," she said as she helped him sit up a little and held a cup of water to his lips.

"Did they hurt you bad?" he asked as he sagged back down on the bed.

"A few bruises and a need to have a good scrubbing, but nothing else," she answered.

"Sorry. I had to wait."

"What?" She pulled a stool up next to the bed, sat down, and smoothed her hand over his brow.

"I saw them get you down on the floor. I waited. Thought it'd be easier to rout them if they were both busy with you."

"It was a good plan. There is nothing for you to apologize for. How did you know where we were?"

"For all we curse the snow, it has its uses." He gave her a weak smile as he tried to focus on her face. "It makes it real easy to follow a trail."

"I was so afraid they had killed you," she whispered, giving in to the urge and touching a kiss to his cheek.

"We Callahans are real tough to kill."

"Thank God for small mercies. Do you think they'll be back?"

"Nope. Not for a while. I took out the gun arm of one of them and they'll want that fixed before they face us again. Maybe we'll get lucky and reach Paradise before that happens."

Deidre prayed they would, but luck had not been with them much so far. Since Tyrone looked as if he had finally gone to sleep, she left him. Heating up some water, she stripped down and scrubbed every part of her the men had touched. She ached to have a long soak in the big metal tub hanging on the wall of the cabin near the sink, but did not think she should take the time for that luxury yet, she decided as she put her robe on. Tyrone would need a close watch until she was sure he was well on the way to recovering.

Bringing the guns nearer to the bed, she sat back down on the stool and watched him sleep. She was terrified, and it was exhausting her to keep that fear at bay, but she had to. Although she suspected Tyrone was right, that Pete's wound would keep the men away for now, she could not relax her vigil. Tyrone was too weak to fight the men again. It was her turn to protect him.

"Deidre?" he called, a note of anxiety in his voice.

"I'm right here," she said, touching her hand to his forehead and stiffening with fear.

"I don't feel so good."

If she had not been so terrified she would have smiled. He sounded like a little boy. He was burning up with fever, however, and that stole all humor from the situation.

"Don't worry," she said, surprised her voice sounded so calm, almost soothing. "I won't let anything happen to you," she whispered, the vow coming straight from her heart.

Chapter Nine

TYRONE SLOWLY OPENED HIS eyes and then grinned. He had heard the sound of splashing water and Deidre softly humming to herself. Even his tired brain had figured out that she was taking a bath, and he was not able to resist a peek. Despite how weak four days of fighting a fever had left him, he felt his body tauten with interest as he watched her.

With her hair haphazardly pinned up and her skin flushed a delicate rose from the heat of the water, she was beautiful. Comparing her to other women he had known was foolish, he decided. Deidre had her own special beauty. If one set her next to the women most of society considered beautiful, it might take a glance or two to see Deidre's loveliness, but a man would have to be stone blind to miss it completely. Tyrone knew a lot of it was

born of the spirit contained in that small, slender body he
was watching with such pleasure.

He clenched his hands into tight fists as he watched her
wash herself, his palms itching with an eagerness to follow
the path of the soapy rag she used. It had been too long
since he had touched that soft skin, since he had held
those small, taut, deliciously sweet breasts in his hands.
Tyrone almost laughed. If he was not careful he would definitely be suffering a relapse. He certainly felt a little feverish.

She rinsed the soap away and put her hands on the
edge of the tub. Tyrone knew she was about to get up and
closed his eyes. Although it was tempting to look, he kept
them closed. Seeing Deidre standing only feet away, naked
and glistening from her bath, was far more delight than he
could endure at the moment. It would only leave him
aching more than he already was and he was too weak to
satisfy that particular hunger.

Tyrone was so busy trying to cool his ardor, he did not
hear her approach the bed, and started when she touched
him. He slowly opened his eyes as she rested her tiny hand
on his forehead. She was frowning and he resisted the
urge to feel his own forehead to see what troubled her.

"Something wrong?" he asked.

"You are feeling a little warm," she murmured.

"Not surprised," he grumbled, then grinned at her.
"You shouldn't go bathing in front of a poor invalid." He
grinned even more when she blushed a brilliant red.

"And you shouldn't be so rude as to watch."

"I wouldn't be human if I didn't at least sneak a peek."

She shook her head and plumped up the pillows behind his back, then helped him sit up. "Rogue."

Her embarrassment was easily shaken off, a hint of excitement slipping to the fore. It made her blood warm to
think of him looking at her as she bathed, but she was not
sure why. His obvious appreciation of the view probably

had something to do with that. Deidre almost smiled. The man was turning her into a wanton even from his sick bed.

"How's it look?" he asked after she had checked his wound, put some more salve on it, and rebandaged it.

"Very good," she replied. "You are obviously a quick healer."

"Quick enough to ride out of here tomorrow?"

"Not that quick. I doubt if you can even stand up without help."

"Let's see. Hand me my pants."

Even as she started to obey that command, she frowned at him. "What are you intending to do?"

He snatched his pants out of her hand and struggled to put them on without standing up right away. "Going to see if I can get to the outhouse without help."

"Tyrone, you've only had one full night free of fever. One night of a restful sleep out of five. You're going to fall flat on your face," she warned as he stood up, clutching the bedpost as he swayed a little.

"Then you better put some boots on so you can come out and catch me," he said as he walked slowly to the back door, yanked on his coat, and stepped outside.

"Stubborn, stupid man," she grumbled as she yanked on her boots and coat and hurried after him.

He made it to the outhouse and she stood outside shivering as she waited. When he stepped back outside, however, he had to accept her help in getting back into the cabin. By the time she got him settled back in bed, he looked a little less pale and she breathed a sigh of relief. He did not, however, look to be in a particularly good humor, so she left him to his sulking and got him some supper.

"I guess it'll be another day, maybe two, before we can leave," he conceded ungraciously as he ate the beans and bacon she served him.

Finishing her own meal and trying not to think too

fondly of steaks and apple pies, Deidre smiled at him. "I'm afraid so. There's been no sign of Pete and Jim, if that is any comfort."

"A little. I just hate losing the time. There's not much left, not if we're going to reach Paradise by Christmas. There's still bad weather lurking as a means to keep us trapped."

"So long as we reach it by the start of the year. That is really all that matters. The rest is just, well, an 'it would be nice.' "

He nodded as she took his plate away and went to the sink to wash out their dishes. Tyrone was not sure why he was so eager to be home at Christmas, and, even better, to have the matter of the ownership of the Callahan lands and mine settled by then. He supposed he looked at it as a Christmas present for him and his brothers and a way to make sure his father rested easy again. The hint of this trouble had been in the air when his father had died and Tyrone knew the man had fretted about it. It would be good to have all his father had worked for secure in Callahan hands again. Christmas just seemed like the perfect time to do it and then celebrate a job well done.

Deidre returned to his side and, for a while, they played cards. Tyrone was a little amused by how well the delicate, ladylike Deidre played poker. If they had been playing for real money, she would own the ranch and the mine by now.

"Enough," he said with a laugh as he tossed his cards down on the bed. "I concede. Remind me never to play for real money. Your father taught you?" he asked quietly as she collected the cards and put them back in her bag.

"Yes." She smiled, pleased to feel only a slight pang, grief slowly being pushed aside by acceptance and fond memory. "He only gambled for money once in a while. Said he had seen too many men go to ruin because of a love for the gambling. However, he was very fond of the game. Maura is even better than I am."

"Good God. Until now, I had always considered myself a good player."

"Oh, you are," she teased, and grinned over her shoulder as she headed out the back door. "It isn't at all easy to beat you."

Tyrone laughed softly as he made himself comfortable in bed. The simple walk to the outhouse had left him weak, but he had recovered from it quickly enough to restore his confidence in his recovery. It would be best to wait until his stitches were removed before riding again, but that was impossible. If they waited at the cabin another week, it would take only one more small delay to ensure that they did not make Paradise by the new year. He could rest all he wanted when he got home.

He was half asleep when Deidre returned. Tyrone listened carefully to her checking all the locks, satisfied that she had not let her guard down. When she slid into bed next to him, he sorely regretted his lingering weakness. He wanted to make love to her, but knew he still did not have the strength to do it right. A soft giggle escaped her and he was just about to ask her what was so funny when two small, very cold feet were placed firmly against his legs.

"Damnation, Deidre," he cried, gasping a little from the shock of it. "Your feet are like two blocks of ice. Did you run through the snow barefoot?"

"No," she said, and laughed, "but it is bitter cold out there. It cut right through my boots and I did forget to put my socks on."

"That shock is enough to wake the dead."

"Sorry."

"No, you're not."

"Well, no, not really. I suppose you're going to make us go back out in that soon."

"I have to. You know that."

She cuddled up to him, pressing her back hard against his front when he slipped his arm around her waist. A faint smile touched her mouth when she felt a gentle nudge of interest against her backside. One part of Tyrone had definitely recovered its full strength.

Deidre was a little disappointed that they would not be making love, and probably would not for a while yet. Not only had he stirred a greed within her with his passion, but their time together was growing alarmingly short. The end of their journey was not far away, and she still had no indication from him that that would not also mean the end of their affair. At times she thought she saw a soft look upon his face, felt a certain tenderness in his touch, but she dared not give those things too much meaning. For all she knew, he always treated women that way. He might actually feel some affection for the women who became his lovers, but affection was not enough.

As his breathing grew slower, she caught his rhythm, her chest rising and falling in time with his. It relaxed her and she closed her eyes. She realized she was going to miss this as much as she would the passion they shared. It was lovely to sleep curled up in his arms, feeling warm and safe. It made it easy for her to delude herself into thinking she was reaching him in some way. Deidre found herself constantly fighting such dreams of harmony and love between them. It was winter. Tyrone might hold her close simply because she was warm. A dog would do as well.

It was funny in a sad way. At the start of this journey all she had been able to think of was how fast she could get to Paradise. Now she dreaded that day. If it was not for the facts that the Martins were quite willing to kill them to stop them, that Tyrone faced utter ruin if they did not get to the land office by the set time, and that Maura might be waiting for her there, Deidre knew she would be doing her best to delay the inevitable. She placed her hand over Tyrone's where it rested against her stomach and sighed. Even this innocent closeness might soon end. Paradise could well prove to be misnamed, at least for her.

Passion swept over Deidre, pulling her from sleep. She threaded her fingers through Tyrone's hair and held him close to the breast he was so avidly kissing. He groaned when he slid his hand between her thighs to stroke his fingers through the hot, damp welcome there and she echoed the soft sound of need. She was more than ready for him when he entered her, wrapping her legs around his slim hips and holding on tightly as he drove them both to the brink of madness.

She was still holding on to him when sanity returned, her still-uneven breaths matching his as her body calmed. It took another moment before she realized the full ramifications of what had just happened. It had only been two days since he had recovered from the fever that had nearly killed him, but recovered he was. Her body was still tingling with the proof of that. She stared at him in consternation when he eased the intimacy of their embrace, propped himself up on his forearms, and looked down at her.

"I have missed that," he whispered, and brushed a gentle kiss over her lips. "Are you about to scold me?"

"For that, no," she replied. "For what I believe you are about to suggest, yes."

Tyrone grimaced faintly as he got out of bed and began to dress. "We can't lose any more time, Deidre."

"I know, but you are still weak. The stitches can't be taken out yet."

"I know I'm not back to my full strength. But we can't stay here until I'm perfectly well and the stitches are removed. We'd never make Paradise in time. I know we won't be able to move very fast and that I might even have to stop earlier than I want to, but at least we'll be getting closer to Paradise, to that damned land office."

Deidre nodded and watched him go out the back door. She got out of bed and began to get dressed, donning all the warm layers of clothes she had been able to set aside for a while. It did not help her mood to see that Tyrone moved with only a hint of stiffness, probably caused more by the tightness of the stitched and healing skin than from any real pain. He would heed no argument she could come up with and she could understand that. Everything he valued, everything his father had built for his family, was at risk.

The moment he returned, she hurried to the outhouse. She wished he had at least taken the time to cuddle a little more after their swift, hungry bout of lovemaking, but she would not complain. If he was even half as hungry for the passion they could share as she was, they might not have left the bed all day if they had not separated quickly. It would have delayed his attempt to get back on the trail to Paradise, but she suspected he would have resented that once the fog of desire had cleared his brain.

The delicious scent of brewing coffee cheered her a little when she returned to the cabin. She greedily accepted the cup Tyrone handed to her, savoring its warmth. His color was good and she tried to let that ease her concern for him. If they took it easy and were not harassed by any more of the Martins' henchmen, she suspected he would be all right.

"Stop worrying about me," he scolded gently, kissing the tip of her nose as he placed their breakfast of bacon and beans on the rough table set before the fireplace.

"I am trying to," she replied as she sat down and began to eat, realizing that she was so bored with the fare that she barely tasted it anymore.

"Deidre, I would much rather stay here, warm and safe, than drag my carcass onto the back of that horse and ride through the cold. I can't do that. Maybe if it was just me, I might take the risk, might take a day or two more of rest and hope I could make it up on the trail. I can't take that risk, can't cheat my brothers of their heritage just because I want to pamper myself."

"I am not arguing with you about the need to get back on the trail. I can't. I would probably do the same thing." She met his brief grin with one of her own, recognizing that her stubbornness matched his own. "Just promise me that you'll take it easy. I don't think you can open your wound again, but who knows? It's more the fact that you are not long recovered from a fever, and that sort of thing can steal a lot of your strength. It can also come back if you let yourself get too tired too soon afterward."

"I know that and, I swear, we will go easy. There's still time enough to do that."

For a while they ate in silence. Deidre could not stop herself from looking for signs that he was indeed recovered enough to travel. She wanted some assurances, ones she found herself and did not just hear from Tyrone's lips. Even if he did not have so much at stake, he was a man, and they were notorious for claiming that they were fine when they most definitely were not. She was not about to let pigheaded pride send him back to bed with a return of his fever.

"How much longer before we get there?" she finally asked, washing the dishes as he packed their things.

"A week, maybe two. If we are forced to go very slowly, I suspect it'll be more like two weeks."

"I did not really comprehend how far away from Missouri Montana was," she murmured.

"Not so far by train or stage. Going on horseback does mean you can take a quicker route sometimes, but it also means you cover the miles a lot more slowly. Yeah, we could push the beasts to a faster pace, but, in the end, that could lose us time, for they'd end up exhausted or lamed.

Especially in this weather. The cold's as hard on them as it is on us."

"I hope you have some very luxurious accommodations for the beasts at your ranch," she said, struggling for a teasing air as she picked up her pack and watched him soak down the ashes in the fireplace.

He smiled and paused to pull her into his arms and kiss her. "I will treat them like kings. After all, if they get me to Paradise in time, they will have saved the day."

"Equine heroes," she murmured as they left the cabin and walked to the small stables.

"I hope Mitchell and your cousin aren't having this much trouble."

Setting her bag down and saddling her horse, Deidre smiled at him. "You put them together again."

"I do that often, do I?" He secured the cinch on the packhorse's saddle and began to strap their badly dwindled supplies on the animal's back.

"Just lately, yes. I hope it's a premonition of some sort. It would be nice to think that Maura has had some protection during her travels."

"Or that the Martins haven't got someone dogging her trail like we do?"

"That would be very fine indeed. Ah, well, I'll just keep telling myself that I'll see her soon."

"You and Maura are close, are you?"

"She is all the family I have left. My mother died when I was only ten and then, one after another, twelve other members of the family followed her. At times it seemed all I ever did was attend funerals." She shook her head and mounted her horse. "Enough of those dark memories. Shall we be on our way?"

"I'm right behind you, ma'am."

Deidre smiled faintly as they rode away from the cabin. Despite her concerns about Tyrone's health, she was not entirely sorry to leave the place. It held too many memories of violence and the fear that Tyrone would die. At least their journey was starting with them both in a good humor. She suspected that would not last for very long and intended to enjoy it. Between the cold, the discomfort of long hours in the saddle, and the monotonous diet they endured, there was not a whole lot else she could enjoy, she thought with a sigh.

Christmas was drawing closer and Deidre wondered if they would make it to Paradise in time to relax and enjoy the holiday. Even if they did, she was not sure she would find much pleasure in it, despite the fact that it had always been her favorite celebration. It would be her first Christmas without her father. She prayed it would not also be celebrated without Maura.

Chapter Ten

DESPITE ALL OF HER efforts not to, Deidre took another peek at Tyrone, who rode silently at her side. He looked exhausted, which was not surprising, but she saw no sign of pain or illness. A week of riding had slowed his recovery from his wound and the fever, but had not stopped it. She prayed that criminal Pete's wound took even longer to heal, for neither she nor Tyrone was in any condition to fight anyone. Even their horses looked exhausted, she thought with a sigh.

"We're almost there," Tyrone said, giving her a tired smile.

"Almost where? Not Paradise?"

"No, not Paradise. We're almost at my friend's ranch. Jason Booker of the Three Angels."

"The Three Angels? An odd name for a man to give his ranch, isn't it?"

"A little. Named it for his aunts who'd raised him and helped him build the place. Sweet ladies. A little odd. Flora, Dora, and Cora Booker."

Deidre laughed. "Oh, dear. How could their mother be so mean? There is nothing wrong with any one of those names, I didn't mean that, but, as a group?"

Tyrone shook his head and laughed as well. "It does make you blink. Still, they seem to have grown into their names. They are a little plump and a little gray now, but they must have been pretty enough when they were young. I've always wondered why not one of them ever got married."

"How many years do you have to subtract to make them young ladies again?"

"Twenty, perhaps? Maybe a little more."

"The war. I suspect the war has something to do with it. A lot of young men died leaving a lot of widows and broken-hearted young maids. I know several women at home who are alone, yet fair enough, genteel enough, to make one wonder why. Each one of them lost the man they planned to marry in that cursed war. You can't turn so many men into cannon fodder without suffering some consequences."

"Well, damn, never thought of that."

"And would never be so rude to simply ask them why they never got married?"

"Ah, but you would?"

"Maybe. I did back home. Curiosity is one of my faults. It soon became clear that men gone to be soldiers was the answer. One woman had been engaged to a man who then chose the wrong side as far as her family was concerned. Her fiancé was banished from her life, went to war where she could not reach him to let him know she was willing to defy her father, and found himself another wife. Very sad. I did wonder from time to time how many other women had just been left behind, slipping into lonely spinsterhood." She shivered and looked around. "Dark thoughts for a dark day. Has it grown colder?"

"No," he answered, saying the word so slowly it grew into two syllables as he, too, looked around. "I'm getting that itchy feeling on the back of my neck."

"Like someone's eyes are fixed there? I just got the shivers," she murmured, meeting his worried gaze and sharing his anxiety. "Think they're back on our trail?"

"Pete could have had time to heal, at least enough to get on a horse again."

"How far away is your friend's ranch?"

"About five miles, maybe a little more."

"Can he handle the trouble that might be following us again?"

"Without question."

Tyrone nudged his mount to a faster pace and Deidre did the same. A part of him felt it was a little foolish to act solely upon feelings they had, but he decided it hurt nothing to be, perhaps, a little too cautious. The fact that, right in the middle of idle conversation, both of them had felt a strong sense of unease added some weight to his decision to hurry. Booker's ranch was close enough that they could give in to that unease without endangering the horses.

A guard at the gates to Booker's ranch was just hailing them when shots rang out. The man went down, wounded in the leg. A second shot creased the left rear flank of Deidre's horse. Tyrone cursed, grabbing out to try to catch the reins, even as he knew it was too late. Her horse bolted, galloping through the gates straight toward Booker's ranch.

Tyrone started after her, then reined in when he saw two of Booker's hands ride up and flank her. Confident that they would be able to help her and get her to safety, he dismounted and sprawled on the ground next to the wounded man. A quick glance at the man's injury assured Tyrone that it was not too serious, the flow of blood already easing.

"Who the hell are you?" the man demanded as he used his bandana to bind his wound.

Catching the glint of the sun off metal, Tyrone knew his enemies were using the trees just beyond the gates for cover. "Name's Tyrone Callahan."

"Ah, heard of you. Friend of Jason. My name's Tom." He briefly shook Tyrone's hand, then scowled toward the trees. "You bring this scum with you?"

" 'Fraid so, although I had thought I'd laid at least one of them low."

"They been chasing you long?"

"For weeks." Tyrone shook his head as he tried to discern enough of a target in the shadows of the trees to take aim at. "Surprised they're being this bold. They've got to know they'll be badly outnumbered here."

"Maybe you've done drove 'em crazy."

Tyrone laughed, but had to wonder if there was some truth behind Tom's jesting words. It was probably Pete and Jim out there and Tyrone would not be surprised if they had become frustrated beyond all common sense. There was also the chance that the Martins were dangling a prize in front of them that was so large they were willing to risk everything to get it. He ducked and cursed as a bullet grazed the ground so close to him the dirt sprayed into his face, chips of rock stinging his cheek.

Tom fired several bullets into the trees in response, then glanced over his shoulder. "Well, your lady friend is safe. Carl and Joe got her horse calmed down and are taking her to the house. And here comes Jason with some men. If those fools after you have any sense, they'll hightail it right outta here. Jason don't like trouble. He'll be eager to stomp it."

Jason Booker reined in his horse beside Tom and Tyrone and looked down at the pair. The tall, fair-haired man, who had always made Tyrone think of Vikings, seemed oblivious to the occasional bullets speeding his way from the trees. Tyrone could not decide if Booker was fearless or just crazy and never had been able to. The way Booker occasionally scowled toward the trees, as if the men shooting at him were little more than a nuisance, did not help Tyrone decide this time, either.

"Want them alive, Ty?" Booker asked, his deep voice rumbling out of his broad chest in the muted roar that, for Booker, passed for a friendly, conversational tone.

"Sad to say, I think dying's the only thing that'll get them to stop hounding me and Deidre," Tyrone replied.

"Just rest here. Be back in a minute."

Before Tyrone could protest this usurping of his duty, Booker snapped a few orders to his men, then charged straight toward the trees, screaming some sort of wild battle cry. His men spread out to the side forming a semicircle. The gunfire they produced was unrelenting and Tyrone felt almost sorry for the men in the trees. He doubted they would escape this time.

"I suppose there is no point in my following him," Tyrone muttered as he sat up and briefly glanced back at his horse.

"Nope," said Tom. "Hell, he'll probably be back and sipping lemonade on the front porch before you even get your ass in the saddle." He cocked his head to the side. "It's over," he murmured as a sudden quiet fell, a quiet made all the more profound coming on the heels of such a furious assault.

Tyrone was helping Tom sit up when Booker returned. Two of his men pulled two horses, a body slung over each saddle. Silently, Tyrone went to look at each dead man and felt a sense of grim satisfaction. Pete and Jim would not be hiring their guns out again. After what they had tried to do to Deidre, he was a little sorry he had not killed them himself, but decided not to argue the matter. The important thing was that they could no longer threaten Deidre or himself.

"Come up to the house and introduce me to your pretty lady," Booker said. "Staying long?"

"Just a night," Tyrone replied. "Two at the most. I've got to get back to Paradise."

As Tyrone hurried to mount his horse, leaving Tom to the care of his fellow ranch hands, he suddenly wondered if coming to Booker's place had been such a good idea. The man seemed a little too interested in Deidre. Tyrone had seen that gleam in his friend's eyes before, a gleam too many women found irresistible. He nudged his horse to a pace that allowed him to catch up with Booker.

Deidre saw Tyrone ride up next to a huge blond man and she hurried to the steps of the porch, looking Tyrone over carefully as he dismounted. "You're all right?" she asked as he stepped up to her.

"Just fine." He smiled reassuringly when she touched his bloodied cheek. "Just a few scratches."

"Jim and Pete?" she asked as she caught sight of the riders leading the horses with the bodies.

"They won't be troubling us again." Tyrone quickly moved to stand next to Deidre, draping a possessive arm around her slim shoulders, as Booker walked up to her. "This is Jason Booker, owner of this place. Jason, this is Deidre Kenney." He frowned when Jason kissed Deidre's hand and she blushed.

"Pleased to meet you, Mister Booker," she said, wondering why the man was grinning so wickedly at Tyrone.

"Call me Jason, darlin'. Come on inside. We'll get you a room where you can clean off the dust of the road and change your clothes. We can have a nice long talk over supper."

Deidre was so pleased at the thought of a bath, she only partly noticed how neatly Jason Booker extracted her from Tyrone's hold and led her into the house. The smell of food welcomed her and she felt her stomach clench in anticipation and appreciation. She smiled her gratitude at her host as a maid led her up the stairs.

By the time Tyrone met Jason in the front parlor for a drink before dinner, he was not feeling very charitable toward his old friend. He had been put in a room far away from Deidre's, the three maiden aunts who lived with Booker set between him and the object of his desire. The thought of making love to Deidre in one of Jason's huge, soft beds was very tempting, but Tyrone doubted he could make it all the way from his room to hers before someone heard or saw him. Since it was obvious that Jason had planned it just that way, Tyrone had to wonder why.

"I'm surprised you didn't put me in the bunkhouse," he drawled as he sat in a chair facing Jason and sipped at the finely aged whiskey his friend served him.

"I considered it," Jason replied, his blue eyes sparkling with barely repressed laughter.

"She's mine, Jason." Tyrone was a little surprised at the hard possessiveness in his voice, but noticed that his friend was not. He suspected that should trouble him, but it did not.

"You're married, are you? You should've said so. I would've put you in a room together." Jason rubbed his chin and looked at Tyrone with a reproval that was blatantly false. "Didn't see a ring, now I think on it."

"No ring, but she is still mine."

"For how long?"

The question was asked softly, but Tyrone felt the force of it. He had no answer, realized he had not taken much time to consider the matter. One or two thoughts had rattled through his head about how, if she continued to please him, he might keep her. They now seemed so arrogant, even callous, he was too embarrassed to repeat them. He would certainly pay dearly if Deidre ever caught wind of them. Jason would probably laugh, and Tyrone decided he was giving the man enough amusement.

"That is between Deidre and me," he finally said, and fought the urge to punch that broad smile off his friend's face.

"It won't be for long. This is still woman-poor country. About the only boundary men honor when it comes to women is the one drawn by a wedding ring." Jason gave Tyrone a slow smile. "Although we both know that doesn't always stop a little delightful poaching. You've never played fast and loose with a maiden before, old friend. Maybe you ought to stop and ask yourself why you did this time." He cocked his head toward the door. "The lady approaches. 'Spect my aunties will flutter in soon, as well."

Deidre's smile wavered slightly as she entered the parlor. Tyrone looked somber, even a little tense. Then Jason smiled and jovially offered her a little wine. When Tyrone smiled as well a moment later, she decided it could not have been anything too serious that had caused that air of tension in the room. Then three nearly identical ladies, all slightly plump, all somewhat pretty with sparkling blue eyes just like their rogue of a nephew's, and all showing the first hints of advancing age, burst into the parlor. Deidre found all of her concerns about Tyrone's mood smothered by their friendly if somewhat scatterbrained chatter. An amiable barrage of questions also kept her so busy that they had all adjourned to the dining room and gone through all the courses except dessert before she realized that the Bookers now knew almost everything. In fact, Deidre was a little surprised she had not been slyly pushed into revealing her relationship with Tyrone.

"My goodness," she said, admiration mixing with amazement as she looked at the Bookers while helping herself to some apple pie. "You people would have made the Spanish Inquisition proud."

Tyrone laughed along with the others, familiar with their techniques. "It's a Booker specialty. Dull your victim's senses with huge quantities of good food and fine wine, then graciously bleed him dry of every tiny scrap of information he might possess."

"One should always know all one can about a situation before acting upon it," said Cora, the aunt dressed in blue. "Cool, calm, and ever deliberate. That is the way to succeed."

"Cool, calm, ever deliberate?" Tyrone grinned at Jason. "Oh, yeah, that's Jason all right."

"The dear boy has his moments."

It was hard, but Deidre hid a smile when Cora called the huge Viking dominating the head of the table a *dear boy*. The mild eccentricities she had already noted in her host were explained from the moment she met the three women who had raised him. She also sensed a frighteningly keen intelligence behind Jason Booker's easy smiles. Some of his questions were mildly voiced, yet so clever they pulled out answers one did not even know one had, and sometimes stirred an insight that had proven elusive.

"I am hoping the last leg of our journey is peaceful, unlike the rest of it, now that Pete and Jim are gone." She sighed and shook her head. "A part of me winces over their deaths, which is foolish, for they would have killed Tyrone or me without blinking. They certainly tried often enough. I suppose I am just appalled at the deaths and violence brought on by greedy men trying to grasp hold of what isn't theirs."

"It has always been so, sad to say," murmured Flora, the aunt in pink.

"We'll have to run the gauntlet of the Martins between here and the land office," Tyrone said, hating to steal away whatever sense of safety the deaths of Pete and Jim had brought Deidre, yet knowing they could not yet relax their guard. "If I were them, even if I thought Jim and Pete still chased us or had caught us, I would be watching closely for our arrival."

"Surely they won't do anything too drastic once we get to town?" Deidre frowned. "They must know that they can't afford too many witnesses. Once caught in a cheat or a crime, all of their other transactions would be questioned. All rumors about them would start to sound like fact."

"But will they?" asked Jason quietly. "If their grip on Paradise is already chokingly tight, people will think twice before they openly accuse the Martins of anything. They might sympathize and want to help, but they've got their own backsides to protect."

"True, but when I left, they were still apt to be cautious in their actions," said Tyrone. "They grasp land and wealth with both hands, using bribery and threats to get them what they want. Only a hint or two of something more, but usually only by their hired men and rarely within the boundaries of Paradise. They seem impervious to suspicion and the hatred of those they crush, but they never give anyone hard proof of their crimes. If they try to kill us too close to home, that proof could be forthcoming. Of course, I'm very close to stealing a big prize out of their hands. It could push them to act rashly."

"Then I will send some of my men with you," said Jason.

Deidre smiled faintly as the two men began to argue. Tyrone was reluctant to pull anyone else into the midst of his troubles, but Jason was just as stubborn as he was. By the time they retired to the parlor for an after-dinner drink, the two men were arguing over just how many men would ride with Tyrone. Since the number of men Jason had originally proposed to send had been very high, a reluctant Tyrone was finally badgered into accepting about half that number. Deidre had the strong suspicion that Jason had planned it that way.

The aunts kept her entertained with their chatter, gently pressing her for any gossip or news she might have. When the men finally settled things between them and joined the conversation, Deidre was amused by the blatant way Jason flirted with her. She found a thread of hope in the way Tyrone glared at his friend. Jealousy and a distinct air of possessiveness might not be borne of the love she craved, but it could mean that his feelings ran a little deeper than passion alone. With the end of their journey looming in front of her, Deidre realized she was almost constantly looking for some sign of those deeper feelings in Tyrone.

Suddenly weary, Deidre excused herself and went to bed. As she crawled beneath the covers, her whole body eagerly welcoming the warm, soft haven, she sighed. She knew she would spend the night alone, but tried to tell herself that was for the best. It would trouble her to carry on scandalously beneath the roof of the Bookers, risking the goodwill of Jason's three aunts, but that was not all of it. A part of her told her that it might be best to start loosening the bonds that tied her to Tyrone Callahan. It was probably the wisest thing to do, even though she doubted any amount of physical distance was going to ease the pain she would suffer if he cast her aside.

Jason smiled as, after his aunts retired for the night, Tyrone cast several longing glances toward the doors. "Not tonight you won't," he murmured.

"Gone prudish on me, have you, Jason?" Tyrone said, not inclined to admit that he had already decided to behave with the utmost propriety tonight, despite all temptation.

"You know I'm as far from that as a man can be yet still claim himself a gentleman, but let's not forget my aunts. I don't think they'd condemn what you've been thinking of, but it could make them uncomfortable."

"Probably make Deidre uncomfortable, too."

"Quite probably. Even though you've seduced the girl, she still carries the mark of a lady and an intriguing touch of innocence. Do you know what I think?"

"No, and not sure I want to, but that won't stop you from telling me, will it?"

"Not at all. Marry the girl."

"Maybe I'm not interested in getting married."

"Maybe not today, maybe you hadn't planned on it, had wanted to wait a while, but I would let go of the reins of bachelorhood, if I were you. You will want to marry someday, just as I will. You'll wake up one morning, look at what you've built, and suddenly want a little spawn of your own blood to leave it to. When that day comes, it'll be that girl you'll think of, I guarantee it. Hell, I don't think she'll get more than ten miles from Paradise before you'll start regretting letting her leave."

"Yeah, I think so, too," Tyrone said on a sigh, then grinned at his friend. "Suppose you'll want an invite to the wedding."

"Damn right. You say she has a cousin?"

"Get that gleam out of your eye. I can't shake the feeling that she's with Mitchell and, if she's half the woman Deidre is, my brother will be planning on keeping her."

"Well, that restores my faith in my own judgment."

"It does? How so?"

"Always thought the Callahan boys were smart little bastards."

"Let's hope Deidre appreciates my finer points enough to say yes then."

"Oh, she will."

"You're so sure of that, are you?"

"Trust me. That girl is just waiting for you to ask."

Chapter Eleven

"A SLEIGH? HOW WONDERFUL!" Deidre cried as she stood outside on the front veranda of Booker's large home and studied the vehicle that would take them the rest of the way into Paradise. "I have only ridden in one once before, but I loved it."

Some of Tyrone's bad mood faded when he looked at Deidre. Snow had fallen the night of their arrival and for a great deal of the next day. Although he still had plenty of time to get to his ranch by Christmas, still two days away, he had not enjoyed two long, lonely nights sleeping in an empty bed. It had been torture of the worst kind to know Deidre was only a few doors away but not be able to go to her. The only close contact he had had with Deidre since arriving had been when she had taken his stitches out, but all three aunts had been there to offer helpful advice. Jason's silent amusement, revealing that he had easily guessed at Tyrone's mounting frustration, had certainly not helped to lighten his mood. But, now, seeing the delight shining on Deidre's small face, he could almost think the frustration and delay he had suffered a small price to pay.

"If the road is clear, with no toppled trees or the like, we should reach Paradise in a few hours," he said, reaching out to take her hand in his, hoping it was not too improper a gesture, but too eager to touch her to care. "If we make very good time, we can collect my brother Stephen and go straight to the land office."

Some of the pleasure Deidre had felt upon seeing the sleigh and the crisp new snow faded at his words. The words *and then what* burned on the tip of her tongue, but she held them back. If he did not choose to speak of the future, if his grand plan was to just let things go along as they were until he was bored, she would not lower herself to nag him about it. Deidre decided she would stick around until Maura joined her and then, if Tyrone still had not presented some plan for the future that went further than how many times they could make love in one night, she was leaving. She would not linger, constantly hoping for more than an affair, and certainly not until he grew bored and gave her her congé. Who knew, she mused with a silent chuckle that held an unsettling bitterness, maybe if he found the sweet shop closed, he would realize how much he craved it.

After saying farewell to the Bookers and thanking them for their help and hospitality, Deidre got into the sleigh. She smiled faintly as Tyrone sat down next to her and tucked her up so firmly in several blankets she felt cocooned. Such concern for her comfort and well-being were good signs, she supposed.

Shortly after they started on their way, Deidre was glad of all her heavy clothing, the blankets, and the heated stones the Booker ladies had placed beneath her feet. It was bitterly cold, and the high, sloped sides of the sleigh provided only a little protection. As she huddled up against the side, little more than her eyes exposed to the air, she felt badly for Booker's men and Tyrone, who were so much more exposed than she. Deidre hoped that nothing slowed their progress, that it did indeed only take a few hours to reach Paradise, for she doubted the men could endure much more than that.

When the town of Paradise came into view, Deidre almost echoed the men's expressions of relief, even though she had not suffered as badly as they had. For once, the knowledge that her time with Tyrone could soon come to an end did not trouble her much. She was far more interested in reaching someplace warm.

Tyrone pulled up in front of a pretty two-story house at the edge of town. He got down from the sleigh, silently motioned for Deidre to wait when she moved to follow, and turned his attention to Booker's men. Ignoring their protests, he gave them the funds to go to a hotel to get warm and dry, fill their bellies with some hot food, and rest, waiting until the morning to return to the Three Angels if they chose to. He reassured them that their job was done, that he had only needed the extra protection while still upon the trail, thanked them, and sent them on their way.

Even as Tyrone turned to help Deidre out of the sleigh, the front door of the house was flung open. From where she stood there was no mistaking the man's relationship to Tyrone, for he had the same dark, dangerously handsome looks, the same lean grace. She sighed when Tyrone abruptly left her side and raced up the front steps of the surrounding porch to embrace the young man. It was understandable that he would be pleased to see his brother and be excited by his victory over the Martins, so she graciously forgave him his boorish behavior. After several minutes of being ignored while Tyrone told his brother all about their adventures, she began to feel a lot less gracious and marched up the steps to plant herself at his side.

When Stephen's attention was drawn to his right, Tyrone frowned and followed his brother's gaze. He flushed with embarrassment when he saw Deidre, realizing that he had momentarily forgotten her. Taking her by the arm, he nudged her toward Stephen and introduced her. When his brother took her hand in his and welcomed her with what Tyrone felt was a nauseating eagerness, he abruptly tugged her back to his side.

"Do you think the land office is still open?" he asked Stephen.

"It is, and the judge is at home nursing his gout, so we can stop there, too," replied his brother.

"Are you sure we can trust Judge Lennon?" He draped his arm around Deidre's shoulders and was a little annoyed to see the same look of amusement in Stephen's eyes that he had seen in Jason's.

"Very sure. He can't stomach the Martins, openly and loudly complains about them, and heartily bemoans the lack of evidence needed to convict them of any crimes. The Martins can't bribe him because they don't have anything he wants or needs, and they aren't stupid enough to try and threaten a man with so many important friends. Who knows? Maybe the old goat just likes swimming against the tide."

"And you think it's a good idea to show him the papers before we take them to the land office?"

"I do. After all, the others we had mysteriously disappeared from that place. The Martins obviously have a man working for them in there. I think it's Will Pope. Doesn't matter. We can't trust anyone there to keep the papers safe and then show them to a judge to make a decision. So, I say go to the judge first, get a ruling first."

"Agreed." He looked at Deidre. "The papers?"

"I'll need a moment of privacy," she replied.

"Come inside," said Stephen, and led them into his house. "I need to get some warmer clothes on. I'll get Bob to see to the sleigh and the team. This business will take a little while and it's too cold to leave the poor beasts standing there." He ushered them into the parlor.

"The sleigh will be taken back to Booker. Any word from Mitchell?" Tyrone asked as he joined Deidre in standing in front of the fireplace, soaking up the welcome warmth.

"Nope, but then he wasn't supposed to get in touch with us, was he?"

"True. Thought he might do so anyway if there was trouble or he picked up a partner." Tyrone sighed and could see by the look upon Stephen's face that his concerns about Mitchell were shared. "Go and get dressed. Let's get this done and over with."

It was only a few minutes' wait before Stephen rejoined them, just about long enough for Deidre to lift up her skirts, get the papers out of the hidden pocket, and hand them to Tyrone. Although Deidre was reluctant to leave the warmth of the fire, she was pleased when it was decided they would walk. She was tired of horses, eager to stretch her legs despite the cold.

The judge was delighted to see them and cackled gleefully when they showed him the papers. Judge Lennon promised to inform everyone he could think of that the Callahans had proven their claim to the ranch and the mine to his complete satisfaction. He also gave them a signed witness statement they could turn in at the land office along with their deeds.

Tyrone and his brother were in high spirits as they strode away from the judge's home and headed to the land office. They readily included her in their joy, and so Deidre was a little surprised when it suddenly fled, both men stopping, their bodies tensed. Following the direction of their identically cold stares, she saw three burly men blocking their way. She needed no introductions to know that these were the Martins and she inched a little closer to Tyrone.

"Heard you left town, Tyrone," said the larger of the three, his thick brown hair well sprinkled with gray. "Safe trip?"

"I survived, Walter," Tyrone replied, his voice hard and cold. "Others didn't."

"Sorry to hear that."

"I imagine you are."

"Going somewhere?" asked the leaner, shorter, of the three. "Bit cold for a stroll."

"We've got some business to attend to, John." Tyrone subtlely stepped in front of Deidre when John rested his hand on the gun he wore.

"At the land office?"

"As a matter of fact, yes. So, if these pleasantries are at an end, we'd like to be on our way." For a moment Tyrone feared the Martins were going to prove him wrong and openly battle him in the street, but then Walter stepped aside, signaling his sons John and Michael to do the same.

"This isn't over yet," said Walter as Tyrone, Stephen, and Deidre stepped past them.

"Oh, I think it is," Tyrone said in an equally quiet voice. "We've already been to see the judge."

A chill snaked down Tyrone's back as he walked. A quick glance at Stephen and Deidre told him his companions felt that same unease. Walter and Michael had the wits to know they could not do anything, that they had lost their bid on the Callahan holdings, and could lose even more if they reacted to that loss with violence in broad daylight with so many witnesses around. It was John, the hot-tempered son, who really worried Tyrone. It was not until he heard Walter speaking to John in a low, angry voice, however, that he began to relax.

"Thought we'd be shot dead on the spot," Stephen said quietly after they had put a little distance between themselves and the Martins. "Sure we're safe?" he asked, casting a very quick glance over his shoulder.

Tyrone nodded, and took Deidre's hand in his. "I don't think they'll make life very pleasant for us, but they can't take anything from us now. The game has been lost and Walter knows it. He won't like it, but he'll make do with what he has. John's the one who worries me. He'd as soon shoot you as look at you, but I believe his father will keep him in line."

"You've beaten them, but they haven't actually been defeated, have they?" Deidre asked.

"No, sorry to say," replied Tyrone. "That'll take time. We can work against them now, however, and we will. I think it's past time those of us who are against them band together. Walter's been picking us off one by one. Our blindness made it all the easier for him. That will stop now."

Stephen murmured an agreement, and some of the anger Deidre felt, an anger stirred by the cold arrogance of the Martins, was eased. It flared back to life again when they went into the land office. After just a moment of dealing with the clerk named Will Pope, Deidre decided that Stephen was right in thinking that the man worked for the Martins. He was belligerent, arrogant, rude, and openly bullied the other clerk. Deidre was a little amazed that the man made so little effort to hide his affiliations.

"How do I know these are real?" asked Will, a smirk barely visible beneath his greasy blond mustache.

"They look official to me, Will," the too thin clerk named Ted said as he nervously peered over Will's shoulder. The air whooshed out of him, he paled, and hastily stepped back after Will viciously jabbed his elbow into his stomach. "Maybe not," he rasped, and stumbled back to his small desk in the far corner of the office.

"Judge Lennon accepted them." Tyrone slapped the signed statement from the judge down upon the counter.

"That old man?" Will drawled, but his anger was revealed by the flush upon his cheeks, and his eyes were narrowed so much they nearly disappeared into the fleshy folds of his face.

"That old man is a highly respected judge in this county, even in the state. And, before you think of just losing that little piece of paper," Tyrone said in a hard, cold voice as he leaned closer to Will, "maybe you ought to know he's sending statements like this and an interesting personal note to everyone he knows, including some officials who may start to wonder what's going on down here."

"Ain't nothing going on down here."

"No? That's fine then, although, if I were you, I'd start making sure my fingerprints weren't all over any of that *nothing*. Now, I'm going to stand right here and watch carefully as you put those papers where they belong and mark them clearly. Then you're going to sign a paper saying you've seen them, seen the judge's acceptance of them as legal and binding proof of ownership, and that you personally filed them away." Tyrone took another paper out of his pocket and set it on the counter.

Will Pope hesitated, then softly cursed, and did as he was told. The Martins might have their hooks in the man, Deidre mused, but it was obviously not deep enough to make him stand firm against two angry Callahans and a wealth of legal papers. She had to hide a smile when a sullen Will signed the paper that neatly took away all chance of his denying the Callahans' claims, and Tyrone had the other clerk come and sign as a witness to it all.

Once outside of the office, Deidre hooked her arm through Tyrone's and smiled up at him. "That last twist of the knife was a very nice touch."

"It was Stephen's idea," Tyrone said, then grinned. "It was good, though. A nice touch indeed."

"Yes, and it might not hurt to boast of it, spread the word, shall we say? After all, if everyone had done the same when they had filed with the land office, maybe the Martins wouldn't have found it so easy to steal so much."

"Damn," both brothers muttered, and Deidre almost laughed at their identical looks of admiration mixed with the usual male irritation over a woman having a clever insight that they had not yet achieved.

When they got back to Stephen's house, Deidre was a little surprised to be left there while Tyrone dragged Stephen back out again. She was settled before the fireplace in a comfortable chair with hot chocolate and food, so it was not quite so bad. Nevertheless, Tyrone had been extremely secretive when she had asked him where they were going. Curling up in the chair and luxuriating in the warmth from the fire, she told herself there was no reason to feel uneasy. Even if she was not imagining the air of secretiveness about Tyrone, it did not have to mean anything bad or dangerous. Maybe, she mused with a sleepy smile, he was going to buy her a Christmas present.

"I hope there is a good reason why you're dragging me out into this cold again," Stephen muttered as, huddled in his heavy coat, he strode back into town at Tyrone's side.

"Deidre and I will be headed back to the ranch as soon as I do this and I realized that this is my only chance to get her a present," Tyrone said, feeling an odd mixture of excitement and anxiety over what he planned.

"Ah, yes, the pretty Miss Kenney. Just what do you plan to do about the fair Deidre?"

"Why do you need to know?"

Before Stephen could answer, they entered the huge mercantile store. Tyrone strode over to where Old Carl kept a glass case filled with an odd selection of jewelry, some pawned or sold by people in need of cash or supplies, and some bought from merchants and traveling salesmen. Ignoring the palpable curiosity from both his brother and Old Carl, Tyrone's gaze fixed upon a small, delicate gold ring set with a single pearl.

"That one," he said to Carl, studying it closely when the man took it out and handed it to him. Relieved to see that it might just be small enough to fit Deidre, he nodded. "I'll take it."

"Is that just a present or is it a farewell gift or, by some chance, is it an engagement ring?" asked Stephen as Old Carl went to find a small box to put the ring in, and Tyrone counted out the money to pay for it.

"Does that matter to you?"

"Well, being the youngest brother, it could cause me a twinge or two to discover that my oldest brother is such an idiot he would let a woman like that get away."

Tyrone grinned then said, "You hardly know her."

"From all you've told me about your travels and from meeting her, however briefly, my gut says you'd be a fool to let this one slip away. That, and the way you look at her."

"How do I look at her?"

"Like she's a sumptuous dessert you can't get your fill of."

"That says it about right." Tyrone paid Old Carl, stuck the ring box into his pocket, and left the store.

Keeping pace with Tyrone, Stephen asked, "So, are you getting married or not?"

"Well, I intend to ask her on Christmas morning. Maybe even Christmas Eve. You'll know if she accepts me when you come to Christmas dinner."

"Oh, she'll accept."

"How can you be sure?" Tyrone appreciated the vote of confidence, although it did not ease all of his uncertainty.

"Because, Brother, she looks at you the same way you look at her."

All the way home to his ranch, Tyrone kept surreptitiously glancing at Deidre, trying to see what Stephen and

Jason did. He could see a warmth in her gaze, now and then, but was not sure it meant any more than friendliness or desire, something he had no doubt she felt as strongly as he did. Now that he was prepared to talk marriage, he realized that he wanted more. He wanted a firm declaration of feelings, ones that ran a little deeper than desire. That touch of cowardice surprised him, but he accepted the need. It explained his nervousness, his uncertainty.

Once at the ranch, he turned Deidre over to the capable Mrs. Horne, the housekeeper at the Sweet Kate for over ten years. He personally saw to the stabling of the horses, ignoring his men's less than kind opinions of the sturdy packhorse. The animals had served him well and had more than earned some special care and attention. A hot bath and the promise of a hot meal greeted him when he returned to the house. He wasted no time in washing up and changing into clean clothes. Tyrone found himself almost embarrassingly eager to dine in his home with Deidre, to show her the house and see her reaction to it.

A little of his uncertainty faded when, after a hearty meal they had both enjoyed to the point of groaning, Tyrone took Deidre on a tour of his house. Her appreciation was fulsome, and, he knew at a glance, heartfelt. When she started to talk about how lovely it would all look swathed in Christmas finery, he laughed, swept her up into his arms, and carried her to his room.

"Tyrone," Deidre said, gasping softly with laughter as he tossed her onto his huge four-poster bed and sprawled on top of her. "What will Mrs. Horne think?"

Although she did nothing to stop his skilled, swift removal of her gown, she frowned, a little disturbed by her weakness for the man. Deidre liked the plump, blunt-speaking Mrs. Horne. She did not really want to behave so badly that she ended up disappointing the woman or gaining her disapproval.

"Ah, Deidre, she won't condemn you for this," he said

as he tossed aside her dress, then paused to start yanking off his own clothes, feeling almost desperate to lie in her arms, flesh touching flesh. "I am about to tell you a family secret. Mrs. Horne was my father's mistress for over five of the ten years she has been here. If he hadn't died, I think he would have married her."

"You've never—" she began, then blushed, afraid she had overstepped by asking about his past amours.

"You're the first woman to grace this bed." Naked, finally, he crouched over her and began to finish the delightful chore of undressing her. "And, by God, you do grace it."

When Deidre was naked, her glorious hair undone and spread all around her, Tyrone stared at her. She looked perfect there, flushed with desire and waiting for him. Suddenly, he knew that the bed would never again look so welcoming unless she was in it. As he eased himself down into her arms, he found himself praying that this would indeed be but the first night of many spent in this bed. It frightened him a little to recognize just how badly he wanted that, wanted her. He had never felt so vulnerable before. Tyrone knew that, if Deidre rejected him, it would make those past heartaches seem like no more than pinched vanity. When he felt her passion flare, he relaxed a little. This he understood. This he could control in some ways. As he joined his body to hers, savoring the deep, totally satisfying feel of it, he decided that, if he had to, he would use this passion they shared to hold her until he could win her heart.

Chapter Twelve

DEIDRE SET THE GIFT she had bought for Maura beneath the tree in the parlor, then stepped back to view her work. She had spent most of the day decorating the house. Tyrone's men had graciously gone out and found her what she considered the perfect tree plus a vast quantity of pine boughs to use for decoration. Although busy wading through the correspondence and paperwork that had accumulated during his absence, Tyrone had occasionally wandered by to lend a hand and, she thought with a faint smile, to steal a kiss or a heated embrace.

Taking a deep breath and savoring the scent of pine, she rejoined Tyrone on the settee near the fire. They were alone in the house, Mrs. Horne having left to spend the holiday with her son's family in town, and the hands whose families lived too far away or, sadly, had no kin, were in the bunkhouse. They had tomorrow free to do as they pleased, huge quantities of food, and a few bottles of whiskey to celebrate with, and even a small gift each from the Callahans. She and Tyrone had supped, shared a scandalously satisfying bath, and now relaxed before the fire, warm, content, and wearing only their robes. Deidre felt dangerously happy.

"Are you sure you can manage the cooking for tomorrow?" Tyrone asked as he draped his arm around her slim shoulders and tugged her close to his side.

She touched a kiss to his cheek, then picked up her wineglass from the table next to the settee. "Mrs. Horne did a great deal of preparatory work. It will probably be one of the easiest meals I have ever cooked." She smiled faintly and sipped her wine. "I was the housekeeper at the Kenney home for many years." Suddenly afraid she had gone past the bounds of propriety in all she had done today, she stared into her wine, unable to meet his gaze. "I fear I have a true love for this holiday. I did not mean to get so carried away today."

He briefly tightened his hold on her, giving her a quick hug. "It looks great. I'm glad you got carried away."

"Oh, I must give you your present." She set down her wine and hurried over to take a small package out from under the tree.

"It's only Christmas Eve, Deidre."

"You should always open one gift on Christmas Eve." She stood before him and handed him the package, suddenly feeling nervous and shy. "I know I only got you the one, but traditions should be followed."

"Ah, Deidre, you helped me keep my lands, all my father built. That was more than enough."

"That was business, at least to begin with. I hope you like it," she whispered, realized she was wringing her hands, and quickly clasped them behind her back.

Tyrone smiled at her and wondered if she knew how

that stance caused her robe to open wide enough to reveal the gentle slopes of her breasts. He decided to cater to his more roguish side and not tell her. She looked adorable, standing there tensely waiting for him to open her gift. Unable to hurt her feelings, he prepared himself to act suitably impressed and grateful, no matter what was in the package.

The breath caught in his throat when he opened the shallow, long box. Inside, resting on thick blue velvet was a knife, but no ordinary knife. The handle was a rich, burnished wood inlaid with scrimshaw. The delicate artistry upon the ivory depicted an old whaling ship on one side and whales on the other. Tyrone had the feeling it was an old knife, probably an heirloom. He knew it was not something she would have found in any of the places they had stopped in and looked at her with appreciation touched with curiosity.

"It is a beautiful piece of work." He picked it up, weighing it in his hand. "How did you know I had a liking for such things?"

"Well, I wasn't really sure. The knife you carry with you gave me a hint. An elaborately etched blade and a heavy wood handle decorated with silver? No common knife that. Even the sheath was fancy."

"Where did you find such a fine piece out here?" He frowned slightly. "It must have been costly."

"I suspect it was, but I didn't find it on my way here. It was Da's," she said quietly.

Tyrone stared at her even as he carefully put the knife away and set it on the table next to him. She had given him one of her father's knives, a possession she no doubt prized, for her deep love for her father was clear to see and hear each time she spoke of him. That had to be proof that she felt a lot more for him than simply passion. He reached out and pulled her into his arms, settling her on his lap as he gently kissed her.

"Thank you," he whispered, resting his forehead against hers as he inwardly winced over the inadequacy of the words. "I have something for you, as well." When she sat back a little, he tugged the small box from his pocket and handed it to her.

Deidre slowly opened the little box and gasped. The beauty of the delicate pearl ring prompted some of her reaction, but, mostly, she was seized by a heart-clenching uncertainty. Was this the sort of gift a man gave his lover? Was this, perhaps, a farewell token for good times shared? Or, did it mean more, the sort of more she had hoped for?

"It is beautiful," she said, her voice not much more than an unsteady whisper.

Praying it would fit, Tyrone took the ring and slipped it on her finger. He breathed an inner sigh of relief when the fit proved perfect, then held her hand, staring down at it. It was odd how the sight of that ring on her finger, a ring bought almost on impulse, clarified his thoughts and feelings. The ring was not just a token of the love he now recognized, but of possession. Deidre was his. He grimaced and nervously met her gaze. Or, she would be if he could just spit out the words and convince her to say yes.

"Marry me, Deidre," he said, softly cursing his ineptitude and tightening his hold on her when she jumped so quickly with surprise, she nearly tumbled off his lap.

It took Deidre a moment to overcome her utter shock. This was what she had ached for, yet she had never thought it would happen so abruptly, completely without warning. She had imagined a more tender scene, perhaps a few words of love or, at least, ones of need and caring. Then she tensed. The total lack of any of the softer words was unsettling. She loved him deeply and unrelentingly, and, while she was willing to accept that he might not feel the same just yet, she needed more than passion. She bit back the strong urge to just say yes and let the chips fall where they may.

"Why?" she asked, holding his gaze and struggling to interpret the look there.

"Ah, Deidre, for so many reasons." He pulled her into his arms again, smiling faintly when she quickly relaxed against him.

"Because I was a virgin?"

"I'd be a liar if I said that didn't matter, but it's not the reason."

"The passion?"

"Oh, God, yes. What man wouldn't want to hold fast to something as glorious as what we share?"

"Passion fades."

"I know, but I doubt ours will. I won't drag out sordid tales of my dark past, but, trust me, I've had experience enough to know that what we share is special, extraordinary. I knew it from the moment I first kissed you. True, cad that I was, I simply set my mind to seducing you with no thought to the future or the consequences."

"Cad that you are, you did a very fine job of it," she murmured, smiling faintly, for something in the way he held her, in the tone of his voice, told her that he did care for her. She needed the words, however.

Tyrone laughed softly and kissed the top of her head. He found it easier to speak of his feelings as he sat there just holding her, not looking into her eyes. Shyness and uncertainty, he supposed, although he hated to use those words in regard to himself. It was rather sad that, with the one woman he truly cared about, his usually glib tongue seemed to be tied up in knots.

"Ah, Deidre, I'm a coward." He placed his hand on the back of her head when she started to lift it, and gently held her down. "I want you. I want you by my side. The closer we got to Paradise, the more I realized I couldn't just set you aside and thank you kindly for the pleasure. I'm ashamed to say that Justin and Stephen saw it before I was really prepared to admit it to myself. They both said I'd be a fool to let you go. I want to go to bed beside you each night, see you at the breakfast table each morning, plant my children in you, laugh with you, argue with you, and grow old with you."

"All right." There was still no declaration of love, but Deidre felt certain a man did not want the things Tyrone spoke of from any woman unless he felt something deeper than desire.

Tyrone cupped her face in his hands and tilted it so that he could look into her eyes. "Did you say yes?"

She nodded. "Yes, I will marry you." She felt his grip on her face tighten slightly, then watched him take a deep, unsteady breath.

"Now I'll ask you the same question you asked me— why?"

"Well, it's certainly not because you were a virgin."

He laughed briefly, then brushed his mouth over hers. "Why?"

Deidre stared into his dark eyes, trying and failing to read the emotion there, an emotion that had turned them a turbulent black. What she did sense was a need in him, a need that had him tensed and waiting for her reply. She sighed. They were to be married. Maybe it was time to swallow her pride and bare her soul. After all, if you couldn't tell your own husband that you loved him, who could you say it to? she mused.

"Because, cad and seducer though you are, arrogant and irritating though you can be, I love you."

She squeaked in surprise when he suddenly hugged her almost too tightly. As she wrapped her arms around him, she decided the strength of his reaction to her words was a good sign. It hurt that he did not immediately reply in kind, but the strong emotion she felt in him gave her some ease. At least her feelings were appreciated and welcome. Any hint of arrogance or amusement would have slain her, made her feel exposed and humiliated.

"Ah, Deidre, I wish I had the skill to smother you in pretty words, sweet words that'd bring the tears to those beautiful eyes, but I seem to be tongue-tied." He stood up with her in his arms and walked over to the bearskin rug in front of the fireplace. "There is one thing I feel compelled to do, however."

"You want to do that now? Here? In the front parlor?" she asked as he set her down on the rug and sprawled on top of her.

"You'd rather do it in the kitchen?" Tyrone undid her robe and ran his unsteady hand down her side.

There was a taut urgency in Tyrone that began to infect Deidre. He was trembling faintly from the strength of it. She undid his robe and he yanked it off, tossing it aside. Hers quickly followed. Instinct told her that his passion had been stirred to this fierce height by her words of love. Perhaps, she mused, this was the only way he knew to show her how deeply her declaration had affected him, the only way he knew to express his own feelings. She would prefer words, but decided she would be a fool to dispel this highly emotional moment with demands and complaints.

His touch enflamed her, and soon she was past thinking about what it all meant. His every caress, every kiss, conveyed a sense of cherishing her as well as his own fierce passion. Despite the raging need that flowed from his body into hers, he took his time, leaving no part of her untouched or untasted.

He was unrelenting, yet she did not sense anything domineering or unkind behind it. It was as if he simply wanted to drown her in pleasure, as if he rewarded her in some strange way. He brought her joy with his clever fingers and deep, searing kisses. She had barely finished shaking from that gift when he did it again with his mouth. This time she fully expected him to join her, but he crouched over her, watching her as her release swept over her, flattering her with heated, scandalous words.

"Tyrone," she groaned, clutching at him, her body still tingling with repletion, yet crying out for him. "I want you with me," she whispered, desperately needing the joining of their bodies, especially now after she had opened her heart to him.

Although he shook with need, he hesitated, then eased their bodies together, stopping the moment they were fully joined. He was amazed at his control. Every nerve in his body was screaming for him to move. The way Deidre clung to him, her lithe body squirming against his in eager invitation, was threatening to send him blindly over the edge. But there was one more thing he wanted before he gave them what they both craved.

"Say it again," he urged, brushing his lips over hers. "I want to hear it now, while we're as close as a man and woman can be. Say it, Deidre."

"I love you," she said, and cried out softly in a mixture of surprise and delight as he began to move inside her.

His thrusts were swift and deep. Deidre was astonished to feel yet another release closing in on her. He slid his arm beneath her backside, holding her closer, and she aided him in that goal by wrapping her body even more tightly around his. When the shivers of release began to flow through her, he was there with her, matching her delight with his own, his voice blending with hers as they crested passion's heights together.

"Ah, Deidre mine," he murmured against her ear as they lay sprawled on the rug, too spent to move and still trembling faintly from the power of their shared release. "I love you," he said, finally able to spit out the words he now knew had been resting in his heart for a long time.

Deidre tensed, her heart pounding with the fear that she had just imagined those long-awaited words, and the joy that they were no dream. When he finally eased the intimacy of their embrace, she caught him off guard, shoving him onto his back and sprawling on top of him. He gave her a half-smile, and she was surprised to see that he looked nervous, almost shy.

"You love me?" When he grimaced faintly and turned his attention to idly toying with her long hair that hung around them like a thick, bright curtain, she framed his face in her hands and forced him to look at her. "Do you think it was easy for me to bare my soul?" she asked softly. "You seem to have agreed to hear the words. I do, too."

"Yes, I love you." He laughed softly when she sank down on top of him, trying to hug him with her whole body. "I love you, Deidre Kenney, soon to be Deidre Callahan. Are you crying?"

Since she was blubbering all over his naked chest, she decided that was a stupid question not worth an answer and, instead, asked, "When did you know?"

"A better question would be, when did I admit to it. I think a part of me knew from the start. Love and marriage was not what I thought I wanted, however." When she shivered, he sat up, taking her with him and collected their robes. "Passion I understood, although the strength of what we shared made me uneasy from time to time. Sad to say, this fool did not see the light until we got here." He shook his head as they donned their robes and he led her back to the settee. "It's hard to explain. I saw you in my bed and it looked, well, right. Then I put the ring on your finger. That was when my feelings became clear to me. The reason I think part of me has known it for a while is because that revelation neither startled me nor made me want to run for the hills."

"Yes, you were slow," she said, grinning at him as he poured them each some wine, and she snuggled against his side as they sipped it.

"And when did you know, Miss I-am-so-damned-clever?"

"Just why do you think a well-brought-up virgin would let you seduce her?"

"Because I'm so damned good-looking? Ouch!" He rubbed the spot where she had pinched his thigh.

"There is that, but, trust me, I was warned repeatedly about your sort. Even though it frightened me, even though everything I was taught told me to keep you at a distance, and even though I risked throwing away all chance of a family, I still quickly fell into your arms. That should have given you a clue."

"It didn't feel so quick to me."

"It was only a matter of days." She looked at him. "Just why would you be so cynical about love and marriage?"

"Two sad and sordid incidents in my misspent youth." He kissed the tip of her nose. "I nursed my sense of injury for years. The sad thing is, once I realized what I felt for you, they seemed a pathetic reason to turn so suspicious, to guard my every feeling. I think it was more my pride and my vanity that was hurt than my heart."

She kissed his cheek. "It served its purpose. It kept you free for me to find."

"And just why were you waiting on the vine for me to steal? I can't believe every man in Missouri is blind."

Deidre blushed faintly at the implied compliment. "There were not too many who wanted to hitch themselves to a poor Irish girl. We weren't dirt poor, but there was obviously no fine dowry of land or coin to be had. I was courted a little, but either the man sparked no interest in me or I only sparked annoyance in the man. A few seemed to think I looked like a delicate flower and would behave accordingly, until I opened my mouth."

Tyrone laughed, ignoring her mild scowl. "And showed them that, although you looked like a soft rose, you had some very big thorns?" He brushed a kiss over her forehead when she nodded. "I rather like the thorns, for all I bluster and bellow when they prick me. It adds spice."

"I'll remind you of those words the next time you are

glaring at me." She stared into her wine and said softly, "I have been so afraid that we would reach Paradise and you would send me away, or I would have to leave just to stop myself from becoming some pathetic doormat for you to wipe your boots on."

"I am sorry that my confusion caused you pain," he said, feeling guilty, for he knew he had never given much thought to her feelings through it all.

"It's done and the prize was well worth it."

For a while they sat sipping wine and cuddling in contented silence. Deidre still felt a little stunned and knew it would be a while yet before she fully accepted and believed in her good fortune. As she stared at the Christmas tree, then out the window, she sighed. There was still one shadow on her happiness.

"It will be Christmas tomorrow," she said quietly, "and I've never been away from home at Christmas." She frowned as she realized how easily Tyrone could misinterpret her words. "Of course, this is my home now. I wasn't—"

He turned her face toward his and kissed her. "I know what you mean, or, more precisely, who."

"You have someone still out there, too. I'm being selfish thinking only of my cousin."

"Then I'm guilty of the same selfishness, for I'm thinking only of Mitchell. It's a little hard to add to that worry by fretting over someone you've never met."

"True. Do you still think they are together?"

"Yes, I do, though damned if I know why. Our bumping into each other was improbable. To have Mitchell find Maura as well is impossible, or should be. Yet, I can't shake the feeling that he has."

"It would be wonderful if they both arrived in time for Christmas."

"Mitchell certainly intended to try, just as I did. Just remember, you got here safe and sound. So can Maura."

"Tyrone, will it be all right for Maura to stay with us?"

"Of course, if she wants to. Will what she wants make any difference to our plans?"

"No, not really, selfish wretch that I am. Maura is the last of my family and I will do all I can to keep her close to me, but we both knew, or, rather, *hoped,* to marry some day. Right now, I just want to know that she is safe. She's such a lady, so sweet-natured and kind. I'm just afraid I have thrown a lamb out into the wolf pack."

"I hope she's safe, too, for your sake, if nothing else. So you can have a good Christmas."

Deidre set her wine down and slipped her arms around his neck. "It's a very fine Christmas already. Maura coming home safe will just be icing on the cake. I love you, and you can't begin to imagine how good it feels to finally say it out loud."

"Oh, I think I can. I love you. Forever," he whispered against her mouth.

"Oh, yes, Mister Callahan, for at least that long."

Maura's
Christmas Secret

Chapter One

"Swine! Scum! Release me this instant or I will have you both gelded!"

Maura Kenney struggled in the beefy grasp of the drunken cowboy dragging her into the alley. His equally filthy and drunken companion staggered along with them. She knew what they wanted. She knew she ought to be terrified and she was, deep inside. At the moment, she was mostly enraged.

"Maybe you ought to shut her up, Hank," said her captor's companion, his words so slurred with drink they were barely understandable. "Someone could hear her."

"In this part of town, Lyle?" Hank tightened his grip slightly when Maura nearly managed to slip free. "If anyone hears this bitch caterwauling, they'll just think she's one of the saloon whores in a fight."

She could not believe this was happening to her. Dressed in deep mourning, she had gone to church to pray for her uncle's soul and had obviously walked through the wrong side of town. They should post signs, she thought crossly. And, she could not believe these fools would look at a skinny redhead dressed in black and feel blinded by lust. Maura decided she should have prayed for a little protection while she was on her knees in the little church.

"Let me go or I shall make you very sorry," she snapped, digging her nails into the backs of her captor's dirty hands.

"Yeah? You and whose army?" drawled Hank. "You're just a bit of a thing. If you was a fish, I'd toss you back."

It amazed Maura that, despite the gravity of the situation, she could feel somewhat insulted. "Then do so, you baboon."

When the man staggered up against a wall, his bleary-eyed friend Lyle moved to stand in front of her. "Can't," he said. "Ain't got the money for a whore, but I am feeling powerful randy."

"My heart bleeds for you," she said, the anger she felt making her voice hard.

Furious, she kicked out at the man, then watched in a strange mix of glee and horror as he stumbled backward and fell to his knees, choking. She had meant to kick him in the face or even in his soft belly, but she had gotten him square in the throat. The fact that it had so completely incapacitated the man was something Maura knew she ought to remember. It suited her better to kick a man there than in the shocking place Deidre had once told her to.

And now they had her considering the best way to do violence to a person. She was a lady and they had her screeching words like some soiled dove from the docks. They were touching her as if she was one of those wretched women. It was not easy to continue to behave like a lady when she was not being treated like one.

"You done killed Lyle," roared Hank, and he shook her.

"I should be so lucky," she replied, but her voice was unsteady from the force of the shaking she had just endured.

Hank twisted around and slammed Maura up against the side of the building, easily pinning her there. She could squirm, occasionally punch or kick, and even bite now and then, but she simply could not break free or force him to let her go. Maura thought of all the hours her mother had spent teaching her manners, poise, and grace. It would sorely disappoint her mother to see all of that refinement disappearing layer by layer beneath the attack of these drunken louts. When Hank pulled open her bodice, popping several of the tiny black buttons, Maura felt yet another layer of civilization shred right along with her dress. She fought him even more ferociously, her temper soaring and blinding her to everything except a need to hurt this man. Even while a small part of her reeled in shock, Maura called the man every vile word she could think of. Such violence kept her from thinking too much on how little chance she had of escaping this situation.

"Swamp slug!"

Mitchell Callahan paused right in front of the saloon doors. That was an odd thing for a woman to be yelling out on the streets of town, especially in this part of town. If any woman who was a regular visitor here wanted to spit foul words at a person, she would come up with something a lot more vicious and disgusting.

"Son of a bitch!"

Now, that was far more like it, he mused. He looked at the saloon doors and sighed. He had come here because he was restless and thought an hour or so with a willing woman might ease that. It had been a very long time since he had been with a woman, so long he had considered using a whore despite his fastidious nature. Just thinking about it made him take another step closer to the saloon doors.

"Damnation, Lyle, stop whining and get over here and help me hold this bitch!"

"I will pull your lungs out through your eyes!"

Interesting, he thought, and grinned faintly. He could not ignore what was happening in the alley next to the saloon. It could be just a disgruntled whore, squabbling with some of her customers. That did not explain why the man needed help holding her, however. No woman should be manhandled. He shrugged and started around the corner to lend a hand. If it was one of the saloon girls and she was reasonably pretty and clean, the night might not turn out so badly after all.

There was little light in the alley and it took Mitchell's eyes a moment to adjust to the gloom. What he saw, however, made him curse. The bigger of the two men had a tiny lady pinned to the wall and the other man was weaving his way over there to lend a hand. It appeared as if the little lady was wearing a very prim black dress, but Mitchell told himself that had to be a trick of the light. She was putting up a valiant fight, and that was all the invitation Mitchell needed to lend a hand.

He calmly walked over to the man who was so unsteady on his feet and was making some very strange choking sounds. Mitchell lightly tapped him on the shoulder, and, when he turned, punched him in the face. The man went down without a sound.

"Lyle," growled the other man, cursing when one tiny booted foot caught him high on the leg, "where the hell are you? This was all your damned idea."

"Lyle is otherwise occupied," drawled Mitchell.

Maura felt almost as surprised as Hank looked. It was impossible to see any of the new man's features, but his shadowed form was huge, and Maura did not think it was simply the poor lighting in the alley that made him seem so. Hank took one quick look at Lyle's still form, cursed, and shoved Maura aside. She cried out as she fell down hard on the trash-strewn ground.

"Go find your own honey, mister. This one's ours," said Hank, standing before the intruder with his shoulders hunched and his fists clenched at his side.

"Are you with these gentlemen willingly, ma'am?" Mitchell asked, keeping a close eye on the man in front of him even as he watched the woman stumble to her feet.

"Gentlemen?" Maura knew she sounded a little shrill, but she was too overwrought to care. "They are filthy pigs and they should be tossed back into the swamp they oozed out of."

"I will take that as a no," Mitchell said quietly, the faintest hint of the laughter he tried to swallow in his voice. "The woman wants you to go," he said to her attacker.

"She's just being a tease and trying to make us pay her more than she's worth. Ain't that right, darlin'?"

"Why don't you go somewhere and eat ground glass," Maura bit out through clenched teeth.

Mitchell admired her unique threats and prepared himself for the attack he knew the man was about to make. When it came it was clumsy and the fight was over quickly. One clean blow to the man's soft stomach and another to the jaw laid him out next to his friend.

Maura stared down at the two men who had planned to rape her. The huge man standing there had defeated them with an admirable swiftness. Then she tensed. She had assumed he had come to her rescue, moved to interfere because he had heard her cries, but it might not be wise to just accept that. He could easily prove to be just as dangerous as the other two. Taking another quick look at her unconscious attackers, she amended that thought. This one could be far more dangerous.

"I thank you for your kind assistance, sir," she said,

using her primmest tone of voice even as she tried to pull the torn edges of her bodice together. "I was losing the battle against these ruffians."

"You're not from the saloon, are you," he said, the words a statement of fact revealing he had no doubt about her answer.

"Certainly not." She frowned a little when she heard what sounded suspiciously like a heavy sigh.

"Well, then, you should have known better than to come to this part of town."

"Should I now. How is that, seeing as I do not live here nor have I ever even visited this place before?" She picked up her shawl and secured it over her torn bodice. "I was simply returning from church—"

"Church?" Mitchell wondered how anyone with such a sultry voice could be so prim.

"Yes, church, not that my whereabouts before this fiasco are any of your concern. As I walked home, I was accosted by these two men and dragged in here, obviously for some nefarious purpose."

"Obviously. So, where were you headed before you were attacked? I should walk you there so there won't be any more of these incidents."

"It would be most improper for you to escort me anywhere. Although you are certainly entirely responsible for me escaping this business unscathed, I do not know you, sir."

He tipped his hat. "My name is Mitchell Callahan."

Maura stopped her subtle attempts to get around him and flee the alley. She must have hit her head or been made far more upset and terrified than she had guessed. The man who had walked up to save her in the nick of time could not possibly have just said he was a Callahan. Then she took a deep, steadying breath. Callahan was not such an unusual name. Neither was Mitchell. Just because one of the brothers who had hired her uncle had the exact same name did not have to mean anything, did not have to be any more than a coincidence. Or, she thought, her eyes narrowing, it was a trick.

After subduing a brief twinge of guilt for thinking poorly of a man who had saved her from a gruesome fate, she began to consider the possibility that he was lying or trying to entrap her. So far she had managed to elude the few attempts made to get a hold of her. There was obviously someone on her trail, but staying close to other people at all times had kept her safe. This was the first time she had been alone. Perhaps it was not just ill luck that led to her being attacked or very good luck that led to this man racing to her rescue. What better way to lull someone's suspicions than to save them, to play the big, brave hero. In fact, it was such a good ploy, she did not know why there was a need to use the name of one of the brothers.

"Mitchell Callahan, is it? From where?" she asked, not overly concerned that her question was rapped out as if she was some sheriff and he an accused criminal.

"Paradise, Montana." He held out his hand. "And you are?"

"Why, I am Maura Kenney." She shook his hand, and tried to sound cheerful, almost flirtatious. "It must be because it is so very dark in here, and so I will not take offense that you do not remember me, sir."

"I recognize the name Kenney," he muttered, staring at his hand when she released it, for he could still feel the warmth of her touch. "Knew a fellow name of Patrick Kenney once. A good man."

"Yes, he was." Maura softened for a moment, swept briefly but strongly with a still-fresh grief. "I am sorry you don't recall anything about that dance we shared when you were in Missouri last," she murmured.

"I was only in Saint Louis once and I didn't do any dancing. I was there on business." He grabbed her by the arm and dragged her out of the alley. "Just to be sure, and to prove to you that you don't know me from a hole in the ground, let's take a gander at each other in the light."

She opened her mouth to protest, then quickly closed it again. Getting out of the alley had been what she had been trying to do since she had been pulled into it. It was a little silly to protest because he took her out instead of allowing her to leave of her own volition. Maura just wished he did not tow her along as if she was some rag doll toy. When they stepped out into the light of a fading day, she faced him to rebuke him for his treatment of her, and nearly gaped. In the alley he had been imposing in size and the rich timbre of his deep voice. In the clear light of day he was enough to make any woman's senses swim.

Long and lean and lethally handsome was the first clear thought that entered Maura's head. She tried not to stare, looking him over discreetly as possible. His thick black hair hung over his collar and forehead in gentle waves, softening his features. High, wide cheekbones, a long, straight nose, and a firm jaw made for a somewhat harsh face, but it was softened by the slightly full lips of his mouth—and his eyes. A deep gray, ringed with thick, long lashes, and set beneath vaguely arched dark brows, his eyes were almost mesmerizing. She tried not to let herself be captured by their allure as she patiently waited for him to speak.

Mitchell dragged her out into the light, turned to say she was lying about having met him, and felt the words catch in his throat. Maura Kenney was certainly no saloon girl. Tiny, slender, and standing so straight he felt an urge to see if she had some strange back prop under her gown, she was unquestionably a lady. She was also unquestionably beautiful. Her thick hair, only slightly mussed by her ordeal, was a deep, rich auburn. Her heart-shaped face was dominated by a pair of wide, deep-blue eyes set beneath delicately arched brows and rimmed by the longest lashes he ever had seen on a woman. His gaze rested on her full-lipped mouth. It was a little wide for her face, but that only made it more tempting. When she lifted her head slightly, sticking out her little chin, he realized he had been staring at her too long.

"Now, do you want to repeat that little tale about having danced with me in Saint Louis?" he asked.

"It was worth a try," she replied, not even attempting to deny her trick.

"I am one of the Callahans who hired Patrick Kenney. Is he here?"

"No, he was shot," she said quietly, unable to keep all of the sadness she still felt out of her voice.

"Good God. And Bill Johnson?"

"He was shot a week before my uncle was."

Mitchell did not want to believe what she was saying. They had hired Bill and Patrick to simply deliver some papers. Although they had warned the men that there would be trouble, that the Martins would do their best to see that the papers never reached Paradise, neither he nor his brothers had thought the job would prove fatal. The deeds were going to be soaked in blood by the time they found their way back to Paradise and Mitchell found that a chilling thought.

"Where are you staying?" he asked abruptly, not wanting to continue the conversation in the street.

"At the Depot Hotel," she replied, and immediately wondered if that was a mistake.

"So am I." He took her by the arm and started off toward the hotel.

"I have not agreed to accompany you there," she said, nearly running to keep up with his long strides.

"And I have no intention of letting Patrick's niece run around these dangerous streets alone."

"But I am not alone. I am with you, whoever you are."

"I told you who I am. I'm Mitchell Callahan, one of the brothers who needs those papers." He looked down at her, idly thinking that a brute like him could crush a little thing like her, then wondered why that thought depressed him. "Didn't your little lie tell you that I am speaking the truth?"

"It might have. It might also be telling me that you're clever enough to have seen through my little ploy."

"Fine. If you want some more time to see that I am just who I say I am, you'll have it. You can tell me your decision when we meet for dinner."

Maura almost cursed and that alarmed her. Then she recalled all she had just been through and decided she had just not recovered yet. The anger and fear were still there, still left a bitter taste on her tongue. That was more than enough to encourage a slip in her manners.

"Since you know that I don't trust you, why do you think I would go to dinner with you?" she asked.

"Because you'll want to eat?"

"How droll." Maura was sure there was a little twitch at the corners of his too tempting mouth, but could not tell if it was from anger or laughter.

"Join me for dinner, Maura," he said in a coaxing voice. "If I am who I say I am, I could help you. We are on the same side."

"That is yet to be determined."

She wanted to dine with him and that alarmed her for a moment. Here was the sort of man her mother had warned her about, a tall, dark man who was eager to protect her. The flutter she felt in her heart told her that she was already too keenly aware of him. If he was who he said he was, then she would have to accept his help. That attraction she felt tingling inside her would not make such an association acceptable. Unfortunately, she would have no way to stop him from riding along with her. More complications were the very last thing she needed. And, if he really was a Callahan, just how much should she tell him?

"I will meet you down here at eight," he said as they stepped into the lobby of the hotel.

Maura sighed. She did have to eat and she had to try to decide if he was an ally or an enemy. There was time to have a rest before dinner, to regain her wits and calm herself.

"At seven, sir," she said quietly but firmly as she eased free of his light hold.

"It'll be busy then."

"Exactly."

Mitchell smiled faintly as he watched her go up the stairs. She had spirit. After what she had just been through many another woman would be prostrate. She seemed a prim little thing, but he knew there was fire beneath that oh so proper exterior. He had seen her with her back to the wall, literally. Although he knew she had to be scared when those two men attacked her, she had revealed only anger, and it had been a classic redhead's fury.

Whistling softly, he went to his room, pleased to catch a faint glimpse of black bombazine disappearing into room 10 as he approached it. Little Maura Kenney fascinated him. When he realized he had lost the urge to go to the saloon, he just smiled.

Chapter Two

MAURA SCOWLED AT HER image in the mirror. She had done everything she usually did, but it did not look the same. Her hair was securely fastened in a bun at the back of her head, only a few whispers of curls left free. The collar of her black dress was high and tightly buttoned, revealing not the slightest patch of skin. Yet, something was ever so slightly different.

Shaking her head, she told herself she was imagining things. If there was a light flush to her cheeks or a hint of a sparkle to her eyes, it was because she was still vastly upset over being attacked. None of it had anything to do with a tall, dark man who called himself Mitchell Callahan.

As she stepped out of her room, she gave a delicate little snort of contempt. She could call herself Queen Victoria if she wanted to. It did not make it so. The man

was going to have to give her more proof than his word no
matter how beguiling his smile.

"Hello, Maura," said an already familiar deep voice
from right behind her.

Maura nearly cursed as she jumped in surprise, then
whirled around to face him. "I thought we were to meet in
the dining room."

"I was just headed there."

She just shook her head as he took her by the arm and
started down the stairs. He was obviously a stubborn man,
used to having his own way. If he did prove to be her ally
and they began to travel together, she was going to have to
curb his tendency to take her where he pleased. The fact
that he discussed it with her made no real difference, for,
as he talked, he dragged her right along to where he
wanted to go in the first place.

Once seated in the dining room, he made no attempt
to choose her meal for her, and her annoyance with him
was eased a little. He made idle conversation about her life
in Saint Louis and what she had seen in her travels until
they were served. The amount of food that was set down in
front of him made her eyes widen slightly, but she said
nothing. He was a rather big man, at least a foot taller than
her own five feet two, if not more, and probably required a
lot to keep up his strength. It was not until they were
served their dessert and coffee that he turned the conversation to the matter at hand.

"You still doubt I am who I say I am, don't you," he said,
smiling faintly.

"I have to."

"Yes, I suppose it is wise to be cautious." He took a small
packet of papers from a pocket in his coat and handed
them to her. "This might help you decide."

Letters, bills of sale, and even a short, scribbled message from Bill were amongst the strange assortment of papers. They were all addressed to him, Mitchell Callahan,

or carried his signature. It was the very strangeness of the assortment, the mundaneness of the papers, that convinced her. No one who forged papers would choose such a collection to try to establish an identity. Silently she handed them back, wondering what would happen now.

"Satisfied?" he asked.

"Yes. I know a little man in Saint Louis who does a little forging of papers and he would never think to include things like the bill of sale for a pair of boots. Very expensive ones, too," she murmured.

"An indulgence. When you got feet as big as mine, it's real important that your shoes fit perfectly."

She laughed softly. "Makes sense."

"So, who has the papers I'm after?"

"I do." She concentrated on eating a piece of her apple crisp, afraid that he would see the lie in her face.

"You?" Mitchell made no attempt to hide his shock. "Just you?"

"Who else is there, Mister Callahan? My uncle was murdered and so was Bill. The job passed on to me and my cousin Deidre."

"Ah, so you aren't here alone."

"I am. Deidre has taken a different route. We felt that would make things a little more difficult for the men trying to steal the papers."

"What possessed you to take on such a job?" he demanded. "Two men are already dead. The danger had to be clear to see. It's no job for two young women."

That display of typical male arrogance had Maura gritting her teeth against a sharp reply. "You hired my uncle and Bill to do a job. That job was bequeathed to Deidre and me. Uncle Patrick said the money owed was to be our legacy. I am more than half the way there, am I not?"

"Sheer luck." He noted the glitter in her beautiful eyes and decided it might be wise to temper his words. "All right, you've managed to get this far and not get shot, but there's no longer any reason to put yourself at risk. I can take the papers the rest of the way." Since that would mean she would leave, Mitchell felt a sharp pang of disappointment, but there was no other choice.

"No." Maura was not surprised when that quiet but very firm refusal left him speechless for a moment, and she waited patiently for him to begin blustering again.

"Yes," he said firmly. "This is my trouble, mine and my brothers. If anyone else is going to be shot at, it should be us."

"Mister Callahan, you can argue until you are blue in the face. It will not change my mind. I am taking the papers I hold to Paradise."

"I don't want my victory over the Martins bought with the blood of a young woman."

"And I have no intention of spilling any."

"Why are you being so damned stubborn?"

"Deidre and I were with Uncle Patrick when he died. Fatally wounded, he somehow managed to drag himself home. We promised him, on his deathbed, that we would complete this job."

"Oh, hell," muttered Mitchell, and he took a few sips of his strong coffee in a vain attempt to calm himself down.

A deathbed vow, he mused, and inwardly groaned. Worse, it was not some note left, some written legacy, but a promise made as they watched the man die. She was right. He could not talk her out of going. Mitchell could understand that, but he did not have to like it.

He studied her as she ate the rest of her dessert, obviously waiting for him to try to sort out his thoughts. There was a part of him that was delighted she would not allow him to send her home. It would take a week or more to get to Paradise if they were able to stay on the trains, and that gave him time to get to know her and figure out just what his interest in her was and how deep it went. Instinct was telling him that this was the one, the woman he had been looking for since he had become a man, but he needed time to be sure. Beautiful big blue eyes could be confusing him. He just wished they could travel together without the threat of the Martins' greed dogging their every footstep.

"There is one other thing you should consider, Mister Callahan," she said quietly as she pushed aside her empty plate and sipped at her coffee. "Your enemies already know I am trying to get the papers to you. Sending me home will make little difference. They won't stop having an interest in me until they are sure I don't have what they want, and I do not believe they will be very gentlemanly in trying to ascertain that for themselves."

"No, they won't." He was relieved that she had given him another good reason to take her with him. "The moment you accepted the job you became a target. Damn, I hate this. That land is all my father left us, what he spent his life building for us. I don't want the Martins getting their greedy paws on it, but neither do I want anyone to die to give it to me."

"Two men, good men, have already died." She took a deep breath to still the grief that always filled her when she thought of the murders of her uncle and Bill. "There is already blood on these deeds, but you didn't put it there. The Martins did. Personally, I would like to see them pay for those murders, even if it is only to deny them what they so badly want."

"I can understand that. I want revenge, too, if only because it might ease some of the guilt I feel."

"You have nothing to feel guilty about, sir. I doubt you thought it would go this far. Unfortunately, you really can't change your mind now. The die is cast, so to speak."

"True. We're stuck. Guess we just have to make the best of it. Well"—he rubbed his chin with his hand as he thought over their options—"if we stay on the train it'll take us a week, maybe two, to get where we are going. Depends on the weather and when the trains we need are running."

"Yes, I have lost several days here and there because of just those things. But, what do you mean by *if* we stay on the trains? Why shouldn't we?"

"Trains are easy to follow. I suspect, by now, they know you are traveling on the trains. Had any trouble yet?" He watched her prepare to answer him, could see her thinking of lying, then deciding against it. Mitchell wondered if she knew how easy it was to read her expression, then decided he would be a fool to tell her.

"There have been a few incidents," she reluctantly confessed. "They do know that I am going by train. However, there is some safety to be found there. There are too many witnesses on a train, too many people who have already proven ready and able to shelter a woman in mourning."

"True. I am hoping that is what will allow us to stay on the trains. However, we are getting closer to Paradise every day. They could get desperate enough to start ignoring witnesses."

"Do you happen to know what the Martins are paying their hirelings? What size of reward they may be offering for the papers?"

"No, but they are rich, very rich. I wouldn't be surprised to find out the reward they offer is enough to make a man risk hanging."

Maura sighed. The deaths of her uncle and their friend had made it clear that, whoever the Martins had hired, they were men who found killing too easy. That seemed proof enough that there was a tempting reward offered for the Callahans' proofs of ownership. She really did not understand how anyone could go to such lengths for land, but had to accept that they did. Although she had eluded the few attempts already made to get her, she also knew that her being a woman was not going to prove any protection at all. In fact, what had happened tonight made her realize that she could well face an added danger no man would.

None of that would stop her, however, she vowed with an inner straightening of her shoulders. She had promised her uncle that the job would be done and she had promised Deidre that she would not falter. Patrick and Deidre had taken her into their home without hesitation after her mother died. For five years she had lived on their gracious hospitality and not once had they made her feel like the poor relation, like she was taking charity and ought to be very grateful for whatever they chose to give her. They had made her part of their little family. Patrick had become the father she had never really had, her own a footloose gambler and lecher who had finally been shot by one of the hundreds of husbands he had so gleefully cuckolded. Now was her chance to pay Patrick and Deidre back for all they had done for her.

"You are looking very serious, darlin'," Mitchell said softly, reaching across the table to clasp her tightly clenched hand in his own.

For a moment she stared at that big hand engulfing hers. It was a handsome hand, Maura thought a little dazedly, the fingers long, almost graceful, but that should not be any surprise. Mitchell Callahan was a very handsome man. It made her feel safe, this sense that she would now be protected whether she wanted to be or not. It was what else the touch of that hand made her feel that worried her. Strange feelings. A warmth seeped through her body from the place where his flesh touched hers in an otherwise innocent gesture, a warmth that had her softening, leaning toward him.

"I did not give you permission to address me so informally," she said, pulling her hand free of his.

"Didn't ask for it," he replied with a brief grin, her jolting return to primness amusing him.

She shook her head. In all of her teachings, her mother had never really explained how one dealt with a man who did not follow the rules. Maura was a little disgusted with herself when she realized she found him charming. It was obviously time to give herself a few bracing lectures and shore up her resolve, especially if she was going to be in the man's company for any length of time.

"I was just thinking of my uncle," she said. "He never would have accepted this job if he had known there was any chance of being shot. He was no coward, but he did not think he should be dying for someone else's troubles, no matter how well he was paid."

"Yet he asked you and his daughter to finish it."

"Yes, he was dying and there was not much set aside for Deidre and me. As I told you, he called this our legacy. I think he also wanted to see it done, finished. After all, no man wants to die for nothing. He certainly would not have wanted to die thinking his murderers had won."

"No, that would certainly keep a spirit restless."

"And, I owe the man. He took me in when my mother died, treated me as if I was his own daughter. Deidre also welcomed me like a sister. This is all they have ever asked of me. I intend to see it done."

"And so you shall," he said.

Mitchell hid his surprise. Obviously what kept her little back so straight was the steel in her backbone. She was a tiny, beautiful lady, yet there had been a hard determination behind her words. Even he felt disinclined to argue with it and he was very accustomed to dealing with stubbornness, his own and that of his brothers.

"Well, the train leaves early so we best turn in," he said. "Am I allowed to escort you to your room?" he asked with a grin as he stood up and helped her out of her chair.

"Since you already know where my room is, there is little point in refusing your offer," Maura drawled, her suspicion that he had purposely found out what room she was in clear to hear in her voice.

"Is the black for your uncle?" he asked as he escorted her out of the dining room, casting a mildly frowning look at the almost prudish black dress she wore.

"Yes, although he never favored the ritual of deep mourning. It is also a way to both evoke sympathy and keep some people at a distance. A trick my uncle would fully appreciate."

"It didn't keep those cowboys away this afternoon," he reminded her as they headed up the stairs.

"True, but they were so drunk I am not sure they could see the color of my dress."

Mitchell suspected there was some truth in that. The cowboys had seen a lone woman and grabbed her. Men bent on rape would not be deterred by such things as mourning attire. The severe black also accentuated her delicate beauty. He suddenly had a craving to see her in colors, however, such as a deep blue to flatter her beautiful eyes.

His fascination with the small woman walking serenely at his side was not fading, was in fact growing by leaps and bounds. Mitchell felt excited, as if he had just found something long lost. Despite the teasing of his brothers, especially from the cynical Tyrone, Mitchell had always felt that he would know the woman meant for him almost at first sight. Every instinct within him was saying that Maura Kenney was that woman. There was one test he could make that might well clear up some of his doubt. Or, he thought with an inner grin, get him punched right in the nose and called river scum.

When Maura paused in front of her door, he took the key from her hand, ignoring the cross look she gave him. He neatly caged her against the wall by placing his hands on either side of her head and edging his body close to hers. Mitchell was pleased to see that he was not frightening her. Her fierce scowl just grew fiercer.

"I would like my key, Mister Callahan," she said firmly,

desperately trying to still the odd tingle of anticipation his closeness was stirring in her veins.

"Call me Mitchell," he said softly, and touched a kiss to her forehead.

"If you do not cease this little game, I will call you any number of things, none of them flattering."

"I know. I heard you flaying those cowboys with your tongue."

She blushed as she recalled some of the things she had said. "I was under a great deal of stress."

"Don't look so nervous, pretty Maura. This won't hurt a bit."

Before she could repeat her request that he give her back her key and leave, he touched his mouth to hers. Maura flattened herself against the wall, alarmed and yet intensely curious. She had never been kissed before, not even by the few men who had courted her back home. Following her mother's teachings, she had firmly rebuffed any such advance beyond a chaste peck on the cheek. The way Mitchell Callahan was nibbling at her lips told her that he meant to be anything but chaste.

Perhaps she had been too long away from her mother's firm lessons in propriety, but Maura suddenly found herself thinking that one kiss would not hurt anything. Even her uncle had said that a little kissing was not enough to plunge her into the everlasting fires of hell. As the pressure of Mitchell's lips increased, however, Maura had the wild thought that there could well be some other fires she was dancing a little too closely to.

His tongue nudged her lips and she gasped softly in surprise. Mitchell took quick advantage of her parted lips, sliding his tongue into her mouth to stroke and tempt her. Maura was faintly aware of leaning against him, of clutching the lapels of his coat, as the strokes of his tongue seemed to burn away all good sense. When the feeling that she wanted to crawl all over his big, hard body swept over her, she was so shocked she pushed him away. The look of desire on his lean features almost drew her back into his arms, but she resisted that temptation, and held out her hand. She prayed he did not see how badly it was shaking.

"It's all right. You can retreat for now. I have my answer," he murmured as he placed the key in her hand and walked away whistling softly.

How strange, she thought as she unlocked her door. She hurried into her room, locked the door behind her, and bolted it. Then she slumped against it and struggled to catch her breath.

"So much for one kiss causing no harm," she muttered, then shook herself free of a lingering bemusement and started to get ready for bed.

Maura wondered if that was why her mother had always been so adamant about allowing no familiarities, no matter how small, then shook her head. Instinct told her that she could have kissed every one of her beaux and not felt what Mitchell Callahan made her feel. And that was what made him dangerous. She was not sure how to fight the wantonness he could stir in her, a wantonness that had begun to sweep over her the moment she had guessed he was going to kiss her. Somehow, she was going to have to learn how to hold him at a distance.

Briefly she wondered if he was the one for her, the mate her mother said all women had out there. A soft curse escaped her as she realized she was seriously considering advice on men from her mother. She had loved the woman dearly, but her mother had shown her only the pain that could come from loving a man. Charming and exciting though her father was, he was useless as a husband and continuously hurt her mother with his absences and infidelities. Maura had long ago decided that she would choose a husband based on common sense, on practical reasons, and not on any romantic nonsense. Then, if her husband proved to be like her father, she would not have her heart torn to pieces as her mother had. The kiss she had just shared with Mitchell Callahan told her that he was definitely not the man to choose, that he could too easily possess her body and soul. She refused to make herself that vulnerable. Her mother had always been the best of teachers.

Mitchell got ready for bed, then sprawled naked on top of the blankets, sipping idly on a glass of whiskey. His mind was filled with thoughts of Maura Kenney. She was the one. He had no doubt about that now. The moment he had felt those soft lips beneath his, had savored the fire that raced through his veins despite the inexperience of her kiss, he had known. The problem would be in making Maura see it.

He frowned, unease deadening the last of the pleasure he had gained from the kiss. It was not just modesty that had made her pull out of his hold so abruptly. He was sure he had seen a hint of fear on her small face. It could be just that she had felt the same thing he had and was too innocent to understand, but he had the sinking feeling there was more to it than that. There was some tangle in Maura's way of thinking that he was going to have to unknot.

Maura Kenney also had a secret. Mitchell was sure of it. There had been the hint of reticence in some of her answers to his questions, the occasional pointed attempt not to meet his gaze. If it was that secret that made her want to hold him at arm's length, he was going to have to find out what it was. Maura was going to be his wife. He grimaced as he realized he might only have a week to convince her of that, for he knew in his gut that she was not going to be an easy conquest.

Chapter Three

MITCHELL STRETCHED OUT IN his seat, subtlely crowding up next to Maura. He inwardly grinned when she tsked in annoyance. It had only taken one glance this morning to know that she was going to try to force some distance between them. He did not think the queen herself could have been more correct, more prim, more cold. If Maura thought that would push him away, she was not thinking too clearly. When he chose to be, he could be more stubborn than both of his brothers combined. She was his and, since he might not have much time to make her understand that, he was not going to cater to any whim of hers that tried to hold him back.

"Are you perchance growing?" she asked, her tone of voice far too sweet.

He could not help his grin. "Just getting comfortable."

"Really. I swear you seem to expand with every mile."

"Big breakfast."

Maura rolled her eyes and stared out of the window of the train. This time there was no place for her to move to, to get away from the light touch of his side against hers. Mitchell was indeed a big man, but he was lean. She could not understand how he could take up so much of the seat. Even stranger was how, no matter how many times she moved away, he oozed closer, yet did not seem to move much at all.

She had greeted him politely but coolly this morning, all of her armor donned. The wretch had just smiled, then proceeded to be so charming she had felt the chinks in her armor start to widen. He had obviously seen that she was trying to draw a line in the sand and he was scuffing it out with his big feet as fast as he could. It was not just how easily he could bend her resolve that was disturbing her, but how easily he could read her. One beau had told her that her constantly serene expression made it very difficult, if not impossible, to guess what she was thinking or feeling. Mitchell Callahan obviously did not have that problem.

"What does your cousin Deidre look like?" he asked.

Even his voice worked to seduce her, she thought with some disgust, then sighed. "A bit like me, only she has fiery red hair and green eyes."

"So, there are two beautiful little redheads trying to outrun the Martins. How is she getting to Paradise?"

Fighting not to let the compliment affect her too much, Maura told him as much as she knew about the route Deidre had taken. "She is using the stage, and her itinerary will be more easily changed. It will also take her longer. Although, I have not made very good time. It is almost Thanksgiving and I am only a little more than half the way there. Delays caused by the train and a period of convalescence rather depleted the advantage the speed the train should have given me."

"You were ill?"

"Bad meat, I think. The worst of it came and went quickly, but it took me far longer than I liked to regain enough strength and steadiness to continue my journey."

"Yes, that sort of thing can lay a person low for quite a while. How did you choose which route you would take?"

"We tossed for it. She kept trying to get me to switch with her, for she felt the ones after us would find it too easy to follow the trains. Deidre feels she is stronger than me and is, well, a little more knowledgeable of the rougher side of life. In all honesty, the fact that she felt this route was the more dangerous of the two made me all the more determined to take it."

"You felt a need for some adventure?"

"No, I felt a need to protect Deidre."

"The stronger and more worldly Deidre?"

She smiled and nodded. "Yes, and I pray she doesn't figure that out. She could become cross." She looked up at him, knowing it would not take him long to see how illprepared she was for the job she had taken on, if he had not already, and wanting him to understand what drove her. "As I told you in the dining room, I owe Deidre and my uncle more than I can say. They not only took in a penniless orphan, they treated me as part of the family. Deidre truly is like my own sister. I fear I did not think of who was better suited for which journey, only that Deidre felt this route was the more dangerous. Naturally, once I knew that, I could not switch with her."

"Naturally." He shook his head, but he did understand. "Well, my brother Tyrone is also taking the more convoluted route and, damn his hide, he probably nagged me to switch for the very same reasons. Who knows? Maybe those two will bump into each other just like we did."

"Would he try to make her go back?"

"He would, but he'd also see why she couldn't. If she does meet up with him, he'll get her to Paradise safely."

"It's more coincidence than we can hope for, I think."

"Maybe. Maybe not. We each picked very similar routes. Not that surprising as there aren't that many ways to get from Saint Louis to Paradise, not unless one's on horseback the whole way. Maybe that was the only coincidence and the rest will just fall into place."

"That would be nice. As I said, Deidre's strong, but when one is dealing with killers, a little help could mean the difference between life and death."

Mitchell turned his gaze on their fellow passengers, studying them carefully as he considered all the possible ramifications of Tyrone meeting Deidre Kenney. If Deidre really was as pretty as Maura, Tyrone would be thinking about seduction, probably as fast as Mitchell himself had. Unfortunately, the cynical Mitchell would not be doing it because he felt he had just met his mate for life. If Tyrone and Deidre Kenney paired up for the journey to Paradise, Deidre might reach the town safely, but, quite probably, well bedded. Mitchell winced as he envisioned arriving in Paradise with Maura only to find a seduced and abandoned cousin. And, recalling the flashes of anger he had glimpsed in Maura, probably a thoroughly enraged one as well. Such a thing would not help him in his goal to make Maura want to stay with him. He shook aside that concern, seeing no gain in worrying over something that had not yet happened and might never happen.

His eyes narrowed as he realized that two burly, unwashed men at the front of the car were far too interested in him and Maura. They were trying to be subtle in their observations, but were failing miserably. Maura was enough to draw any man's gaze, but he did not think admiration for a beautiful woman was what prompted the constant glances from these two men. Mitchell was sure the two men were trouble, but just how much and how soon it would strike, he could not guess. He struggled to keep the tension he felt out of his voice and body, not wishing to alarm Maura. Depending upon what the two men did, the comfort and speed of the train might already have been cast aside.

"What do you intend to do with the money from this?" he asked her, hoping conversation would keep her unaware of any possible danger and keep him distracted enough so that he did not act rashly out of fear for her.

"Deidre and I intend to improve our farm," she replied, wondering why that no longer filled her with the interest and urge to plan that it had at the start of her journey. "Since my uncle had a job, we did not need to make the farm produce all that much to live comfortably. Now we shall."

"You and your cousin want to become farmers?" He tried to picture two delicate redheads out in the hot sun seeding, plowing, and reaping. Although pure pigheadedness would probably make them modestly successful, the backbreaking labor would age them far beyond their years. "That is no work for little ladies."

"Deidre and I are not unaccustomed to hard work, Mister Callahan."

The stiffness in her voice told Mitchell that he had offended her, and he grimaced. He had always been one to speak his mind bluntly and he doubted he could change now. He certainly doubted he could change before they reached Paradise. Even as he promised himself he would try to temper his words, Mitchell decided that Maura needed to learn to be far less sensitive. She would hear a lot worse if she followed through on her plans. A lot of people found it highly offensive for a woman to do a man's job. If the two women were successful, they could also count on their fellow farmers making trouble for them. No man could long stomach a woman doing a better job than he did.

"Just because you can do the work, doesn't mean it will suit you," he said, gentling his tone.

"Our families may not have made a great success at farming, but it's all we've known. The house and the land are now ours. It seems logical to make it our living." She shrugged. "We have a mule, a plow, and fertile land. What would you do?"

"Work it, but I'm not a little bit of a female with skin so fair I'd probably light up like a match under a hot sun. I know women can farm. I've seen it. I've also seen how it bends their backs, steals all the youth from their faces, and makes them look far, far older than they are. It's foolish for two beautiful young women to willingly plow their health and youth into the dirt, if you ask me."

"Well, no one asked you," Maura snapped, her annoyance growing when she realized he had made her lose her temper—again. Before the argument could gather strength, however, Deidre was diverted by the slowing pace of the train. "Why are we stopping?"

A little relieved that the quarrel had not continued, for he knew he would just say more things to annoy her, Mitchell glanced out the window. "We're stopping for water."

"So soon?"

"Trains need a lot of water. Want to get out and stretch your legs?"

When she nodded, he stood up and gently helped her out of her seat. She was a little puzzled when he took great care in getting her into her coat, tugging her hat onto her head, and wrapping a heavy scarf around her neck. Maura felt a little bit like a child being prepared to go out and play in the snow. If Mitchell thought of her as little more than a child, it would certainly help her with her goal of maintaining some distance between them. And yet, Maura realized that she did not like the idea at all, was even hurt and insulted by it. Recalling the way he had kissed her, a kiss no man would give a child, actually relieved her mind. She was, she decided, becoming contrary. It was almost sad. She had barely known Mitchell a day, could number the time spent in his company in mere hours, yet he was already having a devastating effect on her carefully constructed facade and her rigorously controlled emotions.

Once outside, she took a deep breath of the crisp, clean air. With each breath she cleaned her nose and lungs of the less pleasant scents of unwashed people, train smoke, and the, thankfully, occasional whiff of a very cheap cigar. She wished she could bottle some of the fresh air so that she could take a sniff each time those unsavory aromas grew too much to bear. At least Mitchell smelled nice, she mused, then cursed herself for even noticing that.

Glancing up at the gray-blue sky, she murmured, "At least there is no hint of snow."

"We're having a mild winter, so far, at least. It's one of the few things working in our favor."

"Is it? If it makes travel easier for us . . ." she began, then grew silent when he cursed.

"It makes it easier for them. I know," he ground out between clenched teeth.

"Sorry. That was obviously something you did not wish to be reminded of," she said as he took her by the arm and they started to stroll the length of the train.

"Actually, it's something I'd be a fool to forget. I fear I've allowed myself to be lulled into complacency because I haven't had to confront any of the Martins' hirelings."

"Well, you were headed the wrong way. Somehow, the Martins learned that Deidre and I had taken on Uncle's responsibilities. I fear they might have even learned when we left. All they had to figure out was which route we took, and I fear they have learned that as well. I suspect they know the same things about you and your brother. You were simply going to find out what happened to the people you had hired, to find the papers, while the Martins knew the deeds had already left Saint Louis and so could ignore you. I suspect there may be someone in Saint Louis assigned to making sure you don't find out about me and Deidre and come back after us. Now that you are with me, they seek you out as well. Perhaps . . ." she began as they reached the end of the train and turned so that they were headed back toward their own car.

"No," he said firmly, looking for the two men who had so keenly aroused his suspicions in the railroad car.

"You cannot possibly know what I was about to say," she protested.

"Yes, I do. You were about to suggest that I allow you to finish the journey without my charming company."

She wanted to deny it but could not. "I may have been thinking that, since the Martins have not yet set anyone on your trail, you might be wise to take your great hulking self off in another direction."

"Hulking?" He pulled a mournful face and placed his hand over his heart. "You wound me, darlin'."

"I doubt it."

"Anyway, there is no point in me leaving your side now. Not only would it be extremely cowardly of me, but I am sure I have already been seen with you. I have no doubt that I am already a marked man."

"They might still think you are, well, just some flirtatious gentleman I met on the train."

"Nope. The Martins have known me and Tyrone for a long time. I'm sure they've passed out real clear descriptions of us and warned all of their men to watch out for us. They don't want us to get back home."

Before Maura could respond to that dire outlook, Mitchell tensed and peered intently between the railroad cars. She was just about to ask him what had caught his attention when he cursed and shoved her aside. Maura cried out as she landed on her back on the hard, snowy ground. Several shots rang out and Mitchell's body landed on top of hers hard enough to push the breath from her lungs. She was faintly aware of screams, shouts, and the sound of people running as the other passengers who had stepped out for a moment ran for safety.

For one brief, horrified moment, she feared Mitchell had been shot dead. A hundred regrets fled through her mind. She wondered a little wildly how she had collected so many in such a short time. Then she felt his hard chest move against hers as he breathed.

"I thought you had been shot!" she cried, torn between a dizzying sense of relief and outrage that he would frighten her so.

"Not at the moment, but there are two fools would sure like to put a bullet in me. You, too, so stay down," he ordered.

As if she could do anything else with so much male flattening her into the ground, she thought. Her heart pounding so furiously she would not be surprised to discover he could feel it even through their heavy clothes, Maura lay as still as she was able so as not to disturb his concentration in any way. She had told herself she was aware of the danger she was in, was ready to face it, and now she knew she had lied to herself. Although she had been chased, even nearly caught once, followed and watched, she had never faced such a blatant attack. Neither had she so clearly seen that this business could cost her her life, that, in truth, her life meant absolutely nothing to these people. Just as her uncle and Bill's lives had meant nothing. Just as the Callahan brothers meant nothing. And all of this killing was considered acceptable in order to gain land, wealth, and prestige.

The icy fingers of terror clutched at her heart and Maura fought them back with a rising fury. This was an appalling situation, and she would not allow these murderers to force her to cower in some corner. She wished she was a man so that she could stand at Mitchell's side and fight these killers, instead of being shielded by Mitchell's large body, pressed against the frozen ground so hard that she could feel the chill of the earth deep in her bones. Although she had spoken of revenge for her uncle and Bill's murders, Maura now knew that she had never truly felt that urge, not deep down in her heart. Now she did.

Mitchell fired, the blast of the gun so close, Maura felt a painful shock in her ear. One brief glance revealed a man who had obviously been stepping between two cars. He slowly sank to the ground, blood soon staining the snow beneath him. She knew she should be horrified, but, at the moment, she felt no more than relief with a hint of grim satisfaction. The sound of a rifle shot pierced the air next. She felt Mitchell jerk with surprise and wondered what would happen next. Maura was just about to ask when he slowly got to his feet, tugged her up on hers, and caught her close by his side when she swayed.

Through the space between the railroad cars, Maura could see a second body sprawled facedown in the snow. Then two railroad guards appeared, pausing only to nudge each body with a booted foot as they walked toward her and Mitchell. Even though she felt steadier on her feet, she kept close to Mitchell. The two lean, hard men might work for the railroad, but they looked neither welcoming nor safe.

"Only two men?" Mitchell asked, not liking the way the two guards studied him and Maura.

"Only two," answered the taller of the two, his neatly cut sandy hair barely visible beneath his big hat. "They were after you and the woman?"

"Yes. I noticed them just before the train stopped and thought they looked suspicious," Mitchell replied. "I hadn't realized there were any guards on this train."

"Which is just the way we like it. Allows us to keep a

closer watch. Man doesn't think he's being watched and he acts natural. You're right. These two acted suspicious." He briefly glanced back at the two dead bodies. "I'd thought they were planning a robbery." His narrowed gaze returned to Mitchell. "Planned a killing instead."

"Don't know how they planned to get away afterward."

"There was a man waiting on them with two horses near the water tower. Winged him, but he rode off."

"Damn. I was hoping this was all of them." He glanced at an avidly listening Maura and inwardly winced.

Maura listened to Mitchell and the tall guard discuss the two dead men. While the second guard stood silently by, Mitchell and the other man played question-and-answer games. Each time Mitchell neatly avoided a direct reply to the man's query, making it clear that he intended to tell the man as little as possible. Both guards began to look grimmer and grimmer, although, if asked, Maura would have thought that impossible. In fact, they began to eye Mitchell as if he was the cause of all the trouble. It was grossly unfair, but instinct told Maura not to argue and she decided to listen to its advice.

"Why is it you don't want to tell me exactly what is going on here?" demanded the guard.

"It's personal and there's really nothing you can do to help me solve the problem," Mitchell replied. "I know who's after me and why, but I've got no proof of my allegations."

"Well, keep your trouble private if it suits you, but you'll do it elsewhere."

"Not here, I hope."

"Nope, you can get back on the train this time. Might as well enjoy it while you can. At the next stop you and the lady will get off and stay off. I suspect you can find another way to get where you're going."

Chapter Four

"BOOTED OFF THE TRAIN. Tossed out like some common criminal. I have never been so—so—" Words failed Maura as she walked beside Mitchell toward a large, very plain, and obviously very new hotel.

"Mortified?" Mitchell cheerfully offered her a possible choice of word to complete her sentence.

"How can you be so blasé about this?"

He shrugged. "Not much choice. We might try getting on another train if there's one passing through anytime soon. Could check at the ticket office."

"I wouldn't bother. I just saw that guard go into the telegraph office. Unless he is sending word to his mother or the like, I think using the trains might soon be a lost option. I do believe he is sending out a warning about us."

She sighed. "It is almost as bad as seeing my face on a wanted poster somewhere."

"Then it's the stage." He glanced down at her. "Or horse?"

"In this cold? I should also confess that I am not a very good rider," she said quietly. "My mother felt proper ladies should only ride in carriages. When I went to live with Deidre, she began teaching me, but I'm not nearly as good as she is."

"Not to worry. We'll think of something." He set their bags down on the rough board sidewalk in front of the hotel and advanced on her until he had her neatly trapped against the side of the building.

"You are behaving most improperly again," she said, blushing when a couple walking by glanced their way and quickened their steps. "I think you are shocking people."

"I just want to talk to you before we go into the hotel."

"And this conversation requires that I be flattened against a wall?"

He grinned briefly, then eyed her with a combination of wariness and determination. "We are getting only one room. We will sign ourselves in as Mister and Mrs. J. T. Booker."

"We will, will we?" Maura did not know if she should be outraged or alarmed.

"Yes, we will, and you can just stop looking at me as if I'm something that oozed out from under a rock." He sighed and then gave her a crooked, almost sheepish, smile. "I won't say that all of my thoughts about sharing a room with you are innocent. They damned well aren't. Seduction isn't why I'm saying we have to do this, however. Someone just tried to kill us. They weren't even sneaky about it, either."

Forcing her thoughts away from his comment about his own less than innocent ones, she thought about the attack on the train. "They had planned a route of escape."

"True. Still, that was a bold move. We're going to have to be more careful now, more watchful."

"We're getting too close," she murmured.

Mitchell nodded. "And the closer we get, the more dangerous things can become. I can't protect you very well if I'm down the hall, two locked doors between us."

There was too much truth to that statement for her to argue with it. No one knew the papers she carried were useless forgeries. She pushed aside the twinge of guilt she felt over hiding that fact from Mitchell and concentrated on the problem at hand. It was going to be awkward to share a room, but it would unquestionably be a lot safer, for both of them. She could not allow modesty and a fear of her own feelings allow her to put them both at risk. Being so consistently close to Mitchell could prove a danger to her, but all that was at risk there was her chastity and her heart. She could survive the loss of those.

"Why the fake name? Do you think it'll fool the men after us?" she asked.

Mitchell breathed an inner sigh of relief, for he knew she had just agreed to his plan. "It might."

"But probably not for long, hmm? Oh, well, it might at least make them hesitate enough to give us some warning. Shall we go inside?"

"What? No warnings to behave myself?" he asked as he picked up their bags.

"Would it do any good?" She followed him into the hotel, finding the inside as stark and utilitarian as the outside.

"Probably not."

Maura supposed there was something good that could be said about his honesty. In an odd way it made her feel more comfortable with the plan. Since she knew, by his own confession, that he was not averse to trying a little seduction, she could not be caught by surprise. As he stepped up to the counter, she donned what her uncle had always jokingly called her princess look. She did not want to expose the lie they were about to tell by even the hint of a blush. Maura stared at the plump clerk with all the hauteur she could produce, almost daring him to question them. It made the man so nervous he did not even notice that neither she nor Mitchell wore a wedding ring.

She was delighted when he got them a room with a private bath, something that was, thankfully, becoming more and more common, but she winced at the cost. Only the more affluent asked for such luxuries, and the price had obviously been set with that knowledge in mind. As she followed Mitchell up the stairs, she began to wonder just how well off the Callahans were. Obviously their land and mine were worth coveting. The Martins were well prepared to kill for them. Oddly, the thought that he might be very rich made her uneasy.

It was not until she stepped inside the room, saw that there was only one bed, that Maura began to be nervous about their arrangement. Instinct told her that Mitchell was a man to heed a no, even if it was not the word he wanted to hear. What she feared was that she would not say the word and she did not understand why she should fear that. She barely knew the man.

The memory of his kiss chose that moment to flood her mind and she nearly cursed. A part of her obviously felt it knew him well enough to cast aside all rules and modesty. She was puzzled that she had never before met this wanton part of her. She had always considered herself the most proper of women, even a little cold. Where the heat Mitchell Callahan could produce came from, she did not know, nor was she sure she wanted to. It was bad enough that he made her feel so wanton, so deeply curious to know just how wild he could make her. She did not want to think that the armor she had placed around her heart had been so quickly pierced by dark-gray eyes and a charming smile.

"I am going to have a bath," she announced abruptly.

As he set their bags down, Mitchell eyed her with curiosity. She had appeared to be calm, had stared down the hotel clerk as if she was royalty. Now, however, he sensed an uneasiness in her. He hoped she was planning on using the bath to restore her calm. She was so tense at the moment he did not dare touch her for fear she would run screaming from the room.

"I will order us some dinner then," he said, keeping his voice as pleasant as he could.

"We will eat in our room?"

"I think it might be best if we try not to show our faces too often."

"Probably."

She opened her bag and started to take out a change of clothes, then hesitated. It was already late and he had just told her that they would not be going anywhere, so what was the point of putting on a dress when she would just have to take it off again in a few hours? Despite Mitchell's presence, she had no intention of sleeping in her day clothes. They were far too binding. Her nightgown and robe were very modest, prim, in fact. Since she and Mitchell were obviously going to be spending a great deal of time in each other's pocket, Maura decided it was time to ease her grip on the reins of her modesty, and she took out her nightgown and robe.

"Do you think we could have some wine with dinner?" she asked as she collected her soap and other bathing needs.

"Of course." He looked at her closely. "Are you all right?"

"Fine. However, I believe I will be even better after a long, hot bath." She gave him a faint smile and headed toward the bathroom. "It has been a long day and perhaps a little more exciting than I can tolerate."

"Yes, getting shot at can make one a little tense."

"Quite."

"Just don't leave everything in there smelling too

pretty," he said as she disappeared into the bathroom. "I'm going to want a bath after you."

Maura smiled faintly as she shut the door, set down her things, and turned the bath taps on. Her uncle had often complained about the strong feminine scents lingering in the bathroom at home. Men clearly did not appreciate the risk of coming out of a bath smelling like roses or lavender. She sprinkled her lavender-scented bath salts over the steaming water and almost laughed at the thought of a big, virile man like Mitchell smelling so sweet.

As the tub filled, she quickly washed her hair under the running water, rubbed it dry enough with a towel to stop it dripping, and then pinned it up. The moment she slid her body into the hot, softly scented water, she began to feel better. Her tense muscles relaxed and her heartbeat and breathing slowed to a more comfortable pace. Somehow, nothing seemed quite so horrible while soaking in a bath.

The attack on the train had obviously upset her more than she realized. She reluctantly admitted that Mitchell Callahan also had something to do with her sudden attack of nerves. She could feel her own weaknesses clawing their way to the surface every time he was near, and, now, he was going to be near her all the time. It was enough to send any maiden into a panic. Mitchell Callahan, with his crooked smiles and big feet, was one tall, dark, handsome threat to her much guarded chastity and she had no idea of how to guard against that.

So, why guard against it at all? asked that wanton part of her. As she slowly washed herself, Maura seriously considered the question. To many a poor girl, marriage was the only way to gain a future, and chastity was usually a requirement for that. But she and Deidre already had a future planned and it was not dependent upon marriage, not dependent upon men at all.

Maura was determined not to follow in her mother's footsteps, not to let love grab such a hold on her that she became little more than a toy for some man, her happiness dependent upon his attentions. Passion, however, was something else again. In the marriage she had planned for her future, passion had not really figured, only practicality and stability, a calm, sensible union that would give her children. So, where was it written that she could not have both? Wild, insensible passion with Mitchell now and her calm, sensible marriage later? Surely every man did not demand that the woman he married was a virgin?

Realizing that she had been sitting in the tub thinking for so long she was beginning to wrinkle and the water had cooled, Maura pulled the plug and got out. She had given herself something to think about. There was time yet to make up her mind. Even the thought of taking a lover, of taking Mitchell as a lover, to be precise, had her feeling an odd blend of excited and terrified. It was a scandalous plan, but that wanton part of her Mitchell had stirred to life forced her not to dismiss it out of hand. As far as the wanton Maura was concerned, the only problem was how to give up her virginity now, yet still hook a husband in Missouri.

"Disgraceful," Maura muttered as she pulled on her nightgown and robe.

As she gathered up her things, she wondered if this job she had taken on, all the threats to her life, had turned her mind. It would explain why she was suddenly looking at herself as if she was two different people—wanton, sassy Maura, and prim and proper Maura. That was probably Mitchell's fault, too, she decided a little crossly as she stepped out of the bathroom.

She had barely got out of the door before Mitchell was striding in past her. He announced that their dinner would arrive in an hour and shut the door behind him. When she heard him muttering about the stink of lavender in the room, she laughed.

Once she had put her clothes away, she sat in a chair

near a small fireplace and brushed her hair dry. In a strange way, the question she was considering concerning Mitchell made her feel more at ease. Maura wondered if that was because she had taken the matter out of Mitchell's seductive hands and put it firmly in her own. Trying to avoid the matter completely had not worked at all. Now she was working on a plan and that, she supposed, was what made her feel so at ease. Scandalous though it was to even consider taking as a lover a man she had just barely met, she was now facing the problem as a mature woman and not shying away from it like some terrified child.

Her sense of ease faded a moment after the food was delivered. She was just sitting down at the table near the window, wondering if she should begin without Mitchell, when he strode out of the bathroom. Her breath caught in her throat at the sight of him. He was bare-chested and rubbing his hair dry with a towel. Despite her efforts not to, she looked him over. His chest was broad and smooth, the muscles easy to see but not too thick. Sliding her gaze down that glorious expanse of bare skin, she saw a thin line of hair beginning just under his belly button and disappearing into the front of his tight pants. When she found herself wondering what the rest of him looked like she nearly groaned aloud. Prim Maura was appalled, but wanton Maura wanted to go over to him and smooth her hands all over that handsome chest. She closed her eyes.

Mitchell grinned as he grabbed his shirt and put it on. He did not think it was vanity that told him he had seen appreciation in her eyes. It had been there long enough for him to recognize it before she had smothered it with her strong sense of propriety.

He sat down at the table, and drawled, "I'm decent now."

Maura slowly opened her eyes and gave him what she hoped was a frown. It was going to take her longer than a minute to get over the sight of him. She turned her attention to her meal, hoping the mundane act of eating would restore her calm.

Thinking that conversation would also help, she began to ask him about his family and about the lands they were all trying so hard to save. He seemed more than ready to tell her anything she wanted to know, but each word he spoke made her realize how different a world he had come from. The Callahans might have started from nothing, but they had come a long way from that. She suspected that their wealth had been firmly established while Mitchell was still a boy. If not for the trouble with the Martins, she would have never met Mitchell, and not simply because they lived so far apart. They would never have met even if he had lived in Saint Louis. They were very clearly from different classes. About all they had in common was that they were both of Irish descent.

Once the meal was done and Mitchell had set the tray in the hall to be collected later, Maura suggested a game of cards. She knew she was just trying to delay the moment when they had to face the problem of only one bed, and the look of amusement in his fine eyes told her that he knew it, too, but he readily agreed.

After she soundly defeated him in the first hand of poker they played, he took the game more seriously.

"Where the hell did you learn to play like that?" he asked much later as he shared out the last of the wine and Maura set the deck of cards aside.

"Sad to say, my father was a chronic gambler," she replied, relaxing in her chair and sipping her wine. "He taught me. He didn't really know what to do with a little girl, I think. So, the few times he wandered home, he would teach me cards. Uncle Patrick furthered my education. He did not gamble much at all, but he did like the game."

"Well, we've eaten, bathed, and played cards. Anything else you want to do before we discuss what to do about the bed."

Maura quelled the urge to slap the grin off his face. "You could sleep on the floor."

Mitchell glanced down at the hard, wood floor covered by only a few small rag rugs. "Would you be so cruel?"

"Not if you promise to behave yourself. Oh, and try not to ooze all over the bed like you did the seat on the train." The idea of both of them in the same bed made her a little nervous, but she could not really see anywhere else for a big man like him to sleep and *she* was not about to sleep on the floor.

He stood up and walked around to her chair, placing his hands on the arms and caging her in her seat. "Are you sure you can trust me to keep my word?"

Trying not to stare at his mouth, which was temptingly close to hers, Maura nodded. "The odd thing is, I do. Then again, I have to. Today showed me that I can't finish this trip alone. That means we'll be watching each other's back all the way to Paradise. If I can't trust your word, how can I trust you to do that?"

"True. All right, once we get into bed, I'll behave myself." He took her empty wineglass out of her hand and picked her up in his arms.

"I think I will go and get into bed now," she said, instinctively wrapping her arms around his neck, yet trying to sound firm in her demand.

"Let me just walk you over there."

The way their bodies subtly rubbed together as he walked had her heart beating so fast and hard she was amazed he did not hear it. He slowly traced her face with soft, teasing kisses until she ached for his mouth on hers. At the edge of the bed he finally gave her what he had made her crave, and she clung to him, eagerly opening her mouth for the seductive invasion of his tongue. She wrapped her legs around his waist to hold him closer and steady herself as he devoured her mouth, making no effort to temper his hunger. He put his big hands on her backside and rubbed her against him. The feel of the hardness in his groin moving against her sent her reeling, but it was the very strength of her reaction that finally gave her the impetus to break off the embrace.

"Put me down," she said, her voice hoarse and uneven.

"Are you sure?"

"Yes."

Mitchell thought it was the hardest thing he had ever been asked to do, but he released her. He found comfort in the fact that, in his arms, she turned to fire, wildfire, in fact. They were like spark to dry tinder when they were close and he could not believe she could keep fighting that. He was just going to have to scrounge up some patience.

He waited until she had shed her robe, smiling faintly at the voluminous nightgown she wore, then stripped down to his drawers and slid in beside her. This was going to be a torture worthy of the Spanish Inquisition, he decided as he sprawled on his back and stared up at the ceiling. Even though they were not touching he could feel her. He could smell her, smell that hint of lavender and her own soft, womanly scent. If he did not get himself in control soon, he would be climbing the walls by dawn.

"You want me," he said after she had turned out the light.

Maura only briefly considered telling him no. Perhaps it was the lying together in the dark that made telling the truth come easily, but she replied, "Yes, I should have thought that was obvious."

"But you intend to fight me."

"As I must."

"I like to win."

"So do I, Mister Callahan. So do I."

"Damn."

Chapter Five

EVEN THOUGH IT MADE Mitchell far too happy for her liking, Maura pressed closer to his side as the stage jerked and swayed over the bumpy, rutted, frozen road. She was seated between him and a skinny, balding man who clearly did not know that one could actually use water to wash with. The one time she had bumped against him, the aroma that had curled up from his body was so strong, it had been enough to make her eyes water.

They had had to linger at the hotel for an extra day just to catch this stage. Maura wished they had waited a little longer. The stage was full and, except for Mitchell, not with the most pleasant of companions. The very hefty, and strangely similar in appearance, Mr. and Mrs. Dixon sat across from her. Maura would have felt sorry for the third person on that seat, a rather slender, graying gentleman, except that he had arrived on the stage in a drunken stupor and somehow managed to linger in that condition. He was pressed so tightly between Mrs. Dixon and the side of the stage that, if the woman shifted slightly or even took a deep breath, he would probably be pressed right out through the wooden side. Yet, with regular sips from a silver flask, the gentleman apparently remained oblivious to his own plight. Maura did wish that he would pass out with a little more decorum. He just flopped there, his head bumping back and forth between the side of the stage and Mrs. Dixon's shoulder, his mouth hanging open and filling the stage with the most unpleasant wet snores she had ever heard.

The man next to Maura shifted his position on the seat, disturbing the aura of stench hanging around him and sending another strong whiff Maura's way. Maura tried to get even closer to Mitchell. While they had been stuck in the hotel room waiting for the stage, he had missed no opportunity to try to seduce her. At every turn he had stolen kisses, or touched her, or pulled her into his arms. In the end, however, he had held to his promise and behaved himself within the confines of the bed they had to share. He had kept her constantly torn between annoyance and excitement. What he was not doing was giving her the time to think over all of her options concerning him and what he made her feel. She was probably giving him the impression that she was over her annoyance of this morning, but she did not care what he thought at the moment. He smelled far better than the rest of the group.

"Perhaps you would like to just climb up on my lap," Mitchell drawled as he wrapped his arm around her shoulders.

She would kill him, she thought, smiling weakly at a chuckling Mrs. Dixon and trying not to be embarrassed by his audacity.

"Newlyweds, huh?" Mrs. Dixon had the sort of voice

that bounced off the sides of the stage, causing those asleep to twitch and those awake to lean back.

"Yes, ma'am." Mitchell kissed Maura's ear, darting his tongue inside and grinning against her skin when she trembled. "She's my little darlin' and I'm taking her home to Montana to show her off."

She would kill him slowly, Maura decided.

"Don't see any rings. You wouldn't be trying to fun with an old lady, would you?"

Although annoyed by the woman's rudeness, Maura used her sweetest tone of voice as she smoothly lied. "I have placed our rings in a safe place, ma'am. I heard so many frightening tales of robberies, and they are my parents' rings. It would break my heart if they were stolen and lost to me forever."

Mrs. Dixon reached over to pat Maura's hand. "Very wise, m'dear." She sat back, folding her plump hands over her well-rounded stomach. "Ah, two such handsome young people. You'll make some very pretty babies."

Maura could feel a deep blush heat her cheeks. To her utter dismay, she could envision it, could see a little boy with thick black hair and deep gray eyes. That was absurd. No matter what happened between her and Mitchell, marriage was not in the plans, not in hers, and most probably not in Mitchell's. When Mitchell proceeded to agree with the woman, indulging her with fanciful descriptions of what appeared to be a veritable horde of children, Maura decided that killing was too good for the fool. As soon as they reached the next stop, she would begin to slowly torture him.

Maura practically fell in the dirt, she got out of the stage so fast. Only Mitchell grabbing her around the waist saved her from an embarrassing fall. She joined him in politely saying good-bye to all of their fellow passengers even as she prayed that they would never have to travel with the people again.

The stage driver directed them to a faintly run-down-looking boardinghouse that grandly called itself a hotel, and Maura let Mitchell lead her there. Out of the corner of her eye she saw the steeple of a church and decided she would have to get herself over there as soon as possible. It was time to send up a few more prayers.

The room was clean, but had little else to recommend it. This time they had to share the bathroom, but fortunately there were only a few other boarders and half of them were headed out on the next stage. It was not as nice as having a bathroom all to oneself, but it was a shade better than trying to share it with a dozen other people.

"Dinner will be ready in an hour or so," Mitchell said when Maura returned from making use of the bathroom.

"Oh, good, then I have time to go to church," she said, and reached for her coat and hat.

"Church?"

Maura was not sure why Mitchell looked so shocked. She had told him that she had been to a church the first night they met, when he had saved her from the drunken cowboys. Although she was not an oppressively religious person, at times like these, she felt a need to say prayers. It made sense to her to get all the help one could get.

"I would like to go and say some prayers. I say one for my uncle and poor Bill every chance I get. At the moment, I also say a few for guidance and a little protection. I haven't been to a church since the night we met, so now I will add one or two for you."

"Going to try and save my soul?" he asked with a grin as he, too, started to put on his coat and hat.

"It might be an idea. You don't have to come with me. I'm not one to expect everybody to do as I do, or even condemn them if they don't."

"Oh, I have no real problem with going to church occasionally, but that's not why I'm coming now. You shouldn't be out wandering the streets alone."

"Ah, of course. Actually, from what little I saw, I think it is only one street."

"Is there a prayer one can say to cure excessive sassiness?"

"Well, perhaps a little one for a return of humility."

He just laughed and led her out of their room. Maura did not tell him, but she also wanted to ask forgiveness for her lies. While it was true that she had never openly lied and told him the papers she had were real when they were not, she had committed the lie of evasion and silence. That she was doing so with him made her feel especially guilty and she hoped a moment or two of contemplation in church would ease her guilt.

Once at the church, Mitchell took a quick look around inside. No one was there, so he left her to her prayers, stepping outside to roll a cigarette. Maura took out the rosary her father had given her shortly before he had been killed and began her prayers. Soon she began to feel the sense of peace that always came over her while engaged in the ritual of prayer. Before she finished, she also asked for forgiveness for the sin she was thinking of committing with Mitchell. Breaking society's rules she could do with no real qualms, but she would also be breaking a few church rules if she gave in to her passions and that did trouble her.

"Not enough to stop me, though," she mused with a hint of self-disgust as she rose and brushed off her skirts.

As she approached the church doors, she became aware of a noise just outside. At first she thought Mitchell was talking to someone, then heard a thud and what sounded like grunts of pain. What it did not sound like now was a passing, friendly chat with some passerby.

Cautiously, she opened the church door and gasped in horror at what she saw. Three men were doing their best to pound Mitchell into the ground. Maura slipped outside, careful not to draw their attention. The only way she could help Mitchell was if she employed the element of surprise. Resting against the side of the church was a shovel and Maura grabbed it. As a weapon for her, it was almost perfect. She idly hoped it was not the one used to dig graves, for the thought of touching that tool gave her the shivers.

Each blow Mitchell suffered made her wince, but she resisted the urge to charge right into the fray. She knew she had a better chance of helping him, of thinning out the odds against him, if she moved stealthily. That resolve faded when they got him pinned to the ground and one of the men pulled out a knife. With a cry that was a mixture of fear for Mitchell and of outrage over this cowardly assault, she rushed toward the men.

The one holding the knife turned just as she swung the shovel. It caught him square in the face. Blood spurted from his nose and she suspected she had broken it. She did not pause to consider the violence she was now directly involved in, however, but swung the shovel again, catching him off the side of his head. He sprawled on the ground at her feet.

A little distracted by her own success, she was almost too slow to respond to the attempted attack by one of the two men left conscious. She swung the shovel, but missed. The man hesitated to get too close to her, however, and she quickly used that to her advantage. Only once did she take her eyes off him as she held him at bay with the shovel, and that was to check briefly on what was happening to Mitchell. To her relief he had thrown off the grip of the third man and was returning some of the pain that had been dealt to him.

Mitchell threw off the man who had been helping the others to hold him still for the kill. He could see Maura trying to hold the other man back and see the third attacker laid out in the snow. Mitchell knew Maura could not hold off a full-grown man for long, however, no matter how well she wielded her shovel, so he worked to quickly dispatch the man facing him. It was tempting to make him hurt as much as he himself did, but Mitchell resisted that temptation. The moment his opponent fell to the ground and did not move, Mitchell turned all of his attention to the man facing Maura.

The moment Mitchell approached, Maura got out of the way. She could hear voices, and a quick look up the street revealed several men running toward them. By the time they reached the church, she doubted Mitchell would still be in need of any help, not the way he was pounding on the man who had come after her. However, she did hope that one of those men was a sheriff. Just once it would be nice to have the men who attacked them be taken up by the law. If they were very lucky, maybe one of them would implicate the Martins.

When she looked back at Mitchell, she saw him slowly fall to his knees next to the man he had just knocked out. "Mitchell!" she cried in alarm, tossing aside her shovel and running over to him. "Did they get you with that knife?"

"Nope, my spade-swinging heroine arrived in the nick of time," he said, but his voice was hoarse with pain and the blood from a small cut on his lips made his smile a little gruesome.

"What's happened here?" asked a barrel-shaped man as the three townsmen slowed their pace somewhat and walked up to her and Mitchell. "Who started a damned brawl outside of my church?"

"Those men did, sir," Maura replied as she helped Mitchell stand up.

"Bounty hunters?" the sheriff asked, narrowing his eyes and lifting his rifle just a little so that it pointed more directly at Mitchell.

"No, sir," Mitchell replied. "Just some men hired by an enemy of mine."

"Seems you got some powerful enemies, son." The sheriff lowered his rifle and signaled the two men with him to go to the men on the ground. "Secure them good, lads," he ordered, then looked at Mitchell again. "Going to be around if they go to trial?"

"I'd like to, but don't think I can. I've got something to do that needs to be done by the new year." Mitchell waved his hand toward the three men on the ground. "These men were just trying to make sure I don't get that little job done."

"I don't need this kind of trouble in my town, son."

"Are you telling us to get out of town?" Maura asked, shock and dismay weakening her voice so much that it was barely loud enough for the men to hear.

"Let's just say I ain't inviting you to make a long stay."

"Weather permitting, we will be gone as soon as we can," Mitchell said, pulling Maura close to his side in a gesture meant to keep her quiet and for a little support as the grogginess he felt was slow to leave him.

Maura knew Mitchell wished her to stay out of the discussion, but she had to bite her lip to help herself concede to his silent command. They had done nothing except keep themselves alive, yet, once again, they were being treated as if it was all their fault. It seemed an appallingly unjust way to keep the peace, but she knew no one would welcome her opinion on the matter. In fact, she had the impression that, if she said too much, she could get them in even more trouble. If word of any of this got back to Saint Louis, she would never live it down.

Keeping only half an ear on the conversation, Maura thought about all she had just been through. She now knew she was very capable of committing violence. The fact that she had done so to save Mitchell only eased her conscience a little. Yet again her manners and gentility had vanished in a heartbeat because of Mitchell Callahan. True, a delicate, ladylike swoon would have been no help to him at all, but she still felt annoyed.

She suspected some of the tension in her came from the fact that she had also had a revelation as she watched that man hold a knife on Mitchell. Her heart had nearly stopped beating and her blood had run cold in her veins. It was a rather strong reaction to have over a man she kept claiming was little more than a stranger to her. Sadly, it was obvious that a lot more than her passion was stirred by the tall, dark Irishman.

One clear thought had popped into her head as she had thought he was about to die. He was being taken away from her before she could taste the fullness of the passion they so effortlessly created each time they touched. He was all right, but that sense of loss and deep regret still lingered. Even though she hated to even consider the possibility, she could not ignore the fact that there would probably be other attempts made and one of them might well be successful.

Maura knew that, in that brief moment when she had seen the knife aimed at Mitchell's heart, she had made her decision. Right or wrong, she was going to allow Mitchell to become her lover. There would be some regrets at the end of the affair, but she now knew that none of them would compare to the regret that would come if she never tasted of the desire they shared.

And an affair was all it would be, she promised herself. She did not think there was much chance that Mitchell would fall madly in love with a skinny, poor redhead, so she would not allow herself to consider the possibilities of a future. There was also her plan to keep herself free of love's choking grasp.

She sighed and inwardly shook her head. It was a trap

she was greatly afraid she had already fallen into. Still keenly aware of the danger he had been in, she felt so afraid for him that she knew he had already made some serious inroads into her well-protected heart. She would have to be careful not to let him know, to keep the whole affair one of passion and passion alone, at least as far as Mitchell knew.

Suddenly, she was impatient to get back to their room, and scowled at the men. They were going over the same bits of information again and again. Maura suspected the sheriff was just trying to be sure he was getting the truth from Mitchell, but it was cruel to keep the battered man standing here in the cold.

"I think this has been discussed quite enough," she said, drawing all eyes her way.

"Just trying to get the facts straight, ma'am," said the sheriff.

"I can understand that, sir, but Mitchell has just been thrashed by three men and I would like to get him back to the hotel to make sure all he suffers from is bruises and scratches."

"Do you think he'll be needing a long time to recover?"

Maura resisted the urge to hit the man. "I cannot be sure, Sheriff. It is dark and he is wearing far too many clothes for me to judge the seriousness of his wounds with any accuracy."

"Well, he looks all right to me."

"How comforting of you to say so."

"Maura," Mitchell whispered, thinking that it would not help their cause at all if she whetted her surprisingly sharp tongue on the sheriff. "Since there is no stage headed where I need to go tomorrow, I will still be here if you think of anything else you wish to ask me," he said to the sheriff.

Since the sheriff was giving her the look some men gave

women they considered uppity, Maura nodded in agreement. "He should be well rested by then," she murmured, trying to act complacent.

"Well, that'll do, I guess. Just not sure I can keep the fellows long if there's no one here to lay charges against them."

"I deeply regret that, Sheriff," Mitchell said, and the truth of those words was clear to hear in his voice. "I will lose too much if I linger, however. I sure as hell don't want them free to come after me again."

"I'll hold them as long as I can."

"Thank you, sir." Mitchell secured his arm more firmly around Maura's shoulders. "Shall we go, darlin'? Our supper is probably served by now and I could use something to eat."

"You always do. Want food, I mean."

After murmuring a word or two of gratitude, Mitchell started toward the hotel, pulling Maura right along with him. She had the feeling he knew she was losing all grip on her temper concerning the sheriff, so she kept her mouth clenched tightly shut and helped keep Mitchell steady as they walked. Her next problem was going to be how to let Mitchell know she was ready to become his lover, and she turned her thoughts to that difficulty.

Chapter Six

"GO GET ON THAT bed," Maura ordered the minute they entered their hotel room.

"You don't know how long I have waited to hear you say that, darlin'," Mitchell said, kissing her cheek.

Maura just shook her head and nudged him toward the bed. She had calmed down a little since the attack, but her fear for Mitchell would obviously be a long time in receding. Seeing any man in such danger was shocking enough, but to be swamped by personal revelations at the same time would probably leave anyone reeling. She collected some clean water, cloth for washing and bandaging, salve, and some basilicum powder in case there was a deep wound. As she walked over to the bed and set the things down on the small chest of drawers next to it, she took several deep breaths to further calm herself. Mitchell could watch her too closely now and she did not want him to be able to read her feelings in her face, her eyes or her touch.

"I am not hurt that bad, Maura," Mitchell said, flashing her a smile as he took off his shirt, using it to wipe himself off, then tossing it aside. "Just a few bruises and cuts."

"Which all need to be cleaned. Neither the ground you were rolling around on nor the fools pounding on you were clean." She shook her head as she wet a cloth and began to wash off each scrape, bruise, and cut. "I can't believe they attacked us at a church."

"Killers like those, just dumb hired thugs, are, generally, probably not church-going fellows."

She laughed softly as she began to smooth salve over his wounds. Despite the pounding he had taken, he was not injured badly. No stitches or bandages were really needed. Even the cut over his eye that had bled so freely did not look deep enough to require anything more than some salve.

It was a minute before she realized she was taking far longer than was needed to tend to his wounds. She was now simply savoring the feel of his skin beneath her fingers. Maura ached to do more, but her innocence kept her from knowing what that more might be. Neither did she know how to tell him that she was more than ready to succumb to his seduction. Lost in her thoughts and her growing desire, she did not see him move so gave a start of surprise when he suddenly clasped his hands around her waist.

"Maura," he whispered, touching a kiss to her nose, his husky voice imbuing that one word with a dozen questions.

"I know," she said, tossing aside the salve and draping her arms around his neck. "It's very strong, almost overpowering."

"Are you sure you know what I want?" he asked even as he began to undo the long line of buttons that ran down the front of her prim black gown.

She smiled and touched a kiss to his forehead, feeling almost too much pride and just a hint of uncertainty. "I believe so. You want me."

"God, yes."

Maura stood still in between his long legs. She ran her fingers through his thick hair and touched little kisses to his ears, his face, his neck, even his broad shoulders, anywhere she could reach. The feel of his soft warm lips against her throat, his teasing kisses pressed against each newly exposed patch of skin, made her blood run hot. There was no real fear in her over the giant step she was about to take. The urge to know all the secrets a man and woman could share was too strong, the passion he bred in her too hot and tempting.

Suddenly, she recalled exactly what was beneath her prim black gown. Deidre had loved to tease her about that little twist in her otherwise prim and proper behavior. It occurred to Maura that, just perhaps, that wanton side of her had always been there just waiting for the right man, a man like Mitchell Callahan, to bring her forth. Maura decided that it was too late to pull away and hide her little secret now, when she felt Mitchell open the front of her gown and heard the breath catch in his throat.

"Oh, my sweet God."

Mitchell stared at what lay beneath Maura's almost prudish gown. Her corset was a deep maroon color trimmed with black lace and stitching. It cupped her breasts, which were teasingly covered with the thinnest, most delicate black chemise he had ever seen, so thin he could see the dark circles of her nipples through it. It, too, was trimmed with lace, maroon lace and delicately embroidered maroon flowers. He had expected clean, serviceable, white cotton, or, at the most, a little red flannel in the petticoats. This was not the underwear of a young maiden from a Missouri farm. This was the style and tempting quality of underthings a fancy courtesan might wear.

"I have shocked you," she said quietly, made a little nervous by the way he just stared and said nothing.

"Stunned might be a better word," he replied, his voice thick and a little hoarse as he tugged off her dress. Once she stepped out of it where it pooled around her feet, he held it up, looking from it to her underthings and back again once before tossing it aside. "I would never have guessed that this," he ran his hands down the silken front of the corset, "was hidden under that oh-so-proper mourning dress."

"I fear such scandalous things are a weakness of mine," she said, catching her breath as he bent forward to touch a kiss to the tip of her breasts through the delicate ruffle of the chemise.

"They could easily become a weakness of mine, too," he said as he tugged off her petticoats only to stop and stare again. "Oh, yes, I believe they already are."

Only a small bit of the chemise hung below the corset, little more than the wide maroon lace trim. No ordinary drawers for Maura Kenney. She wore the finest silk demi-drawers, a beautiful concoction of black silk with more of the maroon trim that stopped just above her stockings. Those, too, were black, reached to a few inches above her knee, and were held up by lacy maroon garters embroidered in black. Mitchell felt he could stare at her for hours except for the fact that his body was demanding a great deal more than a look. This, he thought with a slow grin, was very dangerous underwear.

"Where did a proper little Irish girl find such delicious fancies in Missouri?" he asked, picking her up and seeing her on the bed, then bending to yank off his boots and socks.

Maura leaned against the pillows on the bed, relieved to hear him still calling her proper. It had occurred to her that he might suddenly question her virtue. She knew exactly what sort of woman usually wore this kind of underclothes, especially since the shop where she bought some of them supplied some of the most expensive bawdy houses in Saint Louis. The way he kept looking at her, his eyes nearly hot as they skimmed over her attire, told her just why such women bought such frills.

"My friend owns a small shop of women's fashions," she explained. "Most of what she sells is quite proper. I bought that dress from her. Her less well-known customers are from some of the bawdy houses that serve mostly the very rich, or particular, as she explains it, and those women buy their things from her, too. Things like these," she murmured as she lightly fingered her silken drawers.

Stripped to his drawers, Mitchell sprawled on the bed at her side. He slowly began to unlace her corset, glad to see that she wore one of the front-lacing ones and that she did not lace herself in too tightly. He also decided that he was more than willing to indulge Maura's little eccentricity in this matter. If she could not find what she liked in Montana, he would have her shopkeeper friend send them things. Although Maura clearly knew she was wearing the sort of things only very improper ladies wore, he doubted she had any idea what this knowledge would do to him. Now, every time he looked at her all buttoned up and looking prim, he would be able to see the lace and silk she wore underneath. Mitchell would not be surprised if such knowledge kept him in a permanent state of semi-arousal.

"Ah, my sweet Maura, you are pretty," he murmured as he tugged off her corset and moved to lay half on top of her.

She trembled, the feel of his big body so close to hers taking her breath away. "You're not so bad yourself, Mister Callahan," she murmured, threading her fingers through his hair and tentatively tugging his face down to hers.

"Thank you, ma'am," he murmured against her mouth, but he hesitated before giving her the kiss they both so ob-

viously ached for. "This is your last chance, Maura. I'd like
to say I'm gentleman enough to stop no matter when you
say no, but I'm fair shaking with wanting now. You stir a
madness in me, girl."

"You stir one in me, too." She brushed her lips over his.
"I won't say no. You should know that. After all, I have let
you see my underwear."

He laughed softly and then kissed her. The moment he
slipped his tongue into her mouth the madness he had
spoken of swept over them both. He knew she shared the
fierce hunger that gripped him, could feel it in the way she
clung to him, the way her slender body trembled in his
arms. Mitchell wanted so badly to go slow with her, to be so
skilled and gentle, but he was not sure he had the willpower. The need to mark her as his, the craving to be inside her, made him shake like an untried boy.

"Maybe I should go throw some cold water on my face,"
he muttered as he undressed her, being neither slow nor
seductive in his movements.

"Pardon?" Maura was not sure she heard correctly as
she clung to his forearms when he crouched over her after
tossing aside her demi-drawers. She glanced down at herself, pleased that he so clearly liked what he saw, then noticed that she still wore her stockings. "You forgot my
stockings," she said, her voice shaking as his continued
staring made her feel both passionate and embarrassed.

"Nope. Didn't forget them." He ran a shaking hand up
her side as he eased his body down on top of hers. "I am a
little afraid I will tear them and, to be honest, I think you
look damned enticing in them."

"Is that why you wanted cold water?" She gasped with
pleasure when he covered her breasts with his big hands,
his thumbs teasing the tips into hard, aching points.

"No, I was thinking that I need to slow down. I don't
want to rush you. It's your first time. I should be slow and

gentle, but, damn, everything inside of me is crying out to be fast and furious."

"I know that feeling. I also know that, no matter how slow and gentle you are, you can still hurt me. It seems to me we should just listen to our bodies. If they say fast and furious, well, if the end result is not perfect, we can always try for slow and gentle later."

"Honey, the way you make my blood burn, I'm not sure I'll be seeing the slow and gentle stage for a long time."

He bent down and licked the tip of her breasts and Maura completely understood his feelings. Within her was a hint of maidenly fear, but it was weak, easily burned away by the desire flooding her body. Although she had little knowledge of the subtleties of lovemaking, she knew the basics. She also knew the loss of her maidenhead could be little more than a twinge or a much sharper pain. She simply did not care. Even if the final joining caused her more pain than pleasure, it would be a small price to pay for all he was making her feel now.

When he began to suckle at her breasts, she lost all capacity for rational thought. Fire raced through her, burning away all modesty and restraint. Need was the only thing she was aware of, need and a searing delight over each kiss, each caress. She tried to touch him everywhere, barely able to let go of him when he moved to yank off his drawers. Before he returned to her arms, she caught a quick look at his erection, rising hard and long out of a thicket of black curls. A flicker of alarm went through her, but then he slid his hand between her thighs, and, with one gentle stroke, thrust her back into that mindless state of pure heated need.

Mitchell clung desperately to a few threads of control. Maura was pure fire in his arms, and that threatened to burn away all restraint. He could not believe his good fortune, either. In his mind he had always envisioned that the woman he would marry would enjoy his touch, would have some passion in her soul, but this went beyond his wildest imaginings.

He slid his hand between her thighs and groaned when he found her already wet with welcome. The way she opened to his touch, her soft cries of pleasure, had him breathing so hard he felt his lungs might give out. Her nails scored his skin as she clutched at his shoulders and he savored that sign that she was as lost to her passion as he was to his. When he eased a finger inside her, the hot, tight feel of her made him nearly spill on the sheets and he knew he could not play this game any longer.

Praying that she was as ready for him as she felt to be, he began to slowly join their bodies. "Quick or slow, darlin'?" he asked, surprised he could still speak.

It took Maura a moment to calm her breathing enough to reply. The feel of him easing into her body was too wondrous for words. Despite the knowledge that there would be some pain soon, she found the fact that he was only slightly joined to her an irritant. Recalling a picture she had seen in a scandalous book one of her friends had found, she wrapped her legs around his waist and her arms around his neck. It might not be the correct position, she thought, but it certainly made it difficult for him to pull away.

"Quick," she whispered and arched up against him, instinct telling her that might gain her more of what she craved.

Then, suddenly, he was there, inside her. A brief, sharp, tearing pain skipped through her and was gone. She gasped, a little from the pain, but mostly from pure delight. A sense of rightness filled her as completely as he did. It did not matter that they had only known each other for a few days. It did not matter that neither of them spoke of love or marriage. This was right.

It was not, however, perfect, she thought a moment

later. She knew Mitchell still had to do something, but she was not sure what. She slid her feet down over his taut backside, then used them to push him even closer. He groaned. Maura squirmed and he shuddered.

"Maura," he rasped. "Does it hurt bad?"

"No, hardly at all after the first twinge."

"Thank God," he whispered, and began to move.

That was what she wanted, she thought as she clung to him. As he used his body to stroke hers in the most intimate of ways, first slowly then faster, Maura felt a tight feeling grow inside her. She tried to cling to him even more as that feeling grew. When he lifted himself away ever so slightly, she tried to pull him back, but he held firm. He reached one hand down between them, down to where their bodies were joined, and touched her. Maura screamed and felt the tight knot inside her break apart, flooding her body with blinding sensations. She was only faintly aware of Mitchell moving rapidly for just a second; then he jerked to a stop, his body shuddering as he groaned her name.

Awareness of her surroundings returned slowly to Maura. She glanced down at the man sprawled on top of her, looking as limp and boneless as a puppet with no strings, and smiled. It was flattering to know she had done that to him, and somewhat comforting to know that she was not the only one who had had all strength and sense stolen away by passion. She idly combed her fingers through his badly tousled hair and wondered what happened next. If there were certain rules to follow when indulging in an affair, she did not know them.

Mitchell slowly lifted his head from its far too comfortable resting place upon Maura's small, perfect breasts and looked at her. She smiled a little shyly and he breathed an inner sigh of relief. Although she had said yes, not only with her voice but with her whole delectable little body, he had feared there would be regrets afterward. The passion they shared, the heat that so easily grew between them, could have prompted her compliance and, now that it had left their bodies for the moment, she could have come to her senses and been horrified. There was no sign of that to be seen in her face. She just looked a little nervous. Since it was the first time she had been with a man, that was understandable. He felt a little nervous himself.

He kissed her gently as he eased the intimacy of their embrace. There were things he ached to say, but he decided it was too soon. It could be more than passion that had set her in his bed, but, considering how fierce that passion was, he could not be sure. If he started making possessive noises and spoke of marriage and children, he could easily scare her off. She had spoken of a plan with her cousin to make the farm profitable. He had no idea how firm that plan was or how important it was for her to be with her cousin. He had gotten her in his bed, he was just going to have to be patient and allow the rest to happen as it would.

"All right?" he asked as he touched a kiss to her forehead and then the tip of her nose.

"Fine." She took a moment to fix her mind upon the condition of her body, and, although she felt a hint of a sting, there was no real pain. "Yes, just fine."

"Lord, woman, you drive a man mad with lust," he said, and smiled as he flopped onto his back.

"Is that a compliment?"

"Oh, yeah." He glanced down at himself, saw the tinge of blood on his member, and swore softly. "I'll get something to clean us up with."

Even as she glanced down to see blood on her thighs, he returned with a damp cloth. She blushed as he washed her off, and that embarrassment pushed away the brief touch of fear the sight of the blood had stirred. He tossed the cloth aside and was just getting back on the bed when a knock came at the door. Maura squeaked with alarm and hurriedly reached for her camisole, which had landed on the floor close to the bed.

"Hell, I think that's our dinner," Mitchell said as he yanked on his pants and started toward the door. "I don't think I'll complain that it's late."

Maura laughed softly as she slipped beneath the sheet to hide while he opened the door. The smell of food brought her right back out as soon as he closed the door. She got out of bed, found her demi-drawers, pulled them on, and then went to get her robe out of her bag. Even as she tugged her robe out of the bag, Mitchell appeared at her side. She looked at him with a hint of curiosity when he took her robe from her hands but did not immediately help her put it on.

"I'll probably sound like some kind of lecher, but do you think you could dine with me wearing only what you're wearing now?"

There was such a boyish, pleading look on his handsome face, she almost smiled. For just a moment she felt a little embarrassed, then told herself not to be so foolish. She had just been sprawled beneath the man, naked to his gaze and his touch. Scandalous though her underthings were, they were a lot more modest than what she wore a few minutes ago, she mused with a half-smile.

"I have never dined with a lecher before," she murmured.

Mitchell grinned, dropped her robe back into her bag, and reached out to unpin her hair. "Trust me, darlin', you probably have. He just hid it better than I do." He sighed with pleasure when her rich, dark auburn hair tumbled free, falling in gentle waves all the way to her slender hips. "I can't believe I was so randy I didn't even take the time to let this down."

She blushed faintly, the way he was looking at her a compliment in itself. "I don't know about you, Mister Callahan, but I am hungry."

He grinned and led her over to the table. It only took Maura a few moments to completely get over the fact that she wore so little in front of the man. By the time they finished their food and Mitchell had set the tray out in the hall to be collected later, she was feeling remarkably seductive. He flattered her with every glance as she sipped her wine, and Maura found herself almost preening, trying to arrange herself in her seat in ways that increased the heat in his eyes. When he finally growled, gulped down the last of his wine, and came around the table to stand over her, she laughed softly, filled with a distinctly female sense of victory.

"Maura," he said, dragging her name out as he leaned over her, his hands on the arms of the chair. "You are playing with fire."

"Mmm, it *is* beginning to feel a little warm in here," she murmured, and placed one small foot on his chest, lightly caressing the hard, smooth skin.

The wanton side of her was in full rein and Maura did not care. She sipped her wine, meeting his hot look over the rim of her glass as she inched her foot down over his taut stomach. Her smile grew a little wider as she slid her foot down a little further, letting it rest against the hard ridge of flesh shaping the front of his pants. She set her empty wineglass down on the floor next to the chair and then moved her foot up and down, gently caressing him.

"Definitely warm," she whispered, running her tongue slowly over her suddenly dry lips.

"Oh, God," Mitchell groaned as he reached down and yanked her into his arms, then strode toward the bed. "Even your damned little feet are dangerous."

Maura just laughed as he tossed her onto the bed and came down on top of her. Now that she had taken that first step, now that there was no turning back. she found herself greedy. There was not much time left before they reached Paradise, and then her time with Mitchell would be over. Maura did not want to lose any time in his arms, did not want to forego any chance at pleasure because of ill-placed modesty, because she knew deep in her heart that she would never feel this way again. Being with Mitchell was like some sumptuous dream, and until she walked away from him for good, she intended to revel in it.

Chapter Seven

A SHIVER OF FEAR went down Maura's spine as she stepped out of the mercantile store and did not see Mitchell. He had said that he was stepping out to enjoy a smoke as she looked for a Christmas gift for Deidre, but there was no sign of him. Maura hugged her packages tightly against her chest and wondered what to do, whether to return to the store, go to the hotel, wait where she was, or go looking for him. After he had made such a point of keeping a close guard on her, his disappearance made no sense, and she was sorely tempted to follow the last option. Only a certainty that Mitchell would not like it kept her where she was.

They had been stuck in the little town for a week, the sheriff's scowl getting blacker and blacker whenever he saw them. Although Maura knew she did not regret one minute of the passion-filled hours she had spent in Mitchell's arms, she knew that staying in one place too long was dangerous. Her only consolation was that the bitter cold, the snow, and the icy rain held everyone captive, and that would include the men trying to chase them down.

It was taking them a long time to get to Paradise. Probably as long as it took the early pioneers, she thought as she began to tap her foot nervously. Despite the advances made, the roads, the stages, and the trains, certain places were obviously still hard to get to. And, bad weather had the power to bring all modern progress to a grinding halt. It had halted her and Mitchell for a week, and, despite how delightful their time together had been, neither she nor Mitchell had been able to forget that he had a very limited amount of time left to thwart the Martins.

"So, where the hell is he?" she muttered.

A filthy hand was suddenly clapped over her mouth. Even as she began to struggle, a strong arm was wrapped around her waist and she was dragged back into the alley next to the mercantile store. A screech of alarm escaped her, and she began to struggle more furiously when she was yanked past Mitchell's prone body.

"Ease up, bitch," snapped the man who held her. "He ain't dead. Just sleeping."

"You sure he didn't have the papers on him, Roy?" asked another voice from farther behind her.

"Real sure, but he'll be giving them to us real soon, Mike."

"I feel bad leaving our boys in the jail."

"They won't be there much longer. Callahan ain't pressed charges yet and ain't gonna be here to go up afore a judge. Kinda hard to send a man to prison when there ain't nobody around to say he done wrong. Now, are you right ready to gag this bitch?" he asked. "We can't have her screaming too much."

"I'm ready."

The minute the man removed his hand, Maura tried to scream, but had barely drawn a breath into her lungs when a short, squat man wrapped a filthy rag over her mouth, tying it tightly at the back of her head. Despite all her struggling, the two men soon had her tied up. The one called Roy slung her over the saddle like a bag of grain, the blow forcing all the air from her lungs. Gasping and struggling to breathe again, Maura was only partly aware of the man swinging into the saddle and placing one hand firmly on her back as he nudged his horse out of the alley. Moments later, he spurred his mount on to a faster pace and Maura was back to trying to keep her breath in her body. Even as she began to black out, she thought of Mitchell, and prayed he was all right.

A loud groan sounded in Mitchell's ears and he realized it had come from him. Slowly, he sat up, his head pounding so fiercely it made him nauseous. Standing was far, far worse. For a full minute he had to press himself hard against the side of the building, fighting the almost overwhelming urge to black out. Spots swam before his eyes, his stomach clenched and roiled, but he held himself together through sheer willpower.

As his wits returned, he suddenly realized the full implications of what had happened to him. Staggering slightly and keeping one hand on the rough side of the mercantile store, he moved toward the street. A scattered little pile of packages in front of the store told him the chilling truth. His enemies had Maura.

Just as Mitchell reached the packages and slumped to his knees beside them, the sheriff arrived at his side, demanding, "What the hell has happened to you now?"

A scrap of paper stuck under the string tied around one of the packages caught Mitchell's attention. "What does it look like? Someone knocked me over the head," he snapped, too worried about Maura and in too much pain to deal with the man diplomatically. "Are those three men still in the jail?"

"Yeah, though I won't be able to hold them much longer. It's a week in jail for brawling unless you're going to charge them with more."

"I can't." He eased open the note and, fighting to focus clearly on the nearly illegible scrawl there, he read: *We got your woman. You want her back, bring the papers to the old drover's shack on the southeast corner of the Bar T Ranch, west of town. Tonight. When the moon's up.* "How far is it to the Bar T Ranch from here?" he asked as he collected Maura's things and carefully got to his feet.

"About five miles, maybe less. You know old man Cox?"

"Nope. I just have to get to an old shack on the southeast corner of his land. That's where they took Maura."

"Your woman? That snippy little redhead?"

"Yes, her." Despite how sick he felt, the glare he sent the sheriff made the man take a step back.

"Damn. More trouble. What the hell do you have that they want so bad?"

"Some land. A mine. They want it and we won't sell. Now they're trying to steal it." Taking a deep breath to steady himself, Mitchell started back to the boarding-house. "Where can I get some horses? Saddles?" he asked the sheriff who was close behind him.

"You finally leaving and taking all this trouble with you?"

Mitchell paused in front of the door to the hotel and seriously considered hitting the man. The only thing that held him back was the knowledge that he would probably end up in jail and thus be prevented from helping Maura. He looked down at the smaller, plumper man, all of his contempt clear to be seen in his expression.

"Yes, I will be leaving. First, I will collect my woman and then we will ride on to Montana. Horses?"

"The stables, end of the street. Ed Jenko. Has good stock, fair prices."

"Good. You might want to wander over to that shack on the Bar T tomorrow to collect the bodies."

Before the gaping sheriff could say another word, Mitchell went inside the hotel. He was not surprised when the man did not follow him. Mitchell wondered how such a coward got the job. He just hoped that, if the man did go out to the shack to collect bodies, it would not be his and Maura's he found.

Taking only enough time to toss Maura's packages on the bed, wash the blood from his face, and check his wound, Mitchell then went to the stables. Ed Jenko, a leather-skinned, bow-legged little man, kept looking at him as if he suspected him to keel over. Mitchell decided that he must look as bad as he felt. He bought three horses, one for him, an even-tempered little mare for Maura, and a sturdy packhorse, plus all the needed equipment. Telling the man that he would collect them in an hour or so, he went into the mercantile store and bought supplies, food, warm clothes, and blankets. It was with a hearty sigh of regret that he added some warm but plain underclothes for Maura.

It was as he was packing Maura's things that he realized he was soul-deep afraid for probably the first time in his life. He had no real idea of how he could save Maura. He did not know the lay of the land. He did not know how many men held Maura. He did not even know if she was still alive. Worse, he did not have the papers to trade for her even if he was fool enough to think that could buy them their lives. Maura had them and, unless she was killed before she could tell them anything, the kidnappers did not know that. And, if she was still alive, what were the men doing to her?

Mitchell shied away from that thought. Maura was his. It was a blind, primitive possessiveness he felt. He would never cast her aside because she had been raped, but he would want to rip apart with his bare hands the men who had touched her. Rape could easily kill the passion in

Maura, a passion he had only just begun to enjoy, and for that he would kill them.

The sun was just starting to set by the time Mitchell rode out of town. Out of the corner of his eye, he saw the sheriff watching him leave and idly hoped the good people of this little town never came under any real threat. When Mitchell passed the church, he seriously considered going inside to say a prayer. If luck was not with him this day, he would not only lose all that mattered to him, but give three fine horses and a bundle of supplies to the very men who had killed him and Maura.

Maura groaned and tried to sit up, only to discover that she could not move. For a brief moment, she panicked, terrified that she had contracted some strange paralyzing disease, then her senses returned. She realized she could not move because her wrists and ankles were tied to something. Cautiously, chillingly afraid of what she might see, she opened her eyes. Despite the somewhat perilous situation she was in, she did feel some relief to see that, although she was tied spread-eagled to a rickety wooden bed, she was still fully dressed.

She took a few slow, deep breaths to further calm herself. There was a slight ache in her chest, but she felt sure her rough treatment had not caused her any serious damage. Maura turned her head, looking toward the soft muttering she could hear. Two men sat on three-legged stools at a tiny table playing cards, a half-empty bottle of whiskey between them. She remembered the brief confrontation in the alley, carefully recalling each word spoken. This had to be Roy and Mike, or so she hoped. If not, that could mean that there were more men somewhere to deal with and that could pose a problem for her and Mitchell.

It surprised her a little that she had no doubt at all that Mitchell would be coming to save her. She also knew, deep in her heart, that he would not be doing so because he thought she had the deeds. It was nice to feel such confidence in her lover, but it was also a little worrisome. Any bond between them that went beyond passion could seriously complicate their affair. She did not want Mitchell caring about her, for then he could easily persuade her to take a gamble on love. Such a gamble had such bad odds that even her reckless father would not have taken them.

With a soft curse, she pushed such musings aside. Now was not the time for such puzzles. She blamed her meandering thoughts on a lingering grogginess, and forced her mind to the problem at hand. Somehow she was going to have to get those fools to untie her. Then she would be ready and able to help when Mitchell arrived.

"I need a drink of water," she announced in the most imperious tone of voice she could muster.

"So? You won't notice thirst where you're going," the taller, leaner man snapped back, then grinned when his companion laughed. "'Lessen, of course, you go to the hot place, eh, Mike?"

"Such an amusing fellow you are," she drawled, ignoring his scowl. "A true gentleman would ensure that the condemned prisoner had all the comfort he needed."

"Hell, she thinks you're a gent, Roy." Mike shook his head, his greasy blond hair swishing back and forth over his forehead. "Ain't that a hoot."

"Shaddup, Mike." Roy slowly got to his feet and walked over to the bed. "Do you really need some water?"

"Yes, I really need some water."

He picked up a canteen from someplace behind her head and held it out to her. "Here."

She looked at the canteen, then up at him, wondering how she and Mitchell could have been snared by someone who obviously did not have a brain in his head. Brute cunning, she supposed. "I believe I will need my hands untied, sir."

"Ain't sure you ought to be untying her, Roy," said Mike, frowning when his companion started to undo the ropes on Maura's wrists. "She's a skinny little thing, but she's real squirmy. Ned said she whacked him on the head with a shovel."

"She ain't got a shovel now, does she?" muttered Roy. "And Ned ain't got a scrap of brain in his head."

It did not really shock Maura to discover that these men were compatriots of the men who had attacked Mitchell in front of the church. And the man Ned must be a drooling cretin, she mused, if Roy thought he was stupid. The fact that Roy thought himself smart, probably even considered himself a leader, could prove useful. She was just going to have to figure out how, she thought, as, once her wrists were free, she sat up and begun to try to rub some circulation back into them. She had to bite back a caustic remark when Roy grunted and thrust the canteen in front of her face.

"Thank you, sir," she said, fighting to sound polite and not sarcastic as she took the canteen, wiped the mouth of it off with her sleeve, and, barely touching her lips to it, took a long, slow drink.

"That's enough." He yanked the canteen out of her hands. "We didn't bring much because we don't plan on staying long."

"You are not going to leave me stranded here, are you?" It galled Maura to do it, but she suspected that playing the dim-witted female would work with these two.

"Your man'll be coming for you soon."

"Are you sure? He was unconscious. How could he know where I am?"

"Yup. Left him a note. Told him, if he wants you back, he's gotta bring us them papers."

"Papers? What papers?"

It was very hard to keep her voice light and her expression one of gentle confusion. They were indeed using her

and the quest for the papers to lure Mitchell into a trap.
Mitchell would be risking his very life for a packet of forgeries. It was an appalling situation and she could not help
but feel that it was all her fault. She quickly shook off most
of that guilt. She could not end this game by revealing that
she carried a worthless bunch of copies. Once the Martins
heard that, they would put all of their resources into getting Deidre. She could not throw Deidre's life away just to
save her own. She could only pray that her loyalty to her
cousin did not cost Mitchell his life as well. Maura suspected that telling these men the truth or giving them the
papers would not save her or Mitchell, either.

"Your man has some papers my boss wants. He gives us
those papers, he gets you back."

"Then I am sure he'll be here soon with what you need.
There is no need to keep me tied. I will wait quietly for
Mitchell."

"Don't think you oughta listen to her, Roy," advised
Mike.

"Shaddup. There's two of us, dammit. I think we can
protect ourselves from one skinny redhead."

Maura fought to simply look grateful when he untied
her ankles. She did not want him to guess at the sense of
triumph that was coursing through her veins. Even if she
could not come up with a plan to free herself, she would at
least not be lying helpless when Mitchell arrived. She
watched Roy as he walked back to the table and sat down.
Covertly she measured the distance from the bed to the
door as she rubbed her ankles to try to ease the return of
her circulation. She was fast on her feet, but there was no
way she could get to the door, unbolt it, and dash outside
before either Roy or Mike got hold of her.

"What are you playing?" she asked with a cheerful curiosity she did not feel.

"Poker," replied Roy as he began to shuffle the cards.

"Oh, lovely. Might I play, too?" The way Roy rolled his

eyes and cast her a contemptuous look told her that her ploy was working. Roy thought she was some empty-headed girl and no match for him.

"Do you know how?"

"Whatta you doing now?" grumbled Mike. "She's a prisoner. You don't get friendly with prisoners."

Mike might actually have a brain, Maura decided, and that could make him dangerous. He was not being lulled into a sense of security by her sweet, dumb-as-a-post act like Roy was. Roy might even be getting a few lecherous ideas about keeping her for a little while after killing Mitchell and getting the papers. Mike just wanted her tied up and then gone.

"It ain't gonna hurt nothing to let her sit in on a game or two," said Roy. "Get her a stool."

"Her man's going to be here soon," said Mike, even as he did what he was told.

"I told him not to come until after the moon rises. 'Sides, he ain't gonna try anything with her here."

As Maura sat down on the wobbly stool, she saw Mike roll his eyes. He obviously had wits enough to know Mitchell might not meekly do as he was told, but not enough backbone to argue with Roy. Mike was definitely the one to keep the closest eye on, she decided as she accepted the cards dealt to her and wondered if she could successfully fake a total inability to play the game.

The secret pocket beneath her skirts brushed against her thigh as she shifted her legs into a more comfortable position. If worse came to worst, she supposed she could try to buy their lives with the forgeries. They were, after all, very good forgeries, done by an expert in his craft. Even the Martins might not be able to tell the difference between them and the real thing. She probably would not know if she had not been the one who had paid to have them done.

She glanced at the men flanking her and inwardly

shuddered. Even though they were acting almost friendly now, she knew they would shoot her dead without a qualm if the need arose. It was there to see in their eyes, cold, soulless eyes that told her they had no consciences at all.

This trip was certainly broadening her horizons, she thought as she showed her hand and displayed a fluttering dismay when told that she had lost, that a straight flush did not beat three of a kind. Kidnappers, hired thugs, killers, and card cheats, she mused. A whole new world of people she never would have met at home. She would have preferred to have stayed blissfully ignorant in her little house outside Saint Louis.

Then she sighed. No, she would not have preferred that. Terrifying though some of the journey had been, it had had its compensations. A tall, handsome Irishman was one that came readily to mind. If she had stayed home, she would never have met him, would never have tasted the passion they so effortlessly shared. Her affair with Mitchell would probably leave her heartbroken and, perhaps, unweddable, but she could not really regret that, either.

As Mike told her that three aces did not beat two fours, Maura hoped that Mitchell was as smart as she thought he was, and sneaky, too. She needed him to come and rescue her, the sooner the better. It was getting harder and harder to play a lackwitted ingenue. If she had to endure much more of this blatant cheating, she was going to put everything at risk, and lose her temper. There was, after all, only so much a person could bear before cracking under the strain.

Chapter Eight

❧❦❧

"SHE'S PLAYING CARDS," MITCHELL whispered in utter disbelief as he peered into the cabin through a filthy little window.

He leaned against the side of the cabin and shook his head. He suspected she had some reason for what she was doing, some plan in mind, but damned if he could figure it out. Although he had not really expected to find her terrified, too panicked to act when he moved to rescue her, he had not expected to see her seated at a table playing cards and sipping rotgut with her abductors.

Then he realized that what she was doing could prove very helpful. The two men were completely distracted, lulled into complacency. That could allow him the element of surprise, and, after a little reconnoitering, he knew there were only the two of them, so surprise might be all he needed to win. Unfortunately, Maura was so close to them, she could easily get in the way.

Very carefully, he moved to peer in the window again. If she had the wits to throw herself out of the way when he burst through the door, he could probably take the two men down before they drew their own guns. Just as he was wishing he could warn her somehow, she glanced up and looked right at him. Her eyes widened briefly and then she dropped her gaze back to the cards she held.

He moved away from the window again and tried to think of some clear signals he could give her that would tell her when he would be coming in and what to do when he did. Glancing up, he grimaced. The moon would soon be a bright light in the sky and the men would be ready for him then. He could not believe they had not already set up some sort of watch for him. They clearly thought him fool enough to meekly do exactly as they commanded, to walk passively into their trap like a lamb led to the slaughter.

Finally deciding what message he wanted to relay to Maura, he peered in the window again. It was a minute or two before she glanced his way. Hoping she did not think he was just waving at her, he tried to tell her, with just a few hand signals, that he would be coming through the door in five minutes and, when he did, she was to get out of the way. He was not sure, but he thought she nodded, and he quickly ducked back away from the window. Mitchell took out his watch and, using the faint light from the window as well as the increasing light from the moon, began to wait. It was going to be the longest five minutes of his life.

Maura stared at her cards, not even seeing them, as she tried to remain calm. It had only been a fleeting glimpse, but she was sure she had just seen Mitchell at the window. She desperately wanted to look again, even though she feared she was imagining things, but knew she had to be very careful. If she looked at the window too often or for too long, it could draw the attention of the men with her.

Mike started to complain that Roy was drinking more than his share of the appalling whiskey. Maura took quick advantage of their distraction and looked toward the window again. When she saw Mitchell's face it was all she could do to hide her elation. That faded a little when he mouthed a few words, made a few hand gestures, and then disappeared again. She wondered briefly if the knock on the head he had gotten in the alley had scrambled his brains.

As she turned her attention back to her cards, she thought about Mitchell's actions. He was obviously trying to tell her something, but she was not sure what. *Door* was one word, of that she was sure. He had also pointed to it. A fleeting glance toward the door revealed that Mike had left it unlocked after taking a quick trip outside to relieve himself. If Mitchell really was planning to come straight through the door, it would be easy enough. Five fingers held up and the word *five* was a little harder to understand, then, suddenly, she caught sight of the little watch pinned on her bodice. He was going to spring his attack in five minutes, although, if she accounted for the time it had taken her to figure out his message, it was probably more like four minutes now. The last signal he had made was one she easily understood, especially if she had guessed everything else correctly. That quick slash of his hand meant *move.*

There was a very good chance she was about to see two men die and Maura tried to prepare herself for it. She had seen it happen when they had been attacked on the train, but from a distance. There would not be the shelter of distance this time. It would be nice if, when Mitchell burst through the door, the two men would meekly offer up their arms and surrender, but Maura sincerely doubted that would happen. And so did Mitchell or he would not have told her so forcefully to move.

The problem as she saw it was that Mitchell would have only one gun against two. His would undoubtedly be drawn and ready to fire, plus he would have the element of surprise, but Maura wanted to even up the odds. After a little thought she decided to make use of the knowledge she had gained on the day Mitchell had strode into her life. Just as the five minutes she had been told to wait drew to a close, she curled up one hand into a tight little fist, and, using every ounce of strength she had, she punched Mike in the Adam's apple.

She was yet again surprised at how effective the blow was. Mike immediately began choking so badly, struggling so hard to stop choking, that he fell off his chair. Roy stared at his companion in utter amazement for a moment before turning a narrow-eyed gaze her way. Maura quickly got up and started to move away from the table. After another look at his still-writhing friend, Roy stood up, making himself the perfect target, she thought, and tried to will Mitchell to enter right now.

Even though she had been expecting him, it still stunned Maura when Mitchell kicked in that door at that precise moment. She raced back to the bed as just one gunshot sounded. Praying that Roy had not somehow freed his gun from its holster before Mitchell could even fire his, she glanced back and breathed a hearty sigh of relief. Roy was sprawled on top of the table, his blood staining the cards and his hand still clenched around his gun handle. Mike was still lying there gasping like a fish on a dry land.

Mitchell turned to look at her, and she did not wait for him to come to her. Maura raced into his arms. Except for the ride to the little shack, she had not been hurt, but she had known she was not safe nor would she leave the hut alive. She had been terrified, the feeling twisting her insides beneath her facade of calm, not just for herself, either, but also for Mitchell. Neither one of her captors had made any real attempt to hide their plans to kill Mitchell and they would have added to the horror of her own death by leaving her knowing she had brought Mitchell to his.

"Are you all right, darlin'?" Mitchell asked, smoothing his hands over her body in a mixture of relief and a need to check her for any injuries.

"I'm fine. A little bruised where they tossed me over the saddle, but nothing else."

"They didn't—"

"I've the oddly insulted feeling they did not really even consider it." She grinned when he laughed. "Although, I think the man you shot was slowly coming round to the idea. He was becoming almost, well, pleasant." She looked at Mike who was trying to sit up, and the way he was rasping as he struggled for each breath made her think that she might have seriously injured him. "What do we do about him?"

"Not sure, but I do have a question. Why is it that, when I gallantly rush to your rescue, I always seem to find a man choking?"

"You didn't rush that other time," she murmured, a little embarrassed by the violence she had committed and sure that Mitchell would not really appreciate her efforts to even the odds for him.

"Very amusing. Why?"

"That time we met, I had just kicked the man in the throat. It seemed to work very well at incapacitating him. So, this time, I punched him in the throat." She blushed faintly under his wide-eyed stare.

"Amazing. And probably a better way for a woman to do it sometimes rather than going for his groin. A lot of men anticipate a woman trying to get him in the groin. They'd never think to protect their throat."

"That first time, I couldn't reach his—er—groin. Deidre told me about that other method of bringing a man down, but, when I saw how this worked, I felt it was a little, well, more genteel." She met his wide grin with a frown that did nothing to hide his amusement.

"I'm sure this fellow is right glad he met with a lady who was too delicate to kick him in the balls."

"Mitchell," she gasped, but could not completely suppress a smile as he laughed.

It seemed a little heartless to stand there laughing and grinning while one man lay dead at their hands and another might be wishing he was, but Maura suspected it was a sense of relief that they were still alive that prompted it. She also knew neither man deserved any sympathy or grief over their passing. They would have killed her and Mitchell, had probably killed others. It said a lot about what sort of men the Martins were that they could find such criminals to do their work for them.

She glanced toward Mike, realizing that he did not sound quite as bad as he had a minute ago. It took her a moment to understand the meaning of what she saw. Mike was reaching for something tucked in his boot. She cried out a warning and shoved Mitchell out of the way even as Mike raised his pistol to aim it directly at Mitchell's heart. A burning pain seared its way across the top of her arm and she fell to the floor so hard she was dazed. The sounds of gunfire filled the small shack and she prayed Mitchell was successful once again as she struggled to regain her senses.

Mitchell scrambled to his feet even as Mike sprawled facedown on the floor. He went over to the man, made sure he was dead, and then looked for Maura, intending to soundly scold her for her actions. His heart stopped in his chest when he saw her lying on the floor. Even on her black dress the spreading stain of blood was visible.

"Maura, damn you, you had better be all right," he said, his voice unsteady as he knelt by her side and began to undo her gown.

"Mike?" she asked, peering at him from beneath her lashes.

"Dead. I should have tied the fool up at the start or searched him for weapons."

"Yes, *we* should have thought of that."

Mitchell pulled open her gown and breathed a hearty sigh of relief. It was merely a graze, a furrow cut out of her soft skin by the passing bullet. He searched the cabin for water, found the canteen, and, dampening his handkerchief, wiped the wound clean. Out of the pocket of her gown he got her own handkerchief and wrapped it around the wound. The whole time he worked, Maura lay very still and that worried him a little.

Once he was done, he pulled her up into his arms and just held her. The first sight of her lying there, not knowing how badly she had been wounded, had been one of the worst experiences he had ever had. Mitchell hugged her a little more tightly, savoring the feel of her lithe, warm, and very alive body. Ever since she had been taken, he had been scared to death for her, and, now that they were safe, he was feeling a little unsteady.

Maura began to regain her wits and strength as she rested in Mitchell's rather tight hold. The wound hurt, but she did not need to see it to know it was not a bad one. She decided it was simply the fact that she had been shot that had made her so faint for a moment. This amount of violence was not something she was accustomed to.

She slowly became aware of the strong emotion in the man who held her. It touched a strong chord inside of her, but she fought that connection. A part of her wanted to believe that this meant he might care for her, that if she tried, she might actually find the joy of a shared love.

It whispered that she could trust Mitchell Callahan with her heart. Maura fought the allure of that voice and pulled forward all the harsh lessons learned while listening to her mother weep.

Although she got her own emotions back under control, she still felt disturbed by the ones she could sense in Mitchell's taut frame. Whether it was a fear for her or the realization that he had killed two men, something made him cling to her. Not sure how to make him more at ease, she began to stroke his head.

Mitchell smiled faintly against Maura's bosom. He slowly pulled himself together. Maura was probably a little confused about the way he was acting. Sometime soon they were going to have to have a serious talk about their future, but now, sitting in a cabin with two dead men, was certainly not the time.

"Stop patting me on the head, Maura," he said, laughter in his voice.

"I was being consoling," she said as she watched him stand up.

"More like motherly and, believe me, that is not what I want from you."

There was a strong undertone to his words, as if he was giving her a message. As he helped her to her feet, she decided she was too tired to figure it out. Some instinct told her that she did not really want to, either, that what he wanted from her was not what she wanted to give. It was all there inside her, but she was terrified to set it free.

"What do we do now?" she asked.

"Get the hell out of here."

"Mitchell, it's a little late to go anywhere, isn't it? Or are we going back to the town? That isn't so far away, I suppose."

"Maura, darlin', you have two choices. We can either stay here with these charming fellows or ride."

"Ride? As on horses?"

"As on horses. I got you a very sweet-tempered mare."

"She could be an angel on four hooves, but I suspect I shall still embarrass myself." She glanced at the two bodies. "The alternative is worse. Just why can't we go back to town for the night and then head out in the morning?"

"I don't think the sheriff can hold those three men much longer. Also, this all shows that we have been found. That town is no longer safe for us."

"And riding through the night will be?" She knew he was right, but she hated the thought of getting on a horse now when she would much rather crawl into a soft, warm bed.

"Sorry, darlin'."

"Oh, it's not your fault. Well, let's go then. It's best if I don't have to think about it too long."

He laughed softly, then kissed her on the forehead. "Just wait here a moment. I'll get the horses. You need to get into some warmer clothes."

Warmer meaning ugly, she thought as he left her. Then she realized she was alone in the cabin with two dead men. Fighting the slightly panicked urge to chase after Mitchell, she kept her gaze fixed firmly on the door. Maybe if she did not look at the bodies, she would not be terrified by them.

When Mitchell returned and held out a vast collection of wool and flannel, she sighed. It was sensible to dress as warmly as possible, but that did not mean she had to like it. While he ripped the graying, rat-chewed blankets off the bed to toss over the bodies, she changed into her new clothes. Several times she got the distinct feeling that Mitchell was watching her, but a quick glance over her shoulder never caught him in the act. Carefully folding her silk underwear, she donned the more practical wool and flannel. She hoped there would be a night or two when they reached Paradise where she could wear such things for Mitchell again.

Mitchell watched Maura take off her scandalous lavender underthings and quelled the urge to make love to her immediately. He was going to miss those scraps of silk and lace. They could not get to Paradise and back to a more normal life too soon to suit him.

Once thoroughly bundled up to Mitchell's satisfaction, Maura followed him out to the horses. She put her things in her bags on the packhorse and then got on the mare. She did seem to be a sweet animal, but the horse's nature, no matter how perfect, could not improve Maura's hopelessly inadequate skills.

"What happens with those men?" she asked as Mitchell headed his mount away from the cabin and she quickly fell into a matching pace at his side.

"I told the sheriff there might be some bodies to collect tomorrow, but I don't think he'll be coming here."

That meant the two men would not get a decent burial and that troubled her a little. She beat down her sense of guilt, by reminding herself of just who they had been dealing with. Maura doubted Mike or Roy would have given a second thought to leaving hers and Mitchell's bodies unburied. They probably would not even have taken the minute or two to toss a blanket over them. And now that she considered what Mitchell was saying, the sheriff would not have bestirred himself, either. People had said that the West could be a hard place, she had just never realized how hard.

"Where are we going?" she asked as she struggled to fall in with the rhythm of her horse. "To another town?"

"No, to a little cabin in the hills."

"Oh. One of yours?"

"Belongs to my family. We've got a fair number of stopping places scattered from Paradise all the way to the

Mississippi. Pa didn't completely trust the trains or the stages."

"His mistrust will obviously serve us well now. Is it far?" she asked quietly, dreading the answer.

"I'm afraid we won't get there until nearly dawn." He smiled gently when she groaned. "We can rest there for a day or two before continuing."

"And how far is this cabin from Paradise?"

"About a week's ride."

"So we should be there the week before Christmas. I hope Deidre is there. It will seem strange not to spend Christmas with her. And I am worried about her."

"She'll get there." He smiled faintly when Maura just shrugged. "Look how well you're doing, and you say she's stronger and more worldly than you are."

"But she doesn't have you charging to the rescue when it's needed."

"True, poor girl." He laughed softly when she muttered something about conceited cowboys, then grew serious. "I just feel that she will hook up with Tyrone. Don't ask me why I feel it; I just do. If I'm right, and that's happened, you'll be seeing her soon."

"I hope so. Even beating the Martins would lose its pleasant taste if it cost Deidre's life, or *any* of our lives."

Chapter Nine

"I THINK I AM just one solid block of ice," said Maura as she and Mitchell stumbled into the little cabin just as the sun started to lighten the sky to a dull gray.

"I'll get a fire going," Mitchell said even as he moved to do so.

As he piled some kindling on the logs set in the fireplace, he frowned. The ashes still scattered there looked very fresh. Glancing around as he nursed the fire to life, he noticed that the cabin did not have that unused look it usually did the few times he had stopped in. Everything was clean, too clean, although there was no real sign of a recent occupancy besides that. He prayed that meant Tyrone had used the place, for it would mean he was safe.

"Oh, that is just what I needed," Maura said as she stepped in front of the fire, still bundled up in all of her clothes. "That, and about three days of sleep."

Mitchell laughed as he tugged her down onto the sheepskin rug in front of the fire. They sat there for a while, enjoying the return of some warmth to their bodies. It was not until he began to nod off to sleep that Mitchell decided they needed to move.

"Get your coat and things off," he advised as he stood up and tugged a drowsy Maura to her feet. "I will make us some food. Just bacon and beans, I'm afraid, but we should eat something before we rest."

She nodded and took off her coat, hanging it on a hook near the door. "We should probably just nap a little, then try to stay awake until night. It could thoroughly twist up our schedule if we start sleeping all day and staying awake all night. Uncle always tried to do that when he had a few jobs that required him to watch people all night." Once stripped down to her dress, she went and sat at the table. "Spying, I suppose you could call it, although I cannot understand what one could possibly see at night. Do many people stay up all night?"

"Most people will save their wrongdoing until the dark can hide them."

"Of course. Well, it may be only beans and bacon, but it smells very nice." She took a deep breath. "And the coffee smells like heaven."

When Mitchell set a plate full of beans, bacon, and pan biscuits in front of her, Maura barely took the time to say thank you before she began to eat. Mitchell was surprisingly quiet and she watched him closely. He looked pale, yet there was a disturbing flush high on each of his cheekbones. He had said that he suffered no ill effects from the knock on the head, but she began to wonder.

Once they had finished their meal, she washed the dishes while he spread the blankets over the bed. He was moving slowly, stiffly. Then she heard him cough, a deep, hoarse noise that shook him and caused the blood in her veins to chill. Quickly drying her hands, she hurried to his side.

"Mitchell, you are sick," she said, pushing at him until he sat down on the bed. "You should have said something." She felt his forehead, and the heat there made her even more afraid for him.

"Thought I was just tired. Never been sick a day in my life."

"You've probably never been shot at, beaten up, and banged on the head all in just a few days, either."

"How would getting knocked on the head make me sick?"

She began to tug off his clothes, his passivity simply confirming her diagnosis. A healthy Mitchell would be grabbing her by now and trying hard to return the service. It looked as if they were about to lose a few more days. He would undoubtedly complain, not willing to rest until he was completely well and strong again, but she would tie him to the bed if she had to.

"Such things can leave you weakened enough to catch something like this." She shrugged as she finished stripping off his clothes and gently urged him beneath the blankets. "It is not at all unusual for people who have suffered a serious injury to become sick and feverish afterward."

"Damn. We're going to lose a few more days, aren't we?"

"We certainly are. It's the middle of winter. Until you are well and strong again, it would be suicide to go back outside and stay out in the cold day after day."

"And you're going to be really bossy about this, too."

"I am. If I must, I will tie you to that bed."

"Wait until I'm strong again."

She frowned at him, his words making no sense. Then she saw the slow, lecherous grin curving his mouth. It took only a moment to imagine several interesting things one could do if one's lover was tied to the bed. Maura blushed, more at her own scandalous thoughts than over his outrageous suggestion.

"Rogue," she scolded, and went to see what she could find that would help him.

In her search, Maura found a surprising number of things that could be used to nurse Mitchell. Not only was the cabin stocked with a few supplies, but Mitchell had filled several saddle packs with a vast assortment of goods. To her delight, she found honey and two lemons. Those would make a soothing drink for his throat. Together with her own few medical supplies, she felt confident that she could get him through this.

"I have to ask," Maura said as she made him a hot honey and lemon drink, using the lemon only sparingly so that her meager supply would last longer. "Lemons seem an odd thing to bring along."

"I thought you might get sick," he muttered, and grimaced, rubbing at his temples in a vain attempt to ease the aching in his head. "You're just a little bit of a thing, not much flesh on you. I was afraid riding for days in the cold would make you sicken."

"I am stronger than I look," she said as she sat down on the side of the bed and handed him the hot drink. "There's some of my headache powder in there to help ease any aches and pains you may have."

"My head does hurt. They gave me a good crack on the head. At least I hope that's what is making it ache. If it is, it'll stop soon." He took another drink of the hot honey and lemon. "This is helping. Damn, I really wanted to get back to Paradise by Christmas."

"That is still possible. Just because you feel like death warmed over doesn't mean you'll be ill that long. Some of these illnesses can be very fierce for only a short time, then leave as quickly as they arrived."

Finishing his drink, he handed the cup back to Maura and sank back down onto the bed. "Let's hope it's one of those. And since I suspect I will not be a very good patient, allow me to apologize now for any rotten behavior I indulge in later."

"You could not possibly be any worse a patient than my cousin Deidre. She begins by moaning that she is sure to die, says all her farewells, and at least considers making out her last will and testament. Then, when she doesn't die, she gets increasingly cross with the slowness of her recovery, and *slow* to Deidre can be one afternoon."

Mitchell smiled sleepily. "I don't think I will be that bad; at least I know I won't be that dramatic."

Maura suddenly remembered those words three days later when his fever finally broke and he slept easily for the first time since their arrival. Within hours after speaking them, Mitchell had declared that he was about to die, and cursed the lack of a priest. Maura was now prepared for the ill temper brought on by the slow pace of his return to full strength. He was a big man, strong, and otherwise healthy, so she hoped that return would not be a long, slow one. If nothing else, she, too, had hoped to get to Paradise before Christmas.

She sat by the fire, relaxed after a comforting bath, and brushed her newly washed hair dry. After the first night of trying to get some sleep next to a thrashing, muttering Mitchell, she had made herself a bed on the floor near the fire. Maura was looking forward to sleeping in the bed tonight. A sound from the bed drew her attention and she scowled when she saw Mitchell sitting up and reaching for his pants where they hung on the bedpost.

"And just where do you think you're going?" she asked.

"To the outhouse," he grumbled, struggling into his pants.

"There is a chamberpot—" she began.

"No, thank you. I have an urge to regain a little of my dignity." He yanked on his boots and cautiously stood up. "Not too dizzy," he muttered, mostly to himself.

"If you fall down out there, you will have to crawl back," she said as he staggered to the back door and pulled on his coat.

"Don't worry about me."

"Easier said than done," she grumbled after he left. Maura paused only a second before dragging on her coat and putting her boots on. She slipped out the door after him and stood on the little back stoop waiting. If he did collapse, she was going to have the devil of a time trying to get his big body back into bed, but he could not afford to take a bad chill now.

"Didn't think I could do it, huh?" he said as he walked back.

Following him back inside, she noticed that, although his step was a little unsteady, he appeared to be holding his own. "I was just there to make sure I could move the rocks out of your way if you had to do some crawling."

"So kind."

He yanked off his clothes, and fell back into bed. Pure bravado had carried him that far, and the last of that was gone. Mitchell smiled faintly as he heard her muttering while she picked up his clothes. By the time she came back to the side of the bed to pull the covers over him, he had regained enough strength to shift his body in an attempt to assist her in the chore.

"And just what did that prove?" she asked as she stood by the bed, her hands on her hips and her small foot tapping on the wooden floor in a gesture of pure annoyance.

"That I'm on the mend?"

"Really? I thought it was a demonstration of just how pigheaded you can be."

"That, too," he said, grinning at her.

"You could have made yourself feverish again."

"We can't stay here too much longer, Maura. I needed to see just how bad I was. I'm weak, no doubt about it, but at least I can stand upright for a little while. Another night's sleep and I'll be even better. I am hoping we can leave before a full week has passed."

"It's so cold out there," she murmured, knowing he was right, yet fearful for him.

"It's not much farther to Paradise." He gave her a coaxing smile. "Do you think I can have some more of that drink you concoct?"

"Of course, although it will be a little weak on the lemon. I've nearly stretched it as far as it will go."

He watched her leave to make him his potion. She had taken very good care of him, the memories of her gentle hands clear despite his fevered state. She also displayed an encouraging concern for his welfare. That implied that her feelings for him went deeper than passion, but he discovered that he was too much of a coward to flat out ask her what she felt. If she still kept her own feelings well hidden by the time they reached Paradise, he was going to have to take the first step. Mitchell hoped that, faced with the possibility that she would return to Saint Louis with her cousin, he would find the strength to do so.

Maura hummed to herself as she finished brushing her hair. Mitchell would return in a minute, having felt a need to go see that the horses were all right. He had improved rapidly in the three days since his fever broke, and they would be back on the trail first thing in the morning. Since she had no idea of what sort of accommodations they would be using, and suspected that she was going to be both tired and aching after riding all day, she did not foresee much chance of indulging their passions again until they reached Paradise. Tonight she intended to indulge them until they both collapsed with exhaustion. There had been a certain look in Mitchell's eyes that told her he was thinking the same thing.

Wanton Maura was back in full control, she mused as she made sure the tie on her robe was secure. Beneath it

she wore a truly scandalous collection of deep-purple underthings, trimmed in black. Mitchell made no secret of
how much he enjoyed her choice of underclothes and
Maura felt certain these would meet with his wholehearted
approval. She just hoped she did not turn cowardly when
the time for the unveiling arrived.

She set out their dinner, a little sorry that she could not
produce something a bit more tantalizing to their senses.
It was hard to make beans, bacon, and pan biscuits romantic. Maura smiled at him when he entered and took off his
coat.

"The horses are still hale and hearty, are they?" she
asked as they sat down and began to eat.

"You've changed your clothes," he murmured, trying,
and failing, to see what she had under her robe.

"I had a quick but thorough wash while you were out at-
tending to the poor beasts, and saw no reason to get all
dressed again."

He just nodded, but covertly watched her as they ate.
She seemed to be sparkling with energy and he wondered
why. Then Mitchell decided the why of it was not particularly important. That energy she was displaying would
serve him well when they went to bed shortly. The fever
and the need to fully recover from its effects had kept him
from making love to her for their entire stay. When he had
awakened this morning, he had felt more than ready to
rectify that little problem, but she had already left his bed.
Tonight, however, would be a different story. Considering
how hard the rest of the trip to Paradise could be, there
would probably be little opportunity or inclination for
lovemaking, and he intended to gather a full harvest of
pleasure to keep him content during the anticipated
drought.

As he sat sipping his coffee, Maura got up to wash the
dishes and he caught his first brief peek at what was under
the robe. A clear but too-soon-gone glance at her stock-

ings made him nearly choke on his coffee. Purple? Not a bright, shocking purple, but a rich, deep one. He did not even know they sold stockings in that color. Several more times as she busied herself around the sink, he saw a tantalizing bit of stocking. Mitchell felt himself growing more and more interested in what the rest of her ensemble looked like. When she came over to wipe off the table, bending over so far that he could peek down the front of her robe and be tempted with even more glimpses of purple, his gaze narrowed and he stared at her.

"Maura, my love, are you taunting me?" he asked.

Maura tossed the cloth in the general direction of the sink, put her hands on her hips, and slowly smiled at him. "Mitchell, how you do malign me."

"Hussy."

"Yes, I am feeling a little hussyish this evening."

He laughed. "I don't think hussyish is a word."

"Perhaps it should be."

"And perhaps it isn't wise to tease a desperate man."

"Desperate, are you?"

"It has been a while."

"Yes, it has."

Maura watched as he peered at the front of her robe as if he could open it through sheer willpower. He began to take another sip of his coffee and she reached for the ties of her robe. What she was wearing was undoubtedly going to shock him. This particular ensemble even shocked her a little. She hesitated, wondering if she should wait until he finished his coffee.

"You're looking at me a little oddly," Mitchell said, thinking that, as soon as he finished his coffee, if she had not removed the robe, he would do it for her.

"I was just recalling how you have reacted to my underthings on other occasions. You do seem to like them."

"I adore them."

"Yes, although one or two of them have seemed to cause

you to act, well, surprised. It might be an idea to set down your coffee."

"Are these better than those pinkish things you wore once?"

Briefly diverted, she asked, "Oh, you liked those pink things?"

"Couldn't you tell? We didn't even make it to the bed that time. Hell, they were so sheer, so thin, it looked like you were naked."

"Oh, well, these are not nearly so sheer."

When she dropped her robe, Mitchell drew his breath in so sharply he nearly choked. She wore no chemise this time. The deep-purple corset was elaborately trimmed with black lace and delicate black embroidery. The thin ruffle of lace at the top of the corset barely covered her breasts. Her little French demi-drawers were also in that rich purple color, and trimmed with black. They were also very short. Since her stockings were tied with a lacy black garter just above her knee, there was a vast amount of lovely white thigh exposed to view.

"I think my fever just came back," he said hoarsely as he rose and went to stand in front of her.

"I believe that is the purpose of these things."

He started to take off his shirt. "Just how hussyish are you feeling?"

"Very. Are you about to make one of your odd and very naughty requests?"

"Oh yeah." He bent down and yanked off his boots and socks. "Take off the little drawers."

That would leave her boldly exposed to view, for the bottom point of the corset stopped just short of what he obviously wanted to look at. Maura thought about it for one minute, just long enough for him to yank off the rest of his clothes. She looked at him standing there, bold and beautiful in his arousal, and decided it would not hurt to grant him his desire. Slowly, trying to be seductive and thinking she might be succeeding if the hot look on his face was any indication, she pulled off her little drawers. She stood up straight, held them out as she looked him plumb in the eye, then dropped them.

"God, Maura," he whispered as he dropped to his knees in front of her, "you cripple me."

He slid his hands up the backs of her thighs and stroked her buttocks, slowly tugging her closer to him. The shock she felt when he kissed the soft curls between her thighs disappeared at the first stroke of his tongue. She threaded her fingers through his hair, obeyed his hoarsely whispered command to spread her legs, and then sank beneath the weight of her own passion. He brought her to release with his intimate kiss, then slowly lowered her sated body down onto the sheepskin rug in front of the fire.

Maura quickly regained her senses and abruptly urged him over onto his back. She covered his strong body with kisses, loving the taste of him, the way he groaned and arched beneath her attentions. When she reached the juncture of his muscular thighs, she proceeded to return the intimate kisses he had given her. Mitchell cried out his approval of her caresses, but he did not allow her to continue them for long. He dragged her up his body and set her on him. Maura revealed her growing skills as she kept them teetering on the edge of release for a long time, before taking them both to the heights. As she collapsed in his arms, she decided there were definite advantages to letting Wanton Maura rule.

Chapter Ten

"THE THREE WHAT?" MAURA asked as she blinked against the glare of the snow and tried to see the gates of the ranch they approached more clearly.

"The Three Angels," Mitchell repeated. "Jason named his ranch in honor of the aunts who raised him. They also helped him with the funds to build this place. All three maiden aunts live with him. Cora, Flora, and Dora Booker."

"Cora, Flora, and Dora. Amazing."

"I don't think it was an intentional thing by their folks."

"They are not triplets?"

"Nope, although they look more and more alike every time I see them."

"Halt!" called a voice, and a man stepped out of a lean-to near the gates, his steadily aimed rifle enough to make them stop. "What do you want?"

"Name's Mitchell Callahan," Mitchell replied. "I've come to see Jason Booker."

"A Callahan, huh." The man relaxed his guard and cradled his rifle in his arms. "Got anyone chasing you?"

"No, not that I know of." Mitchell frowned, growing curious, for it was an odd question.

"Well, go on up to the house. Get out of this cold."

Mitchell nodded and nudged his horse forward. He glanced back once to see the man returning to his small shelter, then shook his head. The man probably just wanted to be sure he could safely return to his little fire.

As they reined in in front of the huge ranch house, Jason Booker himself stepped out. Maura tried not to stare at the man as Mitchell dismounted, then helped her down, but it was hard. She had thought Mitchell was huge, but this man topped Mitchell by several inches and was a bit more muscular. He had thick blond hair that was a little too long, and bright-blue eyes, the color so clear and sharp it could be easily seen even from a slight distance. He made Maura think of Vikings, big, very handsome Vikings.

"Well, Mitchell," Jason said in his deep, somewhat booming voice as he shook Mitchell's hand and clapped him soundly on the back. "Fancy seeing you here, old friend. Bad time of the year to be traveling."

"I wasn't given much choice." When Jason looked at Maura, Mitchell wrapped his arm around her shoulders, tucked her up against his side, and coolly ignored Jason's knowing grin. "This is Miss Maura Kenney from Saint Louis."

"Delighted." Jason took her hand in his and touched a kiss to the back, apparently oblivious to the icy mitten she wore. "I expect you want some warmth, good food, a soft bed, and a hot bath."

"Oh, yes, please," Maura said.

Mitchell dogged Maura's steps all the way up to the room she was shown to. He was acting almost jealous of their host and she tried to ignore the thrill that gave her. It tickled awake the love and need she had for the man, emotions she was desperately trying to keep buried. She did laugh softly, however, at his slightly pouting look when he was taken away to a room far down the hall. Clearly, Jason Booker wanted them to behave properly and she felt that they should honor that wish. Maura knew she would miss Mitchell's big, warm body curled up against hers, but, considering her plans for the future, it was probably for the best that she get used to the loss.

"So, is she the one?" asked Jason as Mitchell entered the parlor a few hours later to share a drink with him.

"It's not something I want to joke about," Mitchell said as he accepted the brandy the man served him and sprawled in a chair facing his friend.

"Actually, for all I teased you, I never really saw it as a joke. Not like Tyrone did, anyway."

"Are you saying that you actually believe a person can recognize his mate for life quickly, almost at first sight?"

"Yes and no." Jason grinned when Mitchell rolled his eyes in mock disgust over his evasiveness. "Have some sympathy. It's not something any man would want to believe. It tastes a little bit too much like female romantic nonsense. And yet, there is a part of me that feels there is some truth to it. I have seen folks who took one look at each other and were married days later, then spent many, many years content and faithful. I have also seen folks who followed all the rules, looked for all the things society says should be considered, and seemed perfectly suited in many ways, yet their marriage failed miserably and they are trapped together. Who knows? I think it may be somewhere in between that the truth lies, or maybe some of us are just blessed with the knowledge."

Mitchell smiled faintly. "Blessed, is it? Maybe so. And, yes, she is the one. Knew it within hours of meeting her.

Hell, I started to get an inkling the first time I heard her sweet voice telling a man that she was going to rip his lungs out through his eyes." He grinned when Jason looked briefly shocked then laughed heartily.

"And such a lady she seemed to be, too."

"Oh, she is that, all right." His smile was sweetly lecherous as he thought of the passion he and Maura shared. "When need be. Sweet, yet tart. Prim, yet . . ." He shrugged. "Yup, she's definitely the one. Now I just have to get up the nerve to ask her."

"You haven't found it in what, about a month?"

"She has this plan to take the money she earns from this job and run the farm in Missouri with her cousin Deidre. If I could be sure she would fail, I'd let her go, then go find her again in a while, say, in the summertime, and see if she had softened up some. But, dammit, I think she could succeed."

"Oh, I shouldn't worry about that plan," Jason said as he sipped at his drink.

Mitchell frowned. There seemed to be some knowledge behind Jason's words, a knowledge Mitchell was not privy to. Jason had always been a clever man, sometimes a little sneaky and sometimes a little manipulative. Mitchell had the feeling that the man was being some of each this time. After so many years of friendship, however, Mitchell knew that whatever secret Jason was holding back, nothing would pry it free until Jason wanted to release it.

"You think it is just empty talk?"

"I think you and circumstances can change her mind."

"Well, maybe if I lay my cards on the table, I can change her mind about going to be a farmer, but I don't think that's the only obstacle I need to surmount." Mitchell frowned slightly as he stared into his drink. "I think she keeps a very tight control on certain emotions and the occasional little remarks she makes and tales she related of her childhood make me think it has to do with her mother and father. I may be looking for something she cannot or will not give."

"Ah, you want love and constancy."

"No need to be sarcastic."

"Sorry. I occasionally let my bitterness spew out onto others. I am pleased that you have found the woman you love and hope you will be happy with her," Jason drawled.

"Phew!" Mitchell shook his head and stared at Jason in wide-eyed surprise. "Could you possibly have come up with words any more polite and more totally *not* heartfelt than those?"

Jason suddenly laughed and also shook his head. "Sorry again. I can get moody at this time of the year."

"Fair enough, if you agree to put up with my moodiness tomorrow morning."

"Spending a night alone makes you cranky, does it?"

"When did you get so prudish? Hell, I'm at one end of the hall and my Maura is at the other, with the triple guard of your aunties in between us. It may not have been gentlemanly to seduce the woman, but I do mean to marry her."

"I suspect you do, only a lot can happen between here and the church." Jason just met Mitchell's disgruntled look with a smile. "Mustn't shock my poor, dear aunties." He cocked his head, listening for a moment, before announcing, "I believe your lady approaches."

Maura smiled at the two men as she entered the parlor. She accepted the glass of wine Jason offered and took a seat on a little settee. Her eyes widened slightly with surprise when Mitchell suddenly sat down beside her.

"The chair was pinching you?" murmured Jason, then he met Mitchell's glare with a smile.

A moment later, three plump, graying ladies entered, and Maura was introduced to Jason's aunts. They were sweet, readily welcoming her, yet seemed to be bubbling over with some secret amusement. Maura did not have much time to consider the puzzle as they all moved to the dining room to eat. Between savoring a delicious meal and replying to a barrage of questions from Jason's aunts, Maura was kept very busy. They soon all trooped back to the parlor for an after-dinner drink and the questions asked began to make Maura uncomfortable. Every time the papers were mentioned, she inwardly winced, hating the lying she was being forced to do. Barely a moment after the aunts had excused themselves, Maura did the same. She knew she was simply delaying the inevitable, but she did not care.

Once in her room, she stripped off her clothes and crawled into bed. Her cold, empty, lonely bed, she thought, and sighed. The closer they got to Paradise the harder she had to fight her feelings for Mitchell. Maura found herself thinking of trying to win Mitchell's love. The spectre of her mother weeping over yet another heartbreak delivered by her feckless father was losing its strength. Maura huddled into a tight ball beneath the covers. It was going to hurt like hell when she walked away from Mitchell, but that pain would eventually ease. If she stayed with him, a man who had not once even mentioned the word love, she risked renewing that pain on a regular basis. She was, she realized, a complete coward. She would rather cut him out of her heart with one, swift blow than risk having it taken out piece by tiny piece by trying to hold on to Mitchell.

"Your lady has a secret or two," Jason said as soon as the women had left.

Mitchell sighed, and nodded. "I got that feeling, too. Not sure I want to poke around trying to find out what it is."

"I shouldn't bother. She also tries very hard to keep herself tightly controlled."

"But why?"

"Who knows. There are shields there, however. You're

going to have to get through them to get to her. I think you've already made some chinks in her armor. The reason I saw the shields is because they slip around you and then she has to prop them back up again." He smiled faintly. "Trust me, I am not that good at reading people."

"Better than most of us. Maura was only your guest for a few hours, and you have already seen the problems it took me almost this long to perceive." Mitchell shook his head. "This kind of troubles a man with some skill at words. I'm a blunt speaker."

"That obviously doesn't trouble her."

"True, but plain speaking isn't always the way to pull secrets out of a person."

"I think you'll find a way, although I doubt you'll find it easy. Still, I have the feeling that she might just want you to try."

"Hell, I have to, don't I." He sighed, then shook aside his concerns. "Still have that sled?"

"Yes, I recently loaned it to someone and it has just come back."

"Can I borrow it?"

"Of course, along with some of my men. Don't argue. You are almost there. It would be tragic to get shot now. Also, a few of my men are headed into town for Christmas anyway."

"Ah, yes, Christmas. I wanted to be back for the holiday, wanted to spend it with my brothers. Maura was also hoping her cousin Deidre had made it to Paradise by now. No word, huh?"

"None. But, wasn't that part of the plan?"

"It was, but, right now, I wish Tyrone had broken the rules, bent them just enough to let me know he's alive." He shook his head. "This not knowing anything is a little hard."

"You and Maura have made it through unscathed. I am sure the others will, too."

Mitchell just nodded. He had the feeling Jason truly believed what he said, but the comforting words did little to still his fears for his brother. As he excused himself and made his way to bed, Mitchell prayed he would find good news when he reached Paradise and home.

"We are going to travel in that?" Maura asked as she gazed at the sleigh, barely able to contain her excitement.

Mitchell smiled at her as he picked their bags up off the veranda. "It's suitable for Christmas Eve, don't you think?"

"It has been years since I have ridden in one, but I always enjoyed them."

"It might be a little colder than you are used to."

Maura grinned. "That has been true for most of the trip here."

"Just let me put our bags away and then I shall escort m'lady to her carriage." Mitchell bowed slightly and then went to put their things in the sleigh.

"I want to thank you for your hospitality, Mister Booker," she said, turning to Jason. "And it is very kind of you to let us use the sleigh. Are you sure you won't be missing it come the holiday?"

"It was something my aunts always enjoyed, but they can no longer bear the cold," he replied. "Take it and enjoy."

"Oh, I will. At least until the cold changes my mind."

"There is one thing I would like to say before you leave, Miss Kenney," he said seriously, keeping a coven watch on Mitchell's whereabouts. "A bit of unasked-for advice if you will."

"Well, one should never turn away advice," she murmured, and the way he looked at her, as if he could see right inside her heart, made her nervous.

"Sometimes the lessons we think we learn from our parents are not the right ones."

Her eyes widened slightly, but she struggled to maintain her air of calm interest. "Such as?"

"A child can see things one way, but it would be a wise person who stops one day as an adult and takes another hard look. True, it is foolish to repeat the mistakes we know our parents made. Just be sure you know what those are."

"Thank you, sir. I will give all you say some consideration."

"I wish you would, Maura," he said quietly, smiling gently. "Mitchell is a good friend and I think we could be friends as well. I always find it annoying to see my friends make themselves miserable when there is no need."

Maura was relieved when Mitchell came and got her. Jason made her very uneasy. She began to feel as if those blue eyes could see her every fear and secret.

Once Mitchell had set her in the sleigh, he spent several minutes making sure she was well wrapped up in warm clothes and blankets. She was *so* well wrapped up by the time he was done, Maura felt she could be tossed out of the sleigh and not be hurt. It was rather nice to be so pampered and fussed over, but she finally told him to just get in and take up the reins. The men waiting to ride with them were becoming a little too amused.

It did not take that long for the joy of the ride to slip away. Maura did not completely lose all the pleasure she found in the sleigh, but it was hard to have fun when one was wrapped up like a mummy and the cold still managed to seep through to the bone. She felt bad for the men riding with them, but they seemed to accept it in stride. They were probably far more accustomed to such cold than she was, she mused, and they had chosen to ride to town.

Her thoughts drifted to what Jason had said and she quivered with unease. It was uncomfortable to think that someone you had just met had seen such things in you, especially when those observations were so directly on target. She was acting upon lessons learned from her parents, but she was not sure they were the wrong ones. A part of her was afraid to look over the sad years of her childhood and try to reevaluate what she had seen, but she decided that it might be a good idea to do so. Even if she did not believe Jason was right, she now felt compelled to actually prove him wrong. That would require a bit of soul-searching.

"Cold, darlin'?" Mitchell asked, glancing at her with some concern.

"I could be sassy and say that is a very stupid question," she drawled, and returned his grin.

"You could be," he agreed. "It's not that much farther to Paradise and a nice warm room."

"Do we go to your ranch?"

"Not yet. We'll take a room in the hotel. I need to see my brother, Stephen, and maybe the judge."

She inwardly cringed. He was thinking of the papers again, the very useless, fake papers. "Do you think there will be some word about your brother Tyrone? Maybe about my cousin, too?"

"I hope so. We certainly didn't cross the miles any faster than they could have, despite using the trains for a while. I am really hoping that Tyrone, and maybe Deidre, too, have already arrived."

"Wouldn't they have stopped at Booker's ranch, too?"

"I would have thought so, but obviously not. Don't worry. As soon as I get those papers where they belong, there will be no more danger for Deidre or for Tyrone, and we can openly hunt them down."

After you spit on me and kick me out of town, she thought morosely. She had not given much thought to how it would be when she told him that the papers she had were forgeries. She now decided it was because she had not wanted to think about it. He was going to feel so betrayed, and that feeling would be made all the worse if Deidre and Tyrone had not yet arrived. Maura huddled a little deeper into her blankets, suddenly feeling a chill that she suspected had nothing to do with the weather.

Chapter Eleven

❧◦❧

"YOU DO STILL HAVE the papers, don't you?"

Maura nodded as she sat down on the bed. The moment she had been dreading had finally arrived. The tension she felt had been mounting from the moment they arrived at the hotel, throughout the process of getting a room, and with each step they had walked toward the room they were supposed to share, until it was a hard lump in her stomach. She had thought to spend a passionate night or two with Mitchell before she had to go home, but she had the feeling that what she was about to tell him was going to turn that little dream into ashes.

"Yes, I have them, but there is something I must tell you," she said as she reached beneath her skirts to unhitch the secret pocket holding the papers.

"That's where they've been hidden all this time?" Mitchell asked, slightly amused. "Who thought of that?"

"Deidre." She handed him the papers and said carefully, "She kept her set of papers in a similar one."

Mitchell looked up from the papers he had just been perusing with a slight frown. "What do you mean—her set?"

For a brief moment, Maura seriously considered not confessing to anything, just letting him go off and find out the truth on his own. He had spoken of his brother Stephen, a lawyer, and a certain Judge Lennon. One of those men would surely recognize that the papers Mitchell had were forgeries. By the time he learned the ugly truth she could be long gone. It was cowardly, but it would probably hurt less.

"Deidre and I had a plan. We had tragic proof that the Martins were willing to kill to stop you from getting those papers," she explained, the look of growing suspicion and betrayal that was turning his dark-gray eyes black tearing at her heart. "We decided to split up. Each of us would carry a set of papers to Paradise. It was rather hoped that the Martins would more closely follow the woman who took the train."

"Why? Why was it better if they followed you?"

She could tell by the hoarseness of his voice that he had already guessed what she had done. "Because the papers I carried are worthless forgeries. Deidre has the real ones."

"And you couldn't have told me this?"

"Deidre and I decided that it had to be kept a complete secret."

"Even from me, Maura?"

"If the Martins had found out . . ." she began, and winced when he spat out a vicious curse.

"Dammit, woman, it would've been kinder if you had just cut out my heart with a spoon."

The papers clutched tightly in his hand, Mitchell strode out of the room. Maura jumped slightly when he slammed the door behind him even though she had expected it.

She sat there for a minute in the silence, blindly watching the tears drip onto her tightly clenched hands.

This was what she had wanted, she told herself firmly. The affair was certainly at an end now. Maura just had not anticipated that it would hurt quite so much. She certainly had not considered the possibility that anything she did would hurt Mitchell, but he was hurt, deeply so. It had been there to see in the taut lines of his face, the near blackness of his eyes, and his loss of color. She had the chilling feeling that his parting words held far more truth than bitterness.

Fighting desperately to calm herself, she stood up and went to draw herself a bath. That would soothe her. It always had before. After a while relaxing in the bath, she would be able to get control of her emotions again. This pain and this wrenching sense of loss could be buried right beside the love and need she had not yet been able to rid herself of. Her skill in doing so had wavered lately, but, now that Mitchell was no longer going to be around to play upon her weaknesses, she would regain that skill. It was just a matter of time.

Mitchell stood outside the hotel almost savoring the cold. He glanced at the papers he still held and thought about throwing them away, then decided to keep them. They could become a memento of sorts, a reminder that even when every bone in your body told you you had found the right woman, you could still be wrong.

He strode off down the street. It was tempting to go straight to the saloon and drink himself into a stupor, but he needed to talk to Stephen. The trouble was not over yet. If Deidre Kenney was still out there, then the ranch and the mine were still at risk, not to mention Deidre as well.

His body shaking, Mitchell stopped again and took several deep breaths of the bitingly chilly air in an attempt to calm himself. It was hard when all he could think of was Maura's betrayal. Despite all he had thought they had shared, she had never trusted him, and that cut him to the bone. He had had to get away from her for fear of what he might say or do. It was bad enough that he had revealed how she had hurt him, if only briefly. He certainly did not want her to see how badly he was falling apart now.

It took several more attempts before he made it to his brother Stephen's house. As he reached up to rap on the door, he saw the papers he still clutched in his hand, and cursed. Shoving them into his coat pocket, he banged on the door. Mitchell hoped Stephen had a bottle of whiskey. Maybe two.

"Mitchell!" Stephen cried with delight when he saw his brother at the door, then frowned when he got a good look at the expression on Mitchell's face. "Something wrong?"

"I need a drink," Mitchell said as he strode past Stephen and headed stright for the parlor.

"Mitchell, are you all right?" Stephen asked as he hurried after his brother.

Going straight to the cabinet where Stephen kept his liquor, Mitchell pulled out a glass and a bottle of whiskey. Ignoring his brother's concerned looks, Mitchell poured and quickly drank two whiskeys. He then poured himself a third, yanked the papers out of his pocket, and handed them to Stephen. As his youngest brother looked over the useless sheets of paper, Mitchell yanked off his coat, tossed it over the back of a chair, and then sat down.

"What are these?" Stephen asked as he sat down in the chair facing Mitchell.

"They are supposed to be the papers the Martins want so badly. They are the reason I have been shot at, beat up, and chased for more miles than I care to count. They are the reason I'm sitting here thinking of getting stone-cold drunk."

"I don't understand." Stephen dragged his long fingers through his thick, black hair, tousling it badly. "You can't know, but Tyrone has returned. He also brought papers. Miss Deidre Kenney had them. We took them to the judge, who approved them, then took them to the land office. We even got that crook Will Pope to sign a paper saying he saw them and filed them. So, how is it that you can have papers, too?"

"Tyrone's all right?" Mitchell asked, briefly diverted from his own misery by concern for his brother.

"Fine. So is Miss Kenney. In fact, Tyrone and Deidre plan to be married."

Mitchell cursed and had another drink. "That is just wonderful."

"I would really like to know how you came by these papers. They can't be real, can they?"

"Nope. They are forgeries. That is what Miss Maura Kenney and I have been protecting with our lives for a few hundred miles."

"Oh. You arrived with Deidre's cousin?"

"Yes. She is over at the hotel, or was when I left there." Stephen helped himself to a glass of whiskey. "Something has you wound up tight as an old maid's corset. Now, we can go back and forth and round and round with me asking questions and you biting out little useless answers or you can just tell me what the hell is wrong?"

Mitchell almost smiled. "You're getting sassy, boy."

"You drive me to it."

After taking a deep breath and an equally deep drink of whiskey, Mitchell told him all about what he saw as the grossest of betrayals by the woman he loved. There was not much sympathy on Stephen's face when he was done with his tale, and no outrage. The most prominent expression was one of curiosity, with the slightest hint of admiration. Mitchell hoped that last was not for the traitorous Maura.

"And you believe this Maura Kenney is that fated mate you have been waiting for?" Stephen finally asked.

"It certainly felt like she was, but a true mate would not betray me like this."

"Was Maura right beside you all the way here? Sharing the discomfort and the danger?"

"Well, yeah, but—"

"Did she fight the Martins' hired guns as hard as you did?"

"Well, yeah, but—"

"Did she ever once falter and speak of giving up, perhaps just saying to hell with it, why am I doing this for these Callahans? These papers aren't worth anything anyway?"

"Well, no, but—"

"So, in other words, despite her lack of skills, despite being, how did you put it, a little bit of a thing, despite cold and men trying to kill her, she left Saint Louis to come here, to finish the job her late uncle had started, an uncle killed by our enemies? She stuck it out unto the bitter-end, playing the diversion, putting her life in danger so that Deidre, who had the real papers, might be able to get through and save our land?"

"Dammit, you really are a lawyer, aren't you?" Mitchell said, half in admiration and half in annoyance. "She should have told me that the papers she had were not real. She didn't trust me."

"She gave her word that she would tell no one."

"I am not no one, dammit," he yelled, then took a deep breath and added more quietly, "She could have told me. She should have known that it would be safe to do so."

"Yes, I suppose she should have. Maybe she didn't think too much on how the papers she had were forgeries. It didn't matter to her, did it? Her job was to divert or at least split the Martins' hunters."

Mitchell rested his head against the back of the chair, stared blindly up at the ceiling, and sipped his whiskey. He carefully thought over all his brother had just said. The things Maura had done, when looked at as a whole, did rather reduce the sting of what she had not done—told him about the papers. Mitchell could not even be sure if it showed that she did not trust him. About the only thing he could be sure it revealed was that Maura Kenney would never break a promise.

He had to wonder if some of the strength of his reaction to her lie was because he was so unsure about her. The only thing he was sure of with Maura was that they could make each other burn. Delightful as that was, it was not enough to build a future on. After spending weeks in each other's company, he had hoped to see more, but Maura kept her feelings well hidden.

"I don't know what to do," he whispered.

"It's obvious that you care deeply for this woman or this lie, and that is all it is if you look at it calmly and unemotionally, and it would not have hurt you so much."

"A lie. Do you really think that was all it was?"

"I don't know the woman, but looking at all she has done, I have to think so. If she really thought you could not be trusted with the truth, that would imply she thought you might give in to or help the Martins. Well, everything she's done seems to imply that that thought never crossed her mind. She stayed with you, fought with you, and froze with you. To me that seems to show a great deal of trust."

Mitchell began to feel a great deal better. Stephen had been able to look at the problem with the calm, logical mind that made him such a good lawyer. It could easily be that he had seen betrayal because he simply did not feel secure with Maura. Perhaps he should swallow his pride, go back to the hotel, and try to sort it all out.

"I think there is only one question you should be asking," Stephen said quietly, smiling faintly at his brother. "Is this really worth giving her up completely?"

"Hell, I don't know. I'm not sure anything is, but then, I'm not even sure I have her."

He stayed with Stephen for a little while longer, talking about their victory over the Martins and Tyrone's marriage plans. Mitchell was both sympathetic and pleased to hear that Tyrone was wracked with uncertainty. Unlike Maura, however, Deidre seemed to make no secret about her preference, at least not to anyone who cared to look closely. Maura was obviously far more tightly controlled than her cousin. In fact, Mitchell thought with a rising sense of having a revelation, it was almost as if Maura was afraid, afraid of what she felt, perhaps even afraid of how vulnerable such feelings could make her.

"I believe I will go back to the hotel now," Mitchell said as he tossed off the rest of his drink and stood up.

"We are supposed to go to the ranch for Christmas dinner," Stephen said, standing up as Mitchell put on his coat. "Tyrone's hoping he will be announcing his engagement."

"Well, Jason has lent us the use of his sleigh, so I will stop by here and get you."

"Strange that Jason didn't tell you Tyrone had returned."

"The sneaky bastard probably thought it amusing to keep it a secret."

"Well, good luck," Stephen said as he followed Mitchell to the front door.

"I wish I could say I didn't need it."

Maura lay sprawled on her back on the bed, staring up at the ceiling and wondering why her bath had failed so miserably in making her feel better. Her emotions were not obeying her. They were swirling through her with such force and confusion she felt nauseated. All the tricks she had used in the past to set such emotions deep inside her, to hide them from herself and the world, were not working.

Mitchell, she thought, and cursed him for what he had done to her. It would take a very long time to get over him, to return to some semblance of normalcy. He had pulled her apart, set free feelings that were fierce and frightening. She loved the fool, and she really resented him for making her feel that way.

She closed her eyes and took slow, deep breaths, struggling to bring back that sense of calm she had always had. It was proving depressingly elusive. All she could see when she closed her eyes was the look of devastation on Mitchell's face just before he had stormed out of the hotel room. She had put that look there and she felt weak with guilt.

All of a sudden she thought about what Jason had said. Maybe, in some odd way, she had learned the wrong lessons from her parents. Unless the man was a bland lump of human oatmeal she suspected him of being like her father. Deep in her heart, she knew she had done that to Mitchell and it was grossly unfair. Mitchell was handsome and charming, but that was all he had in common with her father.

And was she like her mother? she asked herself. Maura did not think so. Even as a child, she had often felt the urge to yell at her father, to scold him for what he was doing to her mother, even to strike him. When he would tell them stories of what a fine time he had in New Orleans, she did not ooh and ahh like her mother over tales of ball gowns and beautiful carriages. She had thought instead about the money he had spent, money they could have used to do more practical things, like put a new roof on the house. Maura sincerely doubted that she would have sat there and cried when tales of his infidelities reached her ears. The philanderer would have been run-

ning for his life. No, she was not like her mother. Her
mother had loved a man who had behaved no better than
a spoiled, thoughtless child, who had walked all over her
and left her and their child struggling from day to day in
poverty. As a woman, she could never have wasted years of
her life on such a man. She would have spanked him, told
him to grow up, and left him behind.

The only thing Maura was sure of was that love could
hurt you, could make you feel as if you were bleeding from
a hundred stinging wounds. She was not sure she wanted
that in her life. It was such a terrible vulnerability. There
was always the chance that her mother had started out as
sassy and strong, but love had turned her into that meek,
forever-crying woman who had spent more time looking
out the window waiting for her husband to stop by than
she ever had on her child.

Maura gasped and clapped a hand over her mouth. She
could not believe she had just thought that. She had loved
her mother. Catherine Kenney had been all that a proper
lady should be. Then Maura stiffened her spine and refused to allow herself to back away from the truth.
Catherine Kenney had had little time and no interest in
anything that did not center around her ungrateful husband. That was where Catherine had failed. She had made
a man the very center of her world, her reason for living,
and he had proven to be a clay-footed idol.

With a weary sigh, Maura felt the touch of exhaustion
start to pull her into a sleep state. She decided it was just
what she needed. Although she had not solved any of her
problems, she did feel as if her revelations would be very
helpful in sorting out what to do with Mitchell. That was, if
he even got within twenty feet of her ever again.

The pain she had been feeling since he walked out
tried to surge back to strong, vital life, but Maura forced it
away. She needed to rest. She was so tired, so heartsore, all

her thoughts were doing was circling around one another in her head. A few hours of sleep would help clear her mind. When she woke up, all of the pain would rush back, but she would be a little bit stronger and, maybe, a little more able to deal with it.

way to come here for two o'clock, and that she had come
to him because no driver or show could keep him from his
work. When she woke up, all of this would make sense. It
just had to make sense, or she ... no one, no matter of that
sense, should have said to be.

Chapter Twelve

SOMEONE WAS WATCHING HER. That sharp realization cut its
way into Maura's sleep-dulled mind. Right behind it was
fear and that brought her fully awake. She was painfully
aware of the fact that she was alone and only half dressed.
Was it the Martins? Had they discovered that she had arrived and come to try to take the papers? Was it some
drunken cowboy who had seen Mitchell bring her into the
room, then desert her? Her hands clenched to try to calm
herself, she slowly opened her eyes. What she saw at the
end of the bed did not completely end her sense of unease.

Mitchell sat there, leaning against the tall end post of
the bed. One foot rested on the floor and one on the bed.
His big hands were clasped around his raised knee. In his
fingers dangled her set of papers. She slowly met his gaze

and sighed. There was little expression on his handsome face, no warmth in his beautiful eyes. He watched her as if she was a stranger. That hurt. That hurt a lot.

"They are very good forgeries," he said, tossing the papers down onto the bed. "Stephen was unable to tell if they were real or not."

"I had the best man in Saint Louis do them," she replied, astounded at how calm she sounded, for inside she was twisted into knots of pain and sorrow, and the fear that he was about to add to that. "He is a master forger."

"You know some very strange people."

"My uncle and Bill often had need of such characters to accomplish their jobs."

"Why didn't you tell me, Maura?"

"I promised Deidre."

He sighed and closed his eyes for a moment before looking at her again. "Why? Didn't you trust me?"

"For the first day, perhaps, no, I didn't. Our meeting was very convenient, against all odds, really. And I am well aware of how good forgeries can be, so your papers didn't necessarily ease my mind that much. It was such a strange assortment, however, that I began to believe you were who you said you were rather quickly."

"That I can understand. It was only smart to be cautious. But after that? And, dammit, even after we became lovers, you still couldn't trust me enough to tell me?"

"I had promised Deidre." She winced at the curse he spat and, deciding she felt a little too vulnerable lying there, sat up against the pillows. "I'm not sure even I understand why I didn't tell you at some point along the way. At times I felt horribly guilty about it."

"Good."

Maura sighed. "I was the diversion, if you will. It was my job to pull some of the Martins' attention my way. They had to believe that I might have all or part of the papers and that they were real." She shook her head. "I didn't think you'd betray me to the Martins. Never that. But what if you didn't agree with our plan? What if you decided someone needed to be told that Deidre was coming with the real papers, thinking to get help to your brother and to her, to even notify your brother to set out after her? These were not things I could know until it was too late to take back the truth, and we both know the Martins seemed to know what we were doing as soon as we did it.

"I don't really know how to explain it. Deidre and I came up with a plan. Part of that plan was that absolutely no one but the two of us knew that the papers I carried were forgeries. I promised her I wouldn't tell and I promised my uncle on his deathbed that I'd help finish this job for him. It's all muddled up together. I clutched this grand plan tightly to my heart, seeing it as my only and last chance to pay back my uncle and Deidre for all they had done for me. Nothing was going to make me waver from that plan. Blind stubbornness, I suppose."

Mitchell muttered a curse and dragged his fingers through his hair. In some ways, he did understand. Stephen was right. In Maura's mind it did not really have anything to do with whether or not she trusted him. It was the plan and the promise. She had agreed to the plan, stuck to it doggedly, and mostly because she had promised Deidre. The lingering pinch of hurt he felt came mostly from the fact she had chosen loyalty to Deidre over him, but he was not even sure he was seeing that correctly.

He stared at her, all too aware of how beautifully tempting she was. Her robe was securely tied, but, in the deep vee at her neck, he could see the smallest bit of black lace. Despite how unsettled he still was over why she had never told him of the forgeries and how she might feel about him, he felt his body tighten with interest. Thoughts of what she might be wearing under that robe skimmed the edges of his mind.

None of it really mattered in the end, either, he decided. She had not betrayed him as badly as he had thought she had. Maura had lied through her silence, no more, no less, and it had nothing to do with trusting him or how she might feel about him. If he had pushed her on the matter of the papers, had asked to see them, or even asked a few pointed questions, she might well have told him the truth. He should have acted upon that sense he had had that she was keeping some secret. That was all in the past, however. He shrugged off the last remnants of the pain he had felt, and that was easy enough to do when he accepted how Maura had looked at it all.

What would happen next was what had him nearly shaking in his boots. He loved her, needed her, wanted her for his wife, but had no real idea if she felt the same depth of emotion he did. She had taken him into her bed, but she had also not stopped talking about returning to the farm, going back to Saint Louis and making her life there.

"All right," he finally said. "I'll accept that it wasn't the betrayal I thought it was. You just lied."

Maura blinked, inwardly delighted that he had forgiven her, yet a little irritated by his conclusion. "I didn't really lie," she said, ignoring the way his eyes narrowed. "I didn't have to. You never really asked any questions. I was always worried that you would."

"Because you wouldn't have been able to continue the lie?"

"Probably not. I won't say I wouldn't have tried, but it would've been a poor effort, easily seen through."

"That's some comfort, I suppose," he muttered, then smiled apologetically when she winced. "I believe you. I believe it wasn't a lack of trust in me. That belief will take a little while to salve all the bruises, however. And I still don't like it that, in a way, you lied to me, no matter how much I can sympathize with how you felt. And, hell, the whole thing was for the benefit of the Callahans, no matter what your reasons were for whatever you did. It'd be damned churlish of me not to at least try to understand when you literally put your life on the line and me and my brothers gain the most from that."

"Well, thank you," she said, and added softly, "I'm sorry."

"Apology accepted. Now, for the next item of business."

"Next item of business?"

"We're getting married."

Mitchell inwardly cursed his ineptitude, but knew it was too late to try again. It should have been done more slowly, the question asked amidst a flurry of kisses and love words. He hoped the shock he saw on her face was because of his bluntness. What really troubled him was that he thought he detected just a hint of fear in her eyes.

"I have no wish to marry," she said quietly, ruthlessly beating back that heedless part of her that wanted to throw herself into his arms and say yes.

That hurt, but there was too much at stake to falter too quickly, Mitchell decided. "You don't wish to marry at all, or you just don't wish to marry me?"

"It's not you."

He got up and strode over to the table near the window, pleased to see that the brandy he had ordered when they arrived had been delivered. Mitchell was tempted to tell her that Deidre was here and was probably going to marry Tyrone and stay in Paradise. He resisted the urge. He wanted Maura to stay for him, only him, and not because it would allow her to be close to one of the last members of her family.

"I see," he drawled as, drink in hand, he walked back to stand by the side of the bed. "I'm only good for stud."

"What a horrible thing to say!"

"What else am I supposed to think? You were a virgin. Despite your taste in underclothes, you're a proper lady to the marrow of your bones. I bedded you. Hell, we've burned the sheets for the last few hundred miles. The next logical step is to get married."

The next item of business. The next logical step. Maura hated those words and almost hated Mitchell for using them. They cut into her like knives. Still reeling from the horrible confrontation over the papers, from all the personal revelations that followed, she was unable to deal with this new twist. Maura felt choked by the myriad of emotions swirling through her.

"Maybe I'm not a very logical person," she said. She could hear the way her voice trembled and feared she would soon break into a thousand little pieces.

"Maura, you will marry me. For all you know, I've set a baby in you."

"Oh, so you would marry me for the sake of the child I might be carrying."

Mitchell frowned at her. He knew he was doing this all wrong, but desperation drove him. Tomorrow she would know that Deidre was safe and the job was done, the Martins defeated. Even if Deidre was staying, Maura might still think to go back to the farm. He could not let her go. The way she was reacting to his words, however, seemed unusually strong. Anger, yes, and he felt he could soothe that. Maybe even a little sense of insult because he was not spouting pretty words, was, in truth, almost ordering her to marry him. That, too, he felt he could soothe, given time. But Maura looked almost frantic. She was beginning to tremble, her voice had risen a notch, carrying a faint hint of shrillness, and she was wringing her hands so tightly and consistently that he thought she might be hurting herself.

"Of course I would. I'm not a man to shirk my responsibility."

"Responsibility," she whispered.

"Maura, we could have a good marriage. We like each other, respect each other, and desire each other."

Maura started to shake her head. Business, logic, and now responsibility. She covered her face with her hands.

She was rapidly losing control and was terrified of what she would do or say, yet could not seem to calm herself down.

"No, no, no," she muttered, and she knew she was talking more to herself than to Mitchell.

"Why the hell not?" he demanded.

"I won't marry a man who doesn't love me," she shrieked, the nearly hysterical sound of her voice only somewhat muffled by her hands over her face. "I will not do as my mother did. I won't. I won't. I won't fall into that trap that just slowly sucks the life out of you. I won't be one of those poor pathetic creatures sitting there waiting for what her husband can never give her, spending all of her time and energy trying to make him love her, and crying all night, night after wretched night, because she can never do enough. I won't."

Mitchell stared at her, and suddenly a lot of things made sense. This was what kept Maura so tightly controlled. There were scars here, scars made by watching her parents destroy each other if he was understanding her tearful babble correctly. He set his drink down on the table by the bed. Despite how badly her upset and pain made him feel, he also felt a stirring of hope. She would not be so afraid if she did not care for him, care deeply. He sat down on the bed and pulled her into his arms, holding her firmly for the minute or so it took her to stop fighting him.

"Tell me about your parents, Maura," he commanded gently, smoothing his hands over her hair.

"It's not important," she mumbled, slowly calming beneath his touch and feeling embarrassed by her outburst.

"Oh, but it is. What happened with them is putting a big wall between us and I want it knocked down."

"Mama loved Papa desperately," she began hesitantly.

"And he did not love her?"

"I don't know. He might have in his way. He was a

roamer, a gambler, and a womanizer. They may have been happy in the beginning, but by the time I was old enough to understand things, it was all wrong. Papa would come home and Mama would be so happy. He'd tell tales of his travels, stay a week or two, leave a little money, and be gone again. She would cry. There were always other women. That made her cry, too. She would sit by the window watching for him to come down the road and cry when another day slipped by and he didn't come home. That was her life, all she cared about. Day in, day out. He was her world and it was filled with tears. When he was shot, caught in bed with another man's wife, she still didn't stop. I sometimes think she cried herself to death. Despite all he had done, it was as if she no longer wanted to live in a world where he no longer lived."

"You still lived there," he said, knowing her reply would probably reveal even more scars, but needing to know it all.

"Yes, I did." Her voice was flat, emotionless. "As soon as I was old enough to work around the farm, I was useful in that I gave her more time to watch for Papa, to write letters begging him to come home, and to let her spend every minute with him when he did stop by. She taught me to be a lady because she believed he would soon be rich and we would move in society as equals. But, you see, my being there also meant that she was not free to chase after him. Sometimes she hated me for that. She followed him in the end, though, didn't she."

He cupped her face in his hands and tilted it up to his. "Maura, my love, I am not your father."

There was such a soft look in his lovely eyes, she felt her heart beat a little faster. "No, you're not," she whispered, and felt the truth of those words in her heart and her mind.

"I don't itch to wander the world. I don't gamble except for the occasional friendly game. And"—he brushed a kiss over her mouth—"I don't womanize. Now, get that suspicious glint out of your pretty eyes. I haven't been a saint. Never wanted to be and never claimed to be. But I was also a single man. I'm no great lothario, though, and don't frequent the bawdy houses."

"Somehow I just can't see you being like that, either."

"And you are not your mother."

She sighed. "No, I don't think I am. I have given it a lot of thought lately and I know I would never have put up with Papa's roaming and infidelities. In fact, a few painful memories reminded me that, even as a child, I had little tolerance for them."

"And there's one other difference to consider."

Maura closed her eyes as he brushed tender kisses over her face, letting the warmth of desire chase away the lingering chill of fear and painful memory. "Mmm. And what is that?"

"I love you."

She jerked back so fast he had to tighten his hold on her to keep her from sprawling on her back. Maura stared into his eyes, trying to read the truth there. Her heart was pounding so fast and so hard, she put her hand over it as if, with her touch, she could calm its pace.

"You love me?"

Mitchell smiled, a little hurt that she did not immediately reply in kind, but seeing hope for himself in her expression, which was an intriguing mixture of doubt and exhaltation. "Yes, have done that nearly from the start." He slowly tugged her close again. "You see, I've always believed I would recognize my woman, my mate, almost at first sight. I suspected you were she. That first kiss confirmed it. Now, I won't say I put the word *love* to what I was feeling, not right away. But, I knew it was right between us from that first kiss, knew I had to get you to see it, too, because my plan has always been to marry you."

Maura smiled at him, making no attempt this time to hide her feelings. "Oh, Mitchell, that's so, so romantic," she said, and laughed softly when he blushed.

"I can be romantic from time to time."

"Yes, you can." She touched his cheek with her fingers and bit back an urge to weep, for she knew he might not understand that they were tears of joy. "I suppose that's why I love you so much." She gasped softly when his hold tightened so much that it was nearly painful.

"Maura?" He cleared his throat, his voice so hoarse with emotion he doubted her name had come out clearly. "You love me?"

"Oh, yes. Why do you think I was so upset? I wanted you, wanted to stay with you, but you never spoke of love, and, even though you were proposing marriage, you said no soft words at all. Everything in me wanted to say yes, but I was terrified of staying with a man I loved but who did not love me."

She giggled when he somewhat awkwardly arranged them on the bed so that she was sprawled beneath him. As always, the feel of his big, warm body caused desire to heat her blood. It amazed her a little how three small words could so completely change fear and despair into hope and happiness.

"I swear to you, Maura, you won't regret marrying me," he vowed as he opened her robe, then groaned as he viewed the deep maroon ensemble he so appreciated. "I will love away any doubts you have."

After she helped him shed her robe, she began to undo his shirt, eager to touch his skin. Mitchell was soon helping her take off his clothes. Their kisses and caresses grew more frantic, their need for each other openly desperate. Now that they had expressed what they felt for each other, laid their fears to rest, Maura needed him as she had never needed him before. She wanted to show him how much she loved him with her body as well as her words and she could tell that Mitchell felt that same compulsion. He did not even take time to completely undress her. Once he was naked, he tugged off her little demi-drawers, and thrust inside her.

"Mitchell," she whispered, a hint of a question in her voice when he remained still, ignoring the quaking need of their bodies.

"Ah, Maura, I do love you."

She tugged his mouth down to hers and brushed her lips over his. "I love you, Mitchell Callahan, and always will."

"And this . . ." He pulled back until he was almost out of her, then slowly rejoined their bodies, smiling faintly at the way they both shuddered. "Ah, yes, this is home."

"And it will always be enough?" she asked, unable to completely cast off all her fears.

"More than enough. Hell, sometimes it's almost too damn much."

She laughed, but it was quickly cut off by her rising passion. Maura wrapped herself around him, struggling to hold him as close as humanly possible as he took them to the heights. They found them together, their cries of release blending beautifully. When he slumped down on top of her, she continued to cling to him, savoring all the new rich feelings the acknowledgment of their love gave her. She murmured her regret when he finally eased the intimacy of their embrace, rolling onto his side and pulling her close in his arms.

"Happy, love?" he asked, rubbing his hand up and down her back, and smiling faintly when he realized he had been too eager for her to take all of her clothes off.

"Yes," she replied, and kissed his chest. "There is only one thing that could add to my happiness. I want Deidre here to share it with me. I want her safe and all of your problems solved."

"Ah, well, there is something I have to tell you." He

smiled at her when she lifted her head to look at him, pleased he could ease the last of her concerns.

As Maura listened to all Mitchell had learned from his brother Stephen, she gasped. "Married? Deidre is to get married to your brother?"

"Yes, seems Tyrone is finally going to settle down." He hugged her. "How's a double wedding sound?"

"Wonderful," she replied, still a little stunned; then she laughed and peppered his broad chest with kisses. "This is the best Christmas I have ever had, even with the sad loss of my uncle. I have found you." She kissed his chin. "And Deidre will still be with me. In fact, we will become true sisters by law." She straddled his body, and brushed a kiss over his lips. "Thank you."

"For what? Deidre got here on her own."

"No. Thank you for loving me."

"Oh, no, love, it's me who should be thanking you for loving me."

"Are we going to argue about this?"

"I think so." He slowly eased their bodies together, smiling at the way she gasped with delight. "And I think it just might take forever for us to decide who is more grateful."

"Forever sounds just about right," she whispered.

Epilogue

Christmas Day

"Tyrone, get your hand out of the bonbons and come look out of the window."

Grinning slightly, Tyrone walked over to where Deidre stood by the front window. She had spent a lot of time there since they had finally gained control of themselves and gotten out of bed. He did wonder how she had known he was stealing a little candy, as he was sure she had not even glanced over her shoulder.

"What am I supposed to be looking at?" he asked as he stood behind her, wrapped his arms around her waist, and kissed the back of her neck.

"Isn't that Mister Booker's sleigh coming down the road?"

It took him a minute to make out the distant shape of something coming down the road. "You've got good vision." He narrowed his eyes, but it was another minute before he could make out the shape clearly enough to say, "Yes, I do believe it is Jason's sleigh. Thought that went back to his ranch."

"The only person you are sure will come today is Stephen, isn't it?"

"Yes, and this is about the time he should be arriving."

"Well, there are three people in that sleigh."

"Dammit, how can you see that?"

She shrugged and folded her arms across her chest as she concentrated on the sleigh. Then she tensed, pressing so close to the window she clouded it with her breath and had to wipe it clean with her handkerchief. For a moment she did not dare trust her own eyes, afraid she was seeing just what she needed and wanted to see. As the sleigh drew even closer, there was no further denying the owner of that distinctive dark-auburn hair. Deidre squealed with delight and, broke free of Tyrone's grasp so quickly he staggered. He was still muttering about that inconsideration as he followed her when she raced toward the front door.

"Maura, stop wriggling," Mitchell said, laughter deepening his voice.

"I'm sorry. It's just that I'm eager to see Deidre," she replied. "I want to see with my own eyes that she is safe and sound."

"She looked fine to me," said Stephen.

"And allow me to apologize if I offend here, if it seems that I am calling you a liar, I am not. It's just that, well, I have to see her. I don't know if I could accept the Pope's word unless I saw her."

It was just as Mitchell pulled the sleigh up in front of the doors to the Sweet Kate that Deidre burst out onto the veranda, shouting Maura's name. As she scrambled gracelessly over a laughing Stephen, Maura called out Deidre's name as well. Then they were hugging each other and laughing, relating bits and pieces of their many stories in a way that left the men both shaking their head in bewilderment.

Introductions were made after Tyrone stopped the chatter of the two young women by simply grabbing Deidre in his arms and clapping a hand over her mouth. They all hurried inside out of the cold. Maura helped Deidre serve drinks of mulled cider, then they both hurried into the kitchen to check on the food.

"Do you love him?" Deidre asked Maura as she checked the smoothness of the gravy while Maura added a little butter to the carrots.

"Oh, my, yes," Maura said, and sighed in a way that made Deidre laugh.

"I always got the feeling that you, well, either couldn't or didn't want to fall in love."

"I didn't want to. I was terrified that I would become little more than a toy for my husband to pick up as he pleased, literally enslaved to my love. Then I had a good hard look at myself and realized I am not like my mother at all."

"I wish you had talked to me about this. I could have told you that."

"I think I needed to tell it to myself," she said quietly, and Deidre nodded in complete understanding. "And do you love Tyrone?"

"Yes, despite his flaws."

"He has flaws?"

"Doesn't yours?"

"A few."

"Same here," drawled Deidre and they exchanged a grin. "Well, let's go back in and make sure they aren't eating all the bonbons and drinking all the cider and making themselves too sick to eat all this fine food."

Once back in the front parlor with the men, Deidre and Maura joined in the hearty round of toasts. Once matters quieted down a little, Deidre stood on a footstool and said quietly, "To Patrick James Kenney. It is his legacy to his lovely angels that has brought us all together."

"To Patrick," Mitchell said, and leaned forward to kiss the tears from Maura's cheeks as the others joined in.

It was during another rush to the kitchen by the women that Mitchell and Tyrone looked at Stephen. "You're next, Stephen," drawled Tyrone.

"Oh, really?" Stephen grinned, and shook his head. "And just where do you suggest I look? I begin to think you two grabbed the best."

"You'll have to see come the summer."

"I will?" He frowned at the envelope that Tyrone stuck into his hand. "What's this?"

Mitchell slowly grinned and patted his youngest brother on the back. "Train tickets to Saint Louis."

Hannah Howell introduced readers
to the Murray brothers in
HIGHLAND DESTINY, HIGHLAND
HONOR, and HIGHLAND PROMISE.
Now she delights readers with the stories
of their daughters in a brand-new Highland
trilogy!
Please turn the page for an exciting sneak
peek of

HIGHLAND VOW

available at bookstores!

Chapter One

Scotland
1446

"Pintle head!"

"Dog droppings!"

Cormac Armstrong almost laughed as the angry, childish voices halted his slow, resigned descent into unconsciousness. It seemed a cruel jest of fate that he would slowly bleed his young life away to the sharp sounds of bairns taunting each other. The sound filled him with an overwhelming melancholy. It stirred memories of all the times he had quarreled with his brothers, painfully bringing him to the realization that he would never see them again.

"Ye are ugly!"

"Oh, aye? Hah! Weel, I say that ye are ugly, too, and stupid!"

The sound of a small fist hitting a small body was swiftly followed by the raucous sound of children fighting. More young voices cut through the chill, damp morning air as the other children cheered on their selected champions. It sounded as if there was a veritable horde of children on the other side of the thicket he hid behind. Cormac prayed that they would stay where they were, that none of them would cross to his side of the thicket and innocently become involved in his desperate troubles. A heartbeat later, he cursed, for he realized his prayers were to go unanswered.

Huge brilliant green eyes and a mass of thick raven curls were the first thing he saw as a thin, small girl wriggled through the thicket and knelt at his side. She was an enchanting child and Cormac desperately wished she would go away, far away. He did not think his enemies were still following his trail, but he could be wrong, and this fey child would be brutally pushed aside by them, perhaps even killed or injured.

"Go, lassie," he ordered, his voice little more than a hoarse, trembling whisper. "Take all your wee companions and flee this place. Quickly."

"Ye are bleeding," she said after looking him over.

His eyes widened slightly as she began to smooth her tiny, soft hand over his forehead. Her voice was surprisingly deep for such a wee lass, almost sultry. More voice than girl, he mused.

"Aye," he agreed, "and I will soon be dead, which isnae a sight for those bonny big eyes."

"Nay, ye willnae die. My mither can heal most any hurt, ye ken. I am Elspeth Murray."

"And I am Cormac Armstrong." He was startled when he found the strength to shake the tiny hand she thrust at him. "Ye must nay tell your mother about me."

"Ye need my mither to make ye stop bleeding."

"Lass, I am bleeding because someone is trying verra hard to kill me."

"Why?"

"They say I am a murderer."

"Are ye?"

"Nay."

"Then my mither can help ye."

Cormac desperately wanted to allow the child to fetch her mother to heal his wounds. He did not want to die. He certainly did not want to die for a crime he had not committed, at least not before he could clear that black stain from his name. It was all so unfair, he thought, then grimaced. He realized that he sounded very much like a child himself.

"Ah, poor laddie," she murmured. "Ye are in pain. Ye need quiet. I will tell the bairns to hush." Before he could protest, she rose and walked back to the edge of the thicket, thrusting herself partway through. "Ye can all just shut your wee mouths!" Elspeth yelled in an astoundingly loud, commanding voice. "There is a poor mon bleeding o'er here and he needs some peace. Payton, take your wee thin legs and run. Find Donald or my fither. Get someone, for this laddie sore needs help."

The only thing Cormac could think of to say when she returned to his side was, "I am nay a laddie. I am a mon, a hunted mon." He softly cursed as he watched other children begin to wriggle their way through the thicket.

"How old are ye?" Elspeth asked as she began to smooth her small hand over his forehead again.

"Seventeen." Cormac wondered how such a tiny hand could be so soothing.

"I am nine today. 'Tis why so many Murrays are gathered together. And ye *are* a lad. My fither says anyone beneath one and twenty years is a lad or a lass and some are ne'er any more, e'en if they grow as old and big as he has.

'Tis what he told my cousin Cordell when he turned six-teen and was boasting of what a fine, grand stallion of a mon he was."

"Aye," agreed an amber-eyed child who was even smaller than Elspeth, as she sat down next to him. "Uncle Balfour says a lad needs to gain his spurs, get himself a wife and bairns, and bring honor to both duties ere he can prance about and declare himself a mon. Why is he bleed-ing, Elspeth?"

"Because he has a few muckle great holes in him, Avery." Elspeth briefly grinned when the other children giggled.

"I can see that. How did he get hurt?"

"Someone is trying to make him pay for a murder he didnae commit."

"Lass," Cormac glanced around at what was an astonish-ing array of eleven beautiful children, then fixed his gaze upon Elspeth, "I said I was innocent, but ye cannae be sure I was telling ye the truth."

"Aye, ye are," Elspeth said firmly.

"No one can lie to Elspeth," said a tall, slender boy crouched to the left of him. "I am Ewan, her brother, and 'tis a most troublesome thing, I can tell ye."

Cormac almost smiled, but then fixed a stern gaze on the lad who looked to be a little older than Elspeth. "Then she will also ken that I speak the truth when I tell her I am naught but trouble, deadly trouble, and that she should just leave me to my fate. Ye should all hie away home ere the danger sniffing at my heels reaches your gates."

The boy opened his mouth to speak, then rapidly closed it. Cormac followed his wide gaze to his sister and his own eyes widened slightly. She was sitting very straight, her beautiful eyes fixed unwaveringly upon her hapless brother. There was a very stern, very adult look upon her small face. Cormac could easily sympathize with the boy's reluctance to argue with that look.

"Ewan, why dinnae ye and the other laddies see if ye can find something to make a litter," Elspeth said. "Oh, and ere ye skip off to do as ye are told, ye can give me that wineskin ye took from Donald."

"I ne'er," the boy began to protest, then cursed and handed the wineskin to Elspeth before he and the other boys disappeared.

"There is no real harm in the lad testing his head for wine, lass," Cormac said.

"I ken it, and Donald puts a hearty brew in his wineskin, but I am thinking ye will find more use of it. Ewan can test the strength of his innards for this potion some other day."

She revealed a surprising strength as she slipped one thin arm around his shoulders and helped him sit up enough to take a drink. It was not only surprise that made him cough a little, however, as he took a drink. Wine did not burn its way down your throat and spread such warmth throughout your body.

"Avery, ye go and fetch me some water," Elspeth ordered, then, as soon as her cousin slipped away, she looked at the two remaining girls. "Bega, Morna, one of ye will give me your shift skirt so that I may bind this laddie's wounds. S'truth, I shall need a good piece of both."

"Why dinnae ye use your own?" grumbled the small, fair-haired girl. "I will be scolded."

"Nay for helping a mon stop his life's blood from soaking the ground, Bega."

As the two little girls struggled to tear their shifts, Cormac looked at Elspeth. "Lass, this is no chore for a wee child."

"Weel, it willnae be fun, but we cannae be sure how long it will take Payton to bring help, so we had best stop this bleeding if we can. My mither is a healer. I ken a few things. Have some more wine."

"This isnae wine," he murmured, then took another drink. She smiled and he thought, a little dazedly, that she would be a very beautiful woman when she finished growing.

"I ken it. So do most others. But, Donald's wife had an evil-tempered drunkard for a father and she gets most pious when she thinks her mon is drinking the *uisquebeath*. So, he hides it in his wineskin. Now, we all ken that our Donald will ne'er become a drunkard. He doesnae have that weakness in him. But he does like a warming drink now and then or e'en a hearty drink with the other men, so we all ignore his wee lie. I think his wife kens all of that, too, but the wee lie helps her keep her fear from making her be shrewish toward her poor mon."

"If ye have Donald's wineskin, then he cannae be verra far away. Nay, nor would anyone let so many bairns run about unguarded. So, lass, where is Donald?"

"Ah, weel, I fear we were mean to the poor mon. We slipped under his guard. Aye, I think we were too mean, for we have been gone from Donncoill for a verra long time and my fither may come looking for us. That means that, soon, poor old Donald will hear a question he has come to dread."

"Where are they, Donald?"

Donald shuddered and tried to stand firm before the bellowing laird of Donncoill and his two glaring brothers. Balfour looked ready to beat him senseless and his brothers, Nigel and Eric, looked eager to hold him down while Balfour did so. He heartily wished he had not lost his wineskin along with the children for he could benefit from a long, bracing drink at the moment.

"I dinnae ken," he replied, and hastily stepped back from the palpable fury of the Murray brothers. "They were with me one moment and gone the next. I have been searching for them for nearly an hour."

"Our bairns have been out of your sight for an hour?" Before Donald could think of any reply to that softly hissed question, young Payton trotted up and grabbed his father Nigel by the arm, saying, "Ye must come with me now, Papa."

Nigel grasped his young son by his thin shoulders. "Has something happened to the bairns?"

"Nay, we are all hale." He glanced at a pale Donald. "Sorry for slipping away from you."

"Never mind that now, son. Where are the others?"

"I will show you." He started to lead the men back toward Elspeth and the other children. "Elspeth found a bleeding mon and she sent me to find help."

Nigel cast one quick glance at his two frowning brothers. There were a lot of reasons for a man to be lying wounded in the remote corners of Murray lands. Few of those reasons were good ones. Nigel urged his son to hurry as Donald caught the reins of their horses and followed on behind.

"Sorry to have hurt ye, Cormac," Elspeth said as she dampened a scrap of linen and bathed the sweat from his face, "but I think I have eased the bloodletting a wee bit."

"Aye, ye did a verra fine job, lass," he struggled to say.

"My mither will have to stitch the wound on your side and on your leg."

"Lass, I cannae thank ye enough, but will ye nay heed me and go? I cannae be sure I have slipped free of the men hunting me and 'twould sore pain me to see ye hurt if they came here and found me. They would hurt ye and the others."

"I did heed your warning. 'Tis why Avery, Morna, and Bega are keeping a verra close watch."

"Ye are a stubborn lass."

"Aye, I have been scolded for it a time or two. Ye need help and I mean to give it to you."

"I am a hunted—"

"Aye, I ken it. My aunt Gisele, Avery's mither, was

hunted, too, and we helped her. She was wrongly accused of a murder, too, so we ken that someone saying ye did it and trying to make ye pay for the crime doesnae make it all true."

Before Cormac could recover from his shock over that revelation and continue the argument, Avery appeared at their side and announced, "Our fithers are coming."

The child had barely finished speaking when Cormac found himself staring up at three hard-faced, well-armed men. He instinctively reached for his sword only to find it gone. Cormac inwardly grimaced when the small boy who had arrived with the men handed his sword over to a tall, amber-eyed man. He knew he had no strength left to defend himself and that he could have seriously erred by drawing his sword on men who might well help him. Nevertheless, he did not like the fact that he had been so neatly disarmed by a mere child. As if to add insult to injury, his tiny, green-eyed savior collected the knife tucked inside his boot and handed it to the tall, broad-shouldered man with the brown hair and brown eyes, then returned to gently bathing his face.

Balfour Murray looked down at his small daughter. "Ye slipped away from poor Donald."

"Aye, I did," she replied, and idly handed a grumbling Donald his wineskin.

"Ye ken that ye shouldnae do that."

"Aye, but I fear the naughtiness o'ertakes me sometimes."

"Weel, the next time the naughtiness starts to o'ertake ye, try to recall that 'twill be followed by a harsh punishment." Balfour looked around, seeing only the four lasses. "Where are the rest?"

"Making a litter for this lad," Elspeth replied.

"Do ye expect me to take him back to Donncoill?"

"Aye."

"Ye are cluttering up my lands with a vast array of the broken and the lame, lass."

"He isnae lame, just bleeding."

Balfour stared down at the youth his daughter was so tenderly caring for. Thick, dark-russet hair and clear blue eyes made for a striking combination. The boy's features were well cut and unmarred. His body was long, youthfully lean, but held the promise that he would become a strong man. If looks carried any weight, Balfour suspected everyone would readily call the lad friend and welcome him. Elspeth might be only nine, but Balfour could not help wondering if, this time, his daughter was acting upon more than her usual tendency to clasp all hurt creatures to her heart. The youth of the lad made Balfour feel inclined to help him without question, but he forced himself to be cautious.

"I am Sir Balfour Murray, laird of Donncoill, and these are my brothers, Sir Nigel and Sir Eric." He nodded first to the man on his left and then to the man on his right. "Who are ye, lad, and why are ye bleeding on this remote part of my lands?" Balfour demanded, not revealing even the smallest hint of mercy.

"I am Cormac Armstrong, sir, and here is where I fell as I tried to reach my kinsmen to the south," Cormac replied.

"Where is your horse?"

"Wandered off when I swooned and fell off his back."

"And who cut ye and why?"

"I am being hunted by the kinsmen of a mon I have been accused of murdering." Cormac sighed when all three men gripped their swords and eyed him with renewed suspicion.

"Did ye do it?"

"Nay."

"And why should I believe ye?" Balfour asked even as he eased his tense, cautious stance a little.

"I can only offer my word of honor." Cormac hoped someone would decide on his fate soon, for he was not sure he could remain conscious much longer. "I am innocent."

"The lads are here with a litter," Nigel announced.

"Weel, best see that it is a sturdy one," Balfour said. "We may yet be dragging the lad back to Donncoill." He looked back at Cormac. "Who are ye accused of killing?"

"A Douglas mon." Cormac was not surprised to see both Balfour and Eric jerk as they immediately tensed in alarm.

"A Douglas mon, eh? Do ye have the strength to tell the tale?"

"I will try. I was courting a lass. Her family decided to wed her to a Douglas mon. He had more land and coin to offer. Aye, I didnae take the loss weel, let my tongue clatter too freely, and gave too loud a voice to my anger, and, aye, my jealousy. So, when the mon turned up dead, his throat cut, but a six month after the wedding, all eyes turned my way. I didnae do it, but I have no proof that I was elsewhere when he was killed nor anyone else I could turn the suspicion on. So, I ran and I have been running ever since. For two long months."

"And the Douglases chase ye?"

"Some. One of the smaller branches of the clan, but I willnae be welcomed by any Douglas, nor will they who aid me."

" 'Tis a hard choice ye give me, lad. Do I believe ye and risk angering the powerful Douglas clan by keeping ye alive or do I leave ye to die, mayhap e'en turn ye o'er to the Douglases e'en though ye might be innocent? Ye ask me to risk a lot on nay more than your word."

"He isnae asking, I am," said Elspeth. "And ye do have one other thing to weigh in his favor, Fither."

"Oh, aye. What is that?"

"From the moment I found him, he has been trying to get me to go away, to just leave him to his fate. He hasnae once ceased to warn me that he could be trouble."

"But ye are a stubborn lass."

"Aye, I am."

Balfour smiled at his daughter, then moved to stand at Cormac's feet. "Come, Eric, lend us a hand. We will set this young fool on the litter and drag his leaking carcass back to my Maldie so she can mend him."

"Are ye certain about this, Balfour?" asked Eric as he moved to help carry Cormac.

"Not fully, but what murderer, what hunted mon, turns aside an offer of aid because he fears a silly wee lass will be hurt?"

"I am nay silly," Elspeth muttered as she followed her father.

Eric and Balfour briefly exchanged a grin, then Eric replied to Balfour's question, "None that I ken. Aye, I feel the same as ye do. I just pray we can get this lad healed and away from Donncoill ere the Douglas clan kens what we have done. It sounds cowardly, I ken, but . . ."

"Aye, but. He isnae kin, isnae e'en a friend or the son of a friend." He glanced down at Cormac as he and Eric settled the youth on the litter. "Ye will be mended and made strong again, lad, God willing, but then ye must walk your own path. Do ye understand?" he asked as he studied the youth's gray, sweat-dampened face.

"Aye, I havenae swooned yet," Cormac answered.

"Good. Ye have seen the riches I must protect," Balfour briefly glanced toward the children. "We Murrays are but a small clan. E'en if we call upon all our allies, we are still small, too small to bring the wrath of the Douglas clan down upon our heads." Balfour signaled Donald to attach the litter to his own horse.

"I dinnae think anyone, save the king himself, could pull together enough allies for that battle."

"And, mayhap, nay e'en him. Ye picked a verra powerful enemy."

"Ah, weel, I have e'er believed that one should strive for the verra best in all things," Cormac whispered, then swooned.

"He hasnae died, has he?" Elspeth asked in a soft, tremulous voice as she touched Cormac's pale cheek.

"Nay, lass." Balfour picked up his daughter and, after Donald and his brothers set the smaller children on the horses, took his mount by the reins and started to walk back to Donncoill. "The poor lad has just fainted. I believe he will be fine, for he showed a great deal of strength just to stay awake and speak sensibly for so verra long."

"And when he is strong, ye will send him away?"

"I must, lass. 'Twould be fine to raise my sword and defend your poor bloodied laddie, for I feel certain he has been wronged, but the cost would be too dear. It could e'en set us against our king."

"I ken it." She twined her thin arms around his neck and kissed his cheek. "Ye must choose between all of us and a lad ye dinnae ken at all and have no bond with. And, I am thinking, in this trouble, 'tis best if he goes on alone. He is the only one who kens where to look for the truth which will free him."

Cormac stood on the steps of the Donncoill keep as his saddled horse was brought over to him. The Murrays had healed him and sheltered him for two months and he had regained his strength. He felt a deep reluctance to leave and not solely because he would have to face the trouble with the Douglases once again. Cormac could not recall ever having stayed at a livelier or more content place. He and his brothers were close, but his own home had never felt so content. Some of what had pulled him and his brothers together was the unhappiness that had too often darkened the halls of their keep, shadows caused by parents who loathed each other, and too many deadly intrigues.

He inwardly stiffened his spine. He could not hide at Donncoill. He had to clear his name. Turning to face Lady Maldie, he gracefully bowed, then took her small hand in his and touched a kiss to her knuckles. Even as he straightened to wish her farewell and thank her yet again for her care, a tiny, somewhat dirty hand was stuck in front of his face.

"Elspeth, my love," Maldie said, fighting a grin, "ye must ne'er demand that a mon kiss your hand." She bent a little closer to her tiny daughter. "And I think ye might consider washing a wee bit of the dirt off it first."

"She will be back," Balfour said as he draped his arm around his wife's slim shoulders and watched Elspeth run off. "Ye shall have to play the courtier for her."

"I dinnae mind. 'Tis a painfully small thing to do for the lass," Cormac said. "I would be naught but food for the corbies if she hadnae found me. Truth tell, I have ne'er understood how she did." He idly patted Elspeth's one-eyed dog, Canterbury, as the badly scarred wolfhound sat down by his leg.

"Our Elspeth has a true gift for finding the hurt and the troubled," Maldie replied.

Cormac smiled. "And ye are expected to mend them all."

"Aye." Maldie laughed. " 'Tis our good fortune that she has e'er understood that not all wounds can be healed. Ah, and here she comes." Maldie bit her lip to stop herself from giggling. "With one verra weel-scrubbed hand."

Elspeth stood in front of Cormac and held out her hand. Cormac struggled not to give in to the urge to glance toward Balfour and Maldie, for their struggle not to laugh was almost tangible and would ruin his own hard-won composure. Little Elspeth was still somewhat dirty, smudges decorating her face and gown, but the hand she thrust toward him was scrubbed so clean it was a little pink. He dutifully took her tiny hand in his and brushed his lips over her knuckles. After a few moments of reiterating his gratitude, he hurried away, braced for the battle to clear his name.

Balfour picked up his solemn-faced daughter and kissed her cheek. "He is a strong lad. He will be fine."

"Aye, I just felt sad because I think he will be fighting this battle for a verra long time."

Chapter Two

Scotland
Ten years later

"My fither will hunt ye down. Aye, and my uncles, my cousins, and all of my clansmen. They will set after ye like a pack of starving, rabid wolves, and tear ye into small, bloodied pieces. Aye, and I will spit upon your savaged body ere I walk away and leave ye for the carrion birds."

Sir Cormac Armstrong stopped before the heavy door to Sir Colin MacRae's private chambers so abruptly his muscles briefly knotted. It was not the cold threat of vicious retribution that halted him, but the voice of the one who spoke it. That soft, husky voice, one almost too deep for a woman, tore at an old memory, one nearly ten years old, one he had thought he had completely cast from his mind.

Then doubt crept over him. There was no reason for that tiny Murray lass to be in Sir Colin's keep. There was also the fact that he had not had anything to do with the

Murrays since they had so graciously aided him, nothing except to send them word that he had cleared his name as well as a fine mare for a gift. He could not believe the little girl who had saved his life was not still cherished and protected at Donncoill. His memory could be faulty. And, how could Sir Colin have gotten his hands on her? And why?

"Weel, we ken that at least one of your wretched cousins willnae be plaguing us again," drawled Sir Colin. "That fair, impertinent lad who rode with you is surely feeding the corbies as we speak."

"Nay, Payton isnae dead."

Such deep pain, mingled with fervent hope, sounded in those few words that Cormac could almost feel it and he cursed. It was hard to recall much after so many years, but the name Payton seemed familiar. Placed side by side with that voice, a voice that brought forth a very clear memory of a tiny well-scrubbed hand thrust out for a kiss, made Cormac finally move. He was not sure what he could do, but he needed to know what was going on. This was clearly not a friendly visit, and that could mean that the tiny Murray girl was in danger.

In the week since he had brought his young cousin Mary to Duncorrie for her marriage to Sir Colin's nephew, John, Cormac had made an effort to learn every shadowed corner of the keep. He did not like Sir Colin, did not trust the man at all. When his cousin's betrothal had been announced, he had been almost the only one to speak out against it. He had not wanted his family connected by marriage to a man he had learned little good about.

After assuring himself that no one could see him, he slipped into the chamber next to Colin's. No guard had been placed at the connecting door between the two rooms. Sir Colin was either too arrogant to think anyone would dare to spy upon him or the man simply did not care. Cormac pressed himself against the wall next to the door and cautiously eased it open. He glanced quickly around the room he was in, carefully noting several places he could hide in the event that someone noticed the door was cracked open. One thing he had learned in two long years of running from the wrath of the Douglas clan, and learned well, was how to hide, how to use the shadows and the most meager of cover to disappear from view. Taking a deep breath to steady himself, he peered into the room.

"That untried lad is of no consequence now," snapped Sir Colin.

"Untried?" The scorn in that husky voice made even Cormac flinch. "Even the beardless amongst my brothers and cousins has had more women than ye e'er will."

When Sir Colin bounded out of his heavy oak chair and strode toward his tormenter, Cormac had to tightly clench his fists to stop himself from doing anything rash. To his relief the man halted his advance directly in front of the woman, raising his hand but not delivering the blow he so obviously ached to. Cormac knew he would have lost all restraint if Sir Colin had struck the tiny, slender woman facing him so calmly.

There was no denying what his eyes told him, although Cormac tried to do just that for several minutes. It was hard to believe that Elspeth Murray was standing in Sir Colin's chambers, alone and far from the loving safety of Donncoill. Cormac was not sure he was pleased to see that he had been right all those years ago. Elspeth had definitely grown into a disarmingly beautiful woman.

Thick, wildly tousled hair tumbled down her slim back in heavy waves to stop teasingly at the top of her legs. Her hands were tied behind her back, and Cormac had to smile. Those hands did not look all that much bigger than they had on the day she had soothed his brow as he had lain bleeding into her father's dirt. Her figure was almost too slender, too delicate, yet just womanly enough to stir an interest in his loins. The way her arms were pulled back clearly revealed the perfect shape of her small breasts. Her waist was temptingly small and her slim hips gracefully rounded. Elspeth's face still seemed to be swamped by her thick hair and wide, brilliant green eyes. There was a childish innocence to her gentle heart-shaped face, from the small, straight nose to the faintly pointed chin. The long thick lashes rimming her big eyes and the soft fullness of her mouth bespoke womanhood, however. She was a bloodstirring bundle of contradictions. She was so close to the door he felt he could easily reach out and touch her. Cormac was a little surprised by how hard he had to fight to resist that urge.

Then she spoke in her rich, deep, husky voice and all hints of the child, all signs of innocence, were torn away. She became a sultry temptress from her wild, unbound hair to her tiny, booted feet. Cormac felt the sharp tug of lust. It struck as hard and fast as a blow to the stomach. Any man who saw her, heard her speak, would have to be restrained from kicking down the heavy gates of Donncoill to reach her. If his heart was not already pledged to another, Cormac knew he would be sorely tempted. He wondered if Sir Colin had simply succumbed to her allure.

"What? Ye hesitate to strike a lass?" she taunted the glowering Sir Colin, her beautiful voice heavily ladened with contempt. "I have long thought that nothing ye could do would e'er surprise me, but, mayhap, I was wrong."

"Ye do beg to be beaten," Sir Colin said, the faint tremor in his voice all that hinted at his struggle for control.

"Yet ye stand there like a reeking dungheap."

Cormac tensed when Colin wrapped one beefy hand around her long, slender throat and, in a cold voice, drawled, "So, that is your game, is it? Ye try to prod me into a blind rage? Nay, my bonny, green-eyed bitch, ye are nay the one who will be doing the prodding here." Three of the five men in the room chuckled.

" 'Tis to be rape then, is it? Ye had best be verra sure

when ye stick that sad, wee twig of flesh in me that ye are willing to make it your last rut. The moment it touches me, 'twill be a doomed wee laddie."

Sir Colin's hand tightened on her throat. Cormac could see the veins in the man's thick hand bulge. His own hand went to his sword, although he knew it would be madness to interfere. Elspeth made no sound, did not move at all, and kept her gaze fixed steadily upon Sir Colin's flushed face, but Cormac noticed her hands clench behind her back until her knuckles whitened. Cormac had to admire her bravery, but thought it fool-hardy to keep goading the man as she was. He could not understand what she thought to gain from the man save for a quick death. When Cormac decided he was going to have to interfere, no matter how slim the odds of success, Sir Colin finally released her. Elspeth gasped only once and swayed faintly, yet she had to be in pain and starved for breath.

"Some may try to call it rape, but I mean only to bed my wife," Sir Colin said.

"I have already refused you," she replied, her voice a lit-tle weaker, a little raspy. "Further discussion of the matter would just be tedious."

"No one refuses me."

"I did and I will."

"Ye will have no more say in this matter." He signaled to the two men flanking her. "Secure her in the west tower." Sir Colin brushed his blunt fingertips over her full mouth and barely snatched them away, out of her reach, before she snapped at them, her even, white teeth clicking loudly in the room. "I have a room prepared especially for you."

"I am humbled by your generosity."

"Humbled? Oh, aye, ye too proud wench, ye will soon be verra humbled indeed."

Cormac gently pushed the door shut as far as he dared, stopping just before it latched. A moment later he was in the hall again, using the shadows cast by the torchlight to follow Elspeth and her guards. Only once did someone look back and that was Elspeth. She stared into the shadows which sheltered him, a frown briefly curving her full lips, then was tugged along by her guards. Cormac did not think she had seen him, but, if she had, she clearly had the wits to say nothing. He followed his prey right to the door of the tower room, all the while struggling to devise some clever plan of escape.

Elspeth stumbled slightly when one of the guards roughly shoved her into the room, but quickly steadied herself. She swallowed her sigh of relief when the other guard cut the rope binding her wrists, then fought the urge to rub them, thus revealing how much they hurt as the blood began to flow to them again. As the heavy door shut behind the two men and she listened to the bolt being dragged across it, she then began to rub her chafed, sore wrists, and make a quick but thorough survey of the room.

"It appears that the only way out of this room is if I succumb to the sinful urge to hurl myself from the window and end my poor life," she muttered as she sat down on the huge bed which dominated the room. She frowned and idly bounced up and down on the mattress. "Feathers. The bastard plainly intends to be comfortable as he dishonors me."

Weary, sick with worry over Payton's fate, and knotted with fear, Elspeth curled up on the bed. For just a moment she fought the urge to weep, not wishing to give in to that weakness. Then, as the tears began to fall, she shrugged. She was alone, and a good cleansing of her misery could help her maintain her strength, especially later.

After what she feared was a disgracefully prolonged bout of weeping, Elspeth flopped onto her back and stared up at the ceiling. She felt drained, as if some physician had placed leeches all over her, leeches that sucked all the emotion from a body instead of the blood. It was going to take a while to get her strength and wits back, two things she would sorely need in the days ahead.

She thought of Payton and felt as if she could weep all over again, if she had any tears left. Her last sight of her cousin had been that of his bloodied body lying alongside the two men-at-arms who had accompanied them. Elspeth had needed only one look to know that their two guards were dead, but she could not be so certain about Payton. She did not want to be. She wanted to cling to the hope that he was still alive, no matter how small that hope might be. If nothing else, Elspeth could not bear to think upon the pain her uncle Nigel and aunt Gisele would suffer over the loss of their son. Even though her mind told her that it was not her fault, she knew she might never be able to shake free of the guilt she felt, for it had been her rejected suitor who had brought about the tragedy. It struck her as appallingly unfair that the chilling memories and nightmares she had suffered for three long years might finally be pushed aside by the sight of her cousin's murder. An old nightmare replaced by a new one.

Elspeth closed her eyes, deciding it would not hurt to seek the rest her body craved. She would need it to be able to endure what lay ahead. Although she had no doubt that her family would come after her in force, she also knew they might not arrive in time to save her from all Sir Colin intended. That was in her own hands.

As she felt sleep creep over her, she heard a faint noise at the door. Either someone was bringing her some food and drink or some poor fool had been sent to check to be sure she was still where they had put her. Elspeth resisted the urge to look. She was too tired and too battered to do anything just yet. In truth, she felt almost too tired to even open her eyes. Then someone touched her arm and she tensed, her weariness abruptly shoved aside by alarm even though she felt no real threat from the person she now knew stood next to her bed.

Cautiously, Elspeth opened her eyes just enough to see her visitor through the veil of her still-damp lashes. He was a beautiful man, his long, leanly muscular body bent over her in a strangely protective way. His face was cut in clean lines, and unmarred. A high, wide forehead, high-boned cheeks, a long, straight nose, a handsomely firm jaw, and a well-shaped mouth made for a face that easily took a maid's breath away. His creamy skin was almost too pale and fine for a man, although many a woman would envy it, and the healthy warmth of it begged for a touch. It was the perfect complement to his deep auburn hair. His eyes, however, were what truly caught and held her attention. Set beneath neatly arched brows and ringed with long, thick lashes, they were the rich blue of clean, deep water, a color she had seen but once before in her life. They were eyes that had filled many a maidenly dream and some that were very far from maidenly.

"Cormac," she whispered, smiling faintly at the way his beautiful eyes widened slightly in surprise.

"Ye remember me?" he asked softly, a little shaken by the warm look in her rich green eyes and the soft, enticing smile of greeting she gifted him with.

"Ah, ye dinnae remember me. Ye are but tiptoeing through the bedchambers of Duncallie to see if any hold something ye like. I am devastated."

Cormac straightened up and put his hands on his hips. Her drawled taunt had quickly yanked him free of his bemusement better than a sharp slap to the face. She was even more beautiful close to, and, for just a moment, as he had stared into her wide, slumbrous eyes, he had been seized by the overwhelming urge to crawl onto that bed with her. The way she had whispered his name in her rich, sensuous voice had reached deep inside him, dragging his tightly controlled lusts to fierce, immediate life. The feeling still lingered, but, now, he struggled to cool his heated blood.

"Aye, I recall you," he said. "Ye are a wee bit bigger and sharper of tongue, but ye are certainly Elspeth, my tiny, begrimed savior from years past."

Slowly, Elspeth sat up, then knelt on the bed facing him. Some of those not so maidenly dreams she had had about him were crowding her mind and she fought to push them aside. He had come to rescue her. Elspeth inwardly smiled as she mused that it was a poor time to tell a man that she had loved and lusted after him for ten long years. For all she knew, he was a wedded man with a bairn or two to bounce on his knee. Finding that thought painful, she forced her mind to settle on the matter of rescue.

"And have ye come to be my savior now?" she asked.

"Aye."

Elspeth smiled and abruptly decided to make at least one small dream into a true memory. Cormac could easily think her next action was simply an impulsive expression of relief and gratitude, or be made to think so. She leaned closer and kissed him. His lips were as soft and as delicious as she had always imagined they would be. If he was wed, this stolen kiss would be but a small trespass.

And then, it happened. Her mother had warned her. Elspeth wished she had listened more closely, but she had been too young to be comfortable hearing such words as desire and passion upon her mother's lips.

He trembled faintly and so did she, but she was not really sure where his shiver ended and hers began. His body tightened and she felt a responsive tight ache low in her belly. She felt his heat, could almost smell his desire. Cormac gripped her by the shoulders and deepened the kiss. Elspeth readily opened her mouth to welcome the invasion of his tongue. As he caressed the inside of her mouth, she felt as if he stroked her very soul. She wanted to pull him down onto the bed with her, ached to wrap herself around his lean body. Even as that thought passed through her passion-clouded mind, she felt Cormac dredge up some inner strength and start to pull away from her. Elspeth fought the urge to cling to him, to halt his retreat.

Cormac stared at the young woman kneeling in front of him. He fought the urge to vigorously shake his head in an attempt to clear the haze from his mind. It was not easy to cool the fire in his blood as he looked into her wide green eyes, for he was sure he saw passion there. He had to sternly remind himself that Elspeth was a high-born woman, one he owed his life to, and he was not free. He had come to rescue her, not to ravish her.

"Why?" he asked, then hastily cleared his throat to try to banish the huskiness from his voice.

"Why not?" she asked back. "Are ye wed?"

"Nay, but—"

Elspeth did not want to hear the rest, not when her heart still pounded fiercely and she could still taste him. "A rash act, born of my delight to see ye alive and here. I ken that my kinsmen will soon hunt for me, but 'twould be help that would come too late."

"And if we do not move quickly, my aid could also prove worthless."

"Ye have a plan, do ye, my braw knight?" She took careful note of the fact that he had not yet released her, but was moving his strong, long-fingered hands over her upper arms in an idle but telling caress.

"I do. 'Tis why it took me near to an hour to come and fetch you," he replied.

"An hour?" Elspeth muttered, unable to hide her surprise.

"I had to tend to a few matters that will ease our escape ere I could come here."

"I meant no criticism, Sir Cormac. 'Twas just a wee disappointing to me to realize I had spent so long wallowing in my misery. I hadnae thought myself such a weakling." She frowned when he chuckled. "Ye find my despair amusing?"

"Nay, lass, merely the indication that ye might e'er consider yourself weak." He took her by the hand and tugged her off the bed. "Ye have ne'er been weak. Nay, not e'en as a wee, muck-smeared bairn of nine."

Elspeth flushed a little with pleasure over his remarks even though they were spoken in a jesting tone. "What is your plan?"

"Ye are to wrap yourself in this cloak and we will walk out of here." He handed her a long, heavy, woolen cloak he had set on the bed before trying to wake her.

"That is your plan?" she asked as she donned the cloak.

"Simple is ofttimes the best," he said as he opened the door and dragged her unconscious guard inside.

She watched as he tied and gagged the man, then tucked him into the bed, pulling the covers up so that only a bit of the man's black hair showed over the blankets. "I dinnae think that will fool them for verra long."

"Long enough for us to escape these walls."

"Are ye truly meaning to just walk out of here with me?"

Cormac tugged the hood of the cape over her head, pulling it forward until it covered her hair and shaded her face. "If any ask what I am about, I shall simply say I am taking my wee cousin Mary for a ride."

"Do ye really have a wee cousin Mary?"

"Aye, and she is here. She is betrothed to Sir Colin's nephew John. I brought her here for her wedding. She stays to her rooms, only coming out to dine in the great hall. The next meal isnae for several hours, so this ruse should work."

As he led her out of the room, then shut and barred the door, she asked, "Would it nay be better to creep away, to keep to the shadows? Mayhap ye ken of a bolthole to use."

"All that would be best, but then we couldnae take my horse."

Elspeth started to say something, then quickly closed her mouth. His plan was fraught with the chance of failure, but she had none at all. He was also right in thinking it best to take his horse. They would not get very far on foot.

"Do we take your cousin's horse as weel? Or mine?"

"I fear my cousin doesnae have a horse." He grimaced. "She is a timid lass and willnae ride alone, travels only in a cart or sharing a saddle with another. All here ken it, too. If I suddenly set Mary on a horse 'twould rouse suspicion. To take your horse would also rouse suspicion. I fear we will have to ride two to a saddle."

"Riding is better than walking. Faster."

"Aye, and now I must ask ye to hush."

"Your cousin Mary doesnae talk, either?"

He smiled faintly. "Nay much, although she and John seem to have a lot to say to each other when they arenae both trying to hide from Sir Colin. Nay, I think ye must remain silent because of your voice."

"Something is wrong with my voice?"

" 'Tis too distinctive," he replied, but could see by the look on her face that she did not really understand. "Trust me," he said, and tugged her hood more closely around her face.

Elspeth nodded and quelled the urge to talk to him. She threaded her fingers through his, savoring the simple act of holding his hand as they crept through the halls of Duncallie. It was the only good thing about their walk through the keep, Elspeth tensely worrying about a cry of discovery at every turning. Walking to the stables through the crowded bailey had her stomach knotting with tension so badly it hurt. She stood in the shadows near the door of the stables as Cormac got his horse, astounded at the way he so calmly spoke to the men there, as if he did not have a care in the world. He had obviously developed a few interesting skills in the years since she had seen him last.

Cormac set her on his saddle and mounted behind her, still idly jesting with the men. Elspeth fought the urge to hit him and tell him to get moving. When they finally rode out of the bailey she slumped against him, weak with relief. They were not safe yet, might not be safe for quite a while, but at least they were no longer directly under the gaze of Sir Colin.

"Where do we go now?" she asked, deciding it felt very good to be so close to him, and made herself more comfortable against his broad chest.

"Since Sir Colin will expect ye to try and get back to Donncoill, I believe we will just continue on in the direction I was planning to go after the wedding."

"Sir Colin could think ye are also trying to get me back to my clan."

"Aye, or to my kinsmen who live both south and west of here. So, that gives the mon two or three ways to search for us. He can have no idea of my true destination. I was to stay for my cousin's wedding then leave, but I told no one where I would go once the celebrations ended, not even wee Mary."

" 'Tis a good idea and, yet, how then shall I return to my kinsmen? That is where my continued safety lies, isnae it? Aye, and the means to stop Sir Colin, to make him pay for kidnapping me, killing two Murray men, and hurting Payton."

He noticed that she still refused to consider the possibility her cousin was dead. The Murray clan was obviously still closely bonded. It would probably be best if she faced the cold truth that her cousin was either dead or soon would be, the cold and a loss of blood finishing what Sir Colin had begun, but he found that he did not have the heart to steal her hope away.

"The king's court is verra near where I must go. We can find someone there who can get word to your clan. If we must, we can set ye under the king's own guard. Your clan hasnae done anything to hurt your standing with the king, has it?"

"Nay. That will do. In truth, 'tis near as fine as going straight to my fither."

"It should take us near to a fortnight since we should travel slowly to save our mount's strength. If luck fails us, and Sir Colin sniffs out our trail, it could take longer. Can ye endure such a long, rough journey?" He frowned slightly as he studied the soft delicacy of the woman in his arms.

"Oh, aye, I am stronger than I look."

Elspeth sighed when he made no reply, his doubt so strong she could almost feel it. She knew she was small and delicate in appearance, but she was indeed strong. Sir Cormac Armstrong was going to have to learn that one should not always make judgments based solely on a person's appearance.

Glancing down at his strong, long-fingered hands upon the reins, she found herself wondering yet again if he was wed, betrothed, or in love with someone. She needed some information—needed to know if he was free—and, Elspeth vowed, by the time they stopped for the night she would have it. Then she would have to decide what to do. If he was wed or betrothed, the next few weeks would be a torment as she tried to hide and even kill all feeling for the man. But if he was free, she had a fortnight to try to make him fall in love with her. That, too, could prove torturous, ripping her heart and pride to shreds. Fate had been kind enough to give her some time with the man she had adored for so long, but it was obvious that fate had also decided to make her pay dearly for that gift. All she could do was try, and pray that she had what was needed to win the prize.

ABOUT THE AUTHOR

Hannah Howell is an award-winning author who lives with her family in Massachusetts. She is the author of ten Zebra historical romances and is currently working on HIGHLAND RING, the second book in her new Highland trilogy focusing on the daughters of the Murray brothers from HIGHLAND DESTINY, HIGHLAND HONOR, and HIGHLAND PROMISE. Look for HIGHLAND RING in June 2001. Hannah loves hearing from readers and you may write her c/o Zebra Books. Please include a self-addressed, stamped envelope if you wish a response.